"PETER."

Alice walked back in. "That was the coroner in Epsom. The oddest thing. Seems when Fred Morgan died, a couple of nights before you came, he had almost no blood in his body. Some sort of bizarre bleeding disease. Makes you wonder if they haven't dropped some new, invisible gas, but he's just an isolated case."

Not completely. "I got a message to please come by the Abbotts' farm. Seems the news I've had three years of vet school preceded me. He had a problem with two of his cows. They were wasted, feeble, and when I tried to take a blood sample, thinking maybe somewhere there was a lab that might look at it, it was almost impossible to find a vein—they'd all collapsed. The animals had very little blood in them. Odd to have two strange happenings on top of the bombing."

"Three strange things," she replied. "Don't forget the disappearing injured man."

How could he? That was the reason they met.

Books by Georgia Evans

BLOODY GOOD

BLOODY AWFUL

BLOODY RIGHT

Published by Kensington Publishing Corporation

BLOODY GOOD

GEORGIA EVANS

KENSINGTON BOOKS
http://www.kensingtonbooks.com

KENSINGTON BOOKS are published by

Kensington Publishing Corp.
119 West 40th Street
New York, NY 10018

All Kensington titles, imprints, and distributed lines are available at special quantity discounts for bulk purchases for sales promotion, premiums, fund-raising, educational, or institutional use.

Special book excerpts or customized printings can also be created to fit specific needs. For details, write or phone the office of the Kensington Special Sales Manager: Attn.: Special Sales Department. Kensington Publishing Corp., 119 West 40th Street, New York, NY 10018. Phone: 1-800-221-2647.

Kensington and the K logo Reg. U.S. Pat. & TM Off.

ISBN-13: 978-0-7582-3481-0
ISBN-10: 0-7582-3481-3

First Printing: June 2009
10 9 8 7 6 5 4 3 2 1

Printed in the United States of America

For Kate,
who asked me to write a World War II book, and
for my mother, my grandmother, and my aunts,
who filled my childhood with tales of THE WAR.

Prologue

September 1940
Over SE England

By Fritz Lantz's reckoning they were twenty minutes from the first drop.

They'd been lucky so far: visibility clear and, miraculously, no ack-ack or searchlights looking their way. Not long now and he'd be unloading his odd passengers and heading back to France and breakfast in the verwirrung.

"How are our cargo?" Fritz asked Dieter, his radio operator.

"A rum lot!"

That point they agreed on. "I'll be glad when we turf them out and get back home. They give me the willies."

Come to that the whole mission seemed off a bit. Dropping spies and saboteurs was nothing unusual and Fritz hoped every single one of them gave the Tommies a run for their money. It would be a long time before Fritz Lantz forgot the bombs the damned Brits rained down on Berlin. But these four he was carrying over the channel put the wind up him so much he almost felt sorry for the enemy. He was still puzzling over his orders: No observing when they jumped. Dieter was to open the doors and return to the cockpit and give the signal from there. He was to close the jump doors ten minutes after the last one had left and not before. Then they were to head right home. That last bit wouldn't be hard to follow.

"Never had a drop like this in my life," Dieter said, shaking his head. "As good as snapped my head off when I tried to explain how to put on the parachutes. Serve them damn well right if they don't open for them."

"Almost there," Fritz replied. "Better go back and latch open the cargo door and let's unload them."

The drop orders were straightforward enough: four drop points five–ten kilometers apart in a rough circle. Some town was getting a foretaste of the invasion. It was war after all.

"Want to know something?" Dieter asked a while later as he returned from latching the cargo door after the drop. "They dumped their parachutes on the floor. Never took them!"

"Don't talk rot! They switched with the spares."

Dieter shook his head. "No, they didn't. Our scary boys jumped without."

He had to be kidding, or hadn't counted the parachutes properly.

"They won't give the Tommies much trouble, will they?" Dieter did have a screw loose if he believed that, but hell, it would make a good story over a pilsner when they get back.

Five miles beyond Beachy Head the engine sputtered and died. Fritz stared horrified at the fuel gauge. He'd left with more than enough to get back now it was empty.

"Bail out!" he called to Dieter as he unbuckled his own harness.

They both made it out seconds before the plane plummeted down toward the Channel but, according to special arrangements by the German High Command, their parachutes failed to open. Dieter and Fritz followed their Focke-Wulf to a watery grave.

* * *

After jumping, the four vampires glided down toward their designated landings. Well briefed and with land support waiting, they were more than ready to do their share preparing the way for the coming invasion.

Gerhardt Eiche, Wilhelm Bloch, and Hans Weiss landed safely and each headed for their appointed rendezvous. Paul Schmidt was less fortunate—by mischance, unexpected wind, or inaccurate coordinates, he missed the clear acreage around a dairy fairm, with the potential for restorative warm blood of both humans and animals, and crashed into the ancient cluster of oaks on Fletcher's Hill, impaling himself on the uppermost branches of a tree, hitting his head on the trunk of another, and mercifully cutting off sense and pain before crashing to Earth.

He recovered not long before the dawn. Weak from the wood poison in his system, he struggled to free his flesh of the splinters and bark. As dawn rose, his remaining strength waned. Without blood he would expire before nightfall, his mission unfulfilled. Despair washed over him at the prospect of failing his blood oath. His country needed him. Needed all of them, and he had failed. He would die on this cursed English soil.

Hours later, he heard an engine approach and stop. A car meant a mortal driver, maybe even passengers. He was saved. He'd have his first feeding of English blood and strike a blow to the enemy.

Chapter 1

Alice Doyle was exhausted. Staying up half the night and all day to deliver twins will do that to you. The elation and adrenaline of her first set of twins had carried her this far home, but as she turned into the lane that ran through Fletcher's Woods, weariness set in. It had been a good night's work, though. She wouldn't easily forget the rejoicing in the Watson farmhouse and Melanie's happiness through her fatigue as she breast-fed her lusty sons.

"A fine brace of boys. Gives one hope for the future, doesn't it, Doctor?" Roger Watson said as he smiled at his grandsons. "If only Jim were here to see them."

The Watsons' only son, Jim, was somewhere in Norfolk with the Army and Alice couldn't help worry how Melanie, a Londoner born and bred, would fare with her in-laws in a farm as remote as any you could find in Surrey.

Still, Farmer Watson was right: Whatever the politicians did or however many bombs fell, life went on.

The numerous cups of tea she'd consumed through the night were having their effects and she still had several miles to go over bumpy country roads. She pulled over to the verge and got out. Other traffic was unlikely out here. Few locals enjoyed the supply of petrol allocated to doctors. Even so,

Alice climbed over the gate and ventured into the woods for a bit of privacy.

She was straightening her clothes back when she realized she was not alone. Darn! A bit late to be worrying about modesty. Deeper into the woods, someone crawled toward her. Assuming injuries, Alice called, "I'm coming. I'm a doctor."

It was a stranger. One of the workers from the hush-hush munitions camp up on the heath, perhaps? What in heaven's name was he doing rolling on the damp ground? As Alice bent over him, he looked up at her with glazed eyes. Drunk perhaps? But she didn't smell anything on his breath.

"What happened?" As she spoke, she saw the stains on his sleeve. Blood loss might well account for his weakness. She looked more closely at him and gasped. Part of the branch of a tree was embedded in his upper arm. How in heaven's name? Had to be drunk. If there wasn't enough to do, she had to cope with boozers who impaled themselves on trees. Seemed that was his only injury. No bleeding from the mouth or nose. Heartbeat was abnormally slow but steady, his breathing shallow, and his skin cold to the touch. Shock and exposure would explain all that. Best get him out of the damp.

"Look," she said, trying her utmost to keep the fatigue out of her voice. "I need you to walk to my car. I've my bag there and I'll have a look at your arm. Then I'll take you down to my surgery in Brytewood and call an ambulance."

The odd, glazed eyes seemed to focus. "Thanks," he croaked.

"What's your name?"

He had to think about that one. Definitely recovering from a wild night. "Smith." Really? Aiming for anonymity perhaps? "Paul Smith."

Alice got behind him and propped his shoulders until he was sitting. "Come along, Mr. Smith," she told him. "I'm going to give you a boost and you have to stand. I can't carry you."

They succeeded on the second go and made slow progress

toward her car, Alice supporting Mr. Smith from his good side. He was a lot lighter than anticipated as he slowly staggered toward the road. He supported himself against the hedge as Alice opened and closed the gate, but once they emerged from the shade into the thin afternoon sun, he collapsed.

Thank heaven for her father's old shooting brake. She got her patient into the back so he was lying against the sack of potatoes the Watsons had insisted she take with her.

"Mr. Smith, I'm going to examine your arm. I'm afraid I'll have to cut your shirt sleeve."

Taking the nod as agreement, Alice snipped off the sleeve. The shirt was good for nothing but rags anyway. Her first observation had been right: Several chunks of fresh wood had penetrated the flesh of his upper arm. "How did you do this then?" she asked as she opened her bag and reached for sterile swabs and Dettol.

And cried out as he grabbed her free hand in a viselike grip and bit her wrist.

He was more than drunk. He was insane. Alice tried to push him away but he held on, digging his teeth into her flesh. She finally grabbed his nose until he gasped for breath and released her.

"Behave yourself! I'm a doctor. I'm here to help . . ." She broke off when she saw he'd passed out.

Something was really wrong. Maybe she should take him straight to the hospital in Dorking but she had patients waiting to take care of. She'd call for an ambulance at home.

Throwing a blanket over him, she got into the front and drove home as fast as safety and the twisting lanes permitted.

As luck would have it, Sergeant Pendragon was sitting at the kitchen table with Gran. The sergeant might be getting on a bit, but he was still hale and brawny and had no difficulty getting the semiconscious Mr. Smith to her examining room. Gran pulled back the curtains to let the last of the daylight in.

"Anything else I can do you for, Doctor?" Howell Pendragon

asked. He'd lived in Brytewood forty years but still retained the singsong cadence of his native Anglesey.

Alice shook her head. "Thank you, no. I'll just clean up his wound."

It was easy enough, too. Mr. Smith lay still, muttering as she probed for the deeper splinters, but seemingly still semiconscious. She'd never seen shock quite like this and, not for the first time, she wished her father were here with his lifetime of experience.

But he wasn't.

Alice made her strange patient as comfortable as she could, covered him with a couple of blankets, and carried the used kidney dish and bundle of bloody gauze away.

In the kitchen, Gran handed her bread and cheese. "I know you've had no lunch and it's a while yet before I'll have tea ready."

"Thanks, Gran." Still chewing, Alice picked up the phone. "Dorking 207, please."

"Dr. Doyle?" the telephonist said. "It's Jenny Longhurst. How are things up at the Watsons'?" News traveled fast and working in the telephone exchange, Jenny kept up with most of it.

"Melanie had a pair of beautiful boys."

"Oh! Lovely! Can't wait to tell everyone. Now, the ambulance depot you said? Anyone hurt?"

"Nothing serious." Alice hoped. She was connected in a trice while, no doubt, Jenny and her cohorts spread the news about the Watsons' new arrivals over the wires.

"An ambulance for a splinter in the arm? We're busy down here. There's a war on, you know."

Alice was almost too weary to be polite. Almost, but not quite. Thirteen years of convent education left its mark. "He has massive injuries to his right arm from multiple penetration of wood shards. Also appears to be suffering from shock, aggravated by exposure over an undetermined period. I need an ambulance just as soon as you can get one up here." She never felt comfortable pulling the "Me doctor, you mere subordinate" line, but if needs must . . .

"Alright then, Dr. Doyle. We'll have someone out there to pick him up. Might be late." Better late than never. "You have his particulars?"

"Yes." She'd appropriated his wallet from his jacket pocket. "Name: Paul Smith. Address on the driver's license is Chelmsford, same as his ration book and . . ."

"What's he doing down here then?"

"He's going?" Gran asked as Alice put up the receiver. "Good thing, too. Something's not right about him."

"Yes, Gran, his right arm is injured."

"Not that, my girl. I mean *wrong*." Alice held back the sigh; Gran was starting off again. "Howell Pendragon thought so, too, and if you'd use the talents you were born with, you'd see as clearly as I do. That Mr. Smith has no life presence. No soul."

Alice took a deep breath. She was too weary to deal with Gran's scolding about ignoring her heritage and gifts. "Yes, Gran, we'll talk about it later. How many patients are waiting?" She'd love to tell every last one of them that she'd been up half the night and was dead on her feet but they counted on her and she was still struggling to convince the village skeptics that she was every bit as much a "real" doctor as her father had been.

"Half a dozen by the look of things." Not too bad at all. "One is Mrs. Jenkins." The local hypochondriac who read medical encyclopedias with the enthusiasm other women reserved for a good Mills and Boon.

"Give me ten minutes and send the first one in."

"I'll put a cup of tea on your desk."

God bless grandmothers!

The ambulance arrived somewhere round about seven, just

as Alice was writing out a prescription for stomach powder. She'd let Gran take care of things. "There you are, Mr. Grace. Give it a couple of weeks and if it doesn't help, come back and we'll try something else."

Mr. Grace left with his prescription and Alice put her head round the door to call in the last patient. Someone she didn't recognize. Perhaps one of the evacuees? She was in her twenties, slight, and tired looking.

"Dr. Doyle? I'm June Groves, one of the teachers evacuated with the school children. I hate to bother you but I cut my hand a few days ago and it's gone a bit nasty."

A "bit nasty" wasn't the word. "How did this happen?" Alice frowned at the red, angry wound.

"I was in a hurry one morning. Trying to open one of those tins of dried milk. Like an ass, I used a kitchen knife and it slipped. I washed it off at the time but . . ."

Washing off hadn't been enough. "Do you have any kaolin poultice at home?"

She shook her head. "I've no idea; it's a billet. Mrs. Roundhill has a houseful of us and I hate to cause extra trouble."

So she was up at the vicarage. "Never mind." Alice filled a clean specimen jar with several spoonfuls scooped from a new tin. "Warm this up. An enamel plate balanced over a saucepan of boiling water is the easiest way. Put half on tonight and bandage it up and the other half in the morning. That should draw everything to a head. Come back after school tomorrow and I'll lance it." And hope it works. "If it gets painful overnight, take a couple of aspirin."

"Thanks." June Groves took the bottle. "What do I owe you?"

"We'll sort that out tomorrow."

Alice shut the door behind her, knowing she should have talked to the young teacher more, made sure her charges were settling in, or if they'd returned to London during the quiet months without bombing. She'd make up for that tomorrow when she came back.

"Alice." It was Gran. "The ambulance is here. They need to talk to you."

"Well, then," the surly faced driver asked. "Where is he?"

A very good question.

Four of them, including the rather good-looking driver's helper, crowded into the examining room. Gran looked bewildered—and worried. Sid Mosley, the older driver Alice had met before, shook his head. "Flown the coop has he? Can't have been as hurt as you thought, Doctor."

Obviously. "He certainly had me fooled. He could barely stand a few hours ago. I needed Sergeant Pendragon's help to get him in here." The discarded and bloody dressing tossed on the floor and the crumpled blankets were sure proof she had not dreamed the entire incident. How Mr. Smith had managed to stand and walk, much less disappear, was beyond her.

"He must have gone out through the house," Gran said. "We'd surely have noticed if he'd come through the surgery."

Odd that Susie, her spaniel, hadn't barked but . . . "I'm sorry you had a wasted journey." There'd no doubt be a round of laughs over this. She could just hear Sid Mosley: "You know that new lady doctor over in Brytewood? Called us out there because a chap was half dying and he got up and walked away before we arrived."

"How about a nice cup of tea before you head back?" Gran asked. Trust her to offer the eternal panacea.

Sitting at the kitchen table while the kettle boiled and Gran lined up cups and saucers, Alice had a chance to sum up the other man. Not as young as she'd thought at first—close to her own age probably. Not bad looking either. Not that she was about to start ogling the ambulance crews. Quiet, not quite meeting anyone's eyes, but when she did meet his gaze he returned her look, his calm brown eyes cautious and intelligent.

"I didn't catch your name," she said as Gran put plates and a custard tart on the table. More experiments with dried egg. Alice hoped it tasted better than the mayonnaise last week.

"Why that looks delicious, Mrs. Burrows," Sid Mosley said, all but smacking his lips together.

"It's Watson. Peter Watson," the younger one replied, as if Mosley hadn't spoken.

Alice took the hand he held out. His fingers were long, his grip strong, and when he smiled, his eyes crinkled at the corners. Nice smile too: even down to the little dimple in his chin. Definitely worth looking at twice.

"Watson?" Gran looked up from spooning tea into the pot. "There are a lot of Watsons around here." And two more since last night. "Any connection?" Gran asked as she reached for the boiling kettle.

"No, madam," Peter Watson replied. "My family is from Devon."

The lid met the pot with a loud ding. "Really? Where? I'm from near Dunstead. Came here when my daughter—Dr. Doyle's mother—married."

When Peter Watson smiled his face lit up. "I went to Blundells but my home was in Broad Clyst, down near Exeter."

Gran was positively beaming as she handed him a cup of tea. "The most beautiful county in England. What brought you up here? The war?"

"He's a conscie. A bloody CO!" Sid Mosley muttered.

The tick of the clock over the door was the only noise, apart for the dull sound of a clinker of burned coke shifting in the boiler. Even Gran stared before pouring another cup and handing it to Alice.

As if she wanted to eat and drink at the same table as a coward! Gran should be offering him a white feather not a cup of tea.

"Yes," Peter Watson replied, his voice tight but steady. "I'm a Conscientious Objector. I was a student in London when the war broke out, so I went before a review board in London. Did my nine months in Pentonville. When I got out, they looked at my records, saw I was a couple of years off qualifying as a vet, so decided I was fit to be an ambulance driver."

Alice couldn't miss the irony in his voice, or the tinge of defiance, daring her to pass judgment. Well, darn it, she already had. They should have found him fit to shovel sludge.

"The ambulance service always needs drivers." Trust Gran to break the silence. "And we'll need every one of you if the bombing gets worse. Alice was up in London last week . . ." She shook her head and reached for the custard tart.

They'd have eaten in silence if Gran hadn't kept the conversation going, asking the darn CO about his family. He had two half brothers, his father was dead, and his mother was still living, and, hopefully, suitably ashamed of her eldest son.

Sid Mosley answered Gran, even volunteered or comment or two of his own, but never, Alice noticed, did he say a word to his assistant.

"That was wonderful," Mosley said as he polished of the last few crumbs. "Very welcome before a drive back in the dark." After a fruitless trip out here, Alice added to herself. "But we'd best be back." Without a word or a nod to Peter Watson, he left.

Peter Watson thanked Gran and shook hands and darn it, she even invited him back to talk about Devon. He gave Alice a cautious look. How she felt was no doubt written all over her face. "Thank you." He didn't offer his hand but said quietly, "Don't judge me too harshly."

The cheek of him! Alice gave a curt nod. She'd judge him just however she pleased.

"Gran! How could you invite him to come back?" Alice was close to bursting by the time the ambulance pulled away. "He's a . . ."

"Young man a long way from home and lonely. And I'm an old woman who likes to talk about my home."

Point taken. Deep breath needed. "Gran, Simon is sitting in a prison camp in Germany. Alan is risking his life on the high seas, and you are inviting a coward to tea." She had to make her understand.

"Alice, my love—" Somehow, the soft Devon burr in her voice seemed more apparent that usual. "I lived though the other war and let me tell you, cowardice is usually the last reason for a man to be a CO. The cowards go along with the committed, not willing to stand up and be noticed. Whatever drove that young man to declare himself, it wasn't cowardice. It takes backbone to stand against the opinion of the entire country and be willing to go to gaol for your convictions. You should perhaps talk to him."

Never. "Yes, Gran. Where's Susie? She's usually right here when we're eating." And scrounging shamelessly.

Susie was in the lounge by the open French windows. Stiff and cooling. She'd been Alice's pet for twelve years, and as she picked up the surprisingly light body, she fought back tears.

"I'll help you bury her," Gran said. "Let's put her under the plum tree."

"I wonder what killed her?"

"She was an old dog," Gran replied.

Old but not sick. Maybe she should ask the not-quite-a-vet-conscie to look at Susie. No way in hell!

Chapter 2

Adlerroost, Bavaria

Bela Mestan had expected them sooner. It was several hours since the vampires' departure. This time, they brought a third man with them. He smelled of danger and other people's pain and her heart caught as she feared he was here to kill her.

They did not introduce him; she expected that. She did not even know their names. She'd been instructed to address them as Zuerst and Zweiten, first and second. Was this one Dritten?

"She will tell us what we want to know," Zuerst said to the nameless man. "Go ahead," he told her. "What happened?"

She shuddered and he smiled. They both knew the pain her connection with the vampires caused. It amused them.

"They left the plane," she replied.

"And?" Zweiten asked. "Where are they now?"

She took a deep breath to win a little time to choose her words. They would not be pleased at what happened. "Eiche, Bloch, and Weiss landed safely and dispersed to their contacts." The three men stared at her, waiting for the rest. "Schmidt was injured."

"Badly?" Zweiten asked.

"How is this possible?" Dritten snapped at the other two.

Bela took a brief pleasure in seeing them both quail under Dritten's fury. "He recovered," she said, keeping her voice level. "He fell onto a tree and the wood poisoned him. He was rescued and found blood."

Her own chilled at Zweiten's laugh. "So some peasant found him and suffered in the cause. Good!"

His amusement froze at a glance from Dritten. This man must be the one who drove the entire mission. "Did he kill?" he asked Bela.

"I felt him absorb the life," she replied. "He was weakened. Without it, he might have expired." Would that have mattered? There were three others and vampires were next to indestructible. If they avoided falling on trees.

"He regained his strength?" Dritten asked.

"He was restored and is moving."

"In what direction?"

Would they ever give her peace? She knew the answer to that. She was their tool. Her compliance the price of her family's lives. She looked Zuerst in the eye, knowing it unnerved him. "That I cannot tell. He is not with any of the others."

"Is he approaching them?"

"I will know when he gets near them."

That satisfied them. Until tomorrow, or maybe later that night, when they might visit her again. She was at their beck and call and they all recognized that.

Alone in her cell, Bela looked out of the window toward the mountains on the horizon. Maybe the vampires would prevail. They could fly, had no need to respect frontiers, and guns or weapons could not harm them permanently. But had the foul Germans taken on monsters who would destroy them in return? And how had mere mortals coerced vampires to their cause? Using the same threats they'd used on her? Except fairies were far more likely to succumb to the rigors of the camps than vampires. Maybe the vampires had joined of their own volition, to thrive on the carnage and the killing.

Bela could only guess. Just as she could only guess at the safety or otherwise of her kindred. Who knew if any survived? None possessed her strength of telepathic powers. Maybe they were all dead, but she dare not risk refusing to collaborate, just in case the Germans kept their word and did spare her family.

But the price came hard. Linking with vampires. The filthy undead. Foul was not the word for the dark creatures who'd ripped her skin with their fangs and sucked her blood as she shuddered and struggled under them.

Chapter 3

Paul Schmidt ran through the evening. He was kilometers away from his contact and his safe house, but he was alive. Thanks to the good Samaritan of a doctor and her dog. It hadn't been enough blood to repair all his loss, but killing the doctor seemed rather churlish after she'd saved him, and anyway, it would bring unwanted attention to the area. Orders were to sit tight, take up his job, and mingle unobtrusively with the pathetic inhabitants until he got the signal to move. Once he reached his rendezvous point that was.

At a guess, he was a good twenty-five or thirty kilometers away. Maybe more. It would help if he knew where he was, but painted-out signposts weren't much use, even to vampire sight.

On the off chance, he slipped into the unlighted and unlocked church at the edge of the village. The obscured name board gave no hint, but a stamp on the inside of a tattered hymnal clearly stated PROPERTY OF THE CHURCH OF ST. MICHAEL AND ALL ANGELS, BRYTEWOOD.

It was all he needed.

Back outside, in the shadow of the church wall, he pulled the emergency maps from the inside of his jacket lining. He'd been right, twenty, perhaps twenty-five kilometers, and he'd be in Guildford. A day late but his contact would be waiting. Had to be waiting.

The best way was across country, and, with a little bit of luck, he'd find a handy farm with convenient livestock along the way.

Dead cows wouldn't attract the same attention as a dead doctor.

Paul Schmidt set off across the churchyard, leaping over a couple of gravestones and a crumbling memorial before deciding conserving strength was a better idea. He did vault the gray flint wall and stepped into the middle of the narrow lane, looking up at the canopy of stars to gauge north.

And sensed a brother vampire nearby.

Who?

This was not, he was convinced, some foppish, effete English vampire. This was one of his Aryan brothers. The brain rhythm was strong and reassuringly familiar. He'd sensed the same in his homeland in the Hartz Mountains. Only one other vampire hailed from that part of Germany. Could it truly be Gerhardt Eiche, or as he no doubt posed himself: Gabriel Oak? What a foolish affectation, taking his name from a nineteenth-century English novel. Far more sensible to take a clearly anonymous name. A name matching countless numbers of the enemy.

But foolishness or not. If Eiche were nearby . . .

Paul stood and cast his vampires senses around. Just down the lane on the left was a pair of flint cottages, up on the right a large house, perhaps the vicarage? He sensed mortal life in all of them. The large house was pretty much teeming with it. Children, he suspected from the heartbeats.

What he was searching for was brain activity with a slow, voluntary heartbeat.

He found it behind the green painted door of the first cottage. The sort of bucolic residence featured on calendars and penny postcards and no doubt once inhabited by the sort of yokel represented by Eiche's namesake. Not a trace of light showed through the tightly drawn curtains, but as Paul raised his hand to the brass knocker, a voice asked, "Who's there?"

Female, mortal, old, and nervous. What had Oak been up to? "A friend of Mr. Oak. I need your help."

Eiche opened the door enough to peer out. A slash of light shot into the dark, highlighting the path and the bushes by the door. "What the hell?" he muttered, grabbing Schmidt's arm and yanking him inside, shutting the door behind him. "You've no business here. This is not your contact."

"I was injured on landing and went off course. I was on my way to my contact when I sensed you nearby."

"You're hurt! And your clothes! What happened?"

Glimpsing himself in the mirror over the mantelpiece, Schmidt understood the shock in the mortal's voice. He looked frightful; his shirt and jacket dark with blood, and his arm bare where the doctor had cut off his sleeve. "I was. We heal."

She was tall for a woman and slender. Her hair gray and her face lined. Her eyes bright with the zeal of a mortal on a world-altering mission. "You are a second one?" she asked.

Paul Schmidt nodded and held out his hand. "I am."

"Well, I never! Welcome. I am Jane Waite and honored to aid you and play my part in the victory." Her hand was thin, the skin papery with age, but her clasp was firmer than expected for a mortal of her advanced age.

"Paul Smith, at least in these islands. I apologize if I presume, but I need to rest and stay out of sight. Too many mortals have seen me already."

"You can't hole up here," Eiche said as the old biddy opened her mouth to speak. "This is my safe house."

And he was not about to share. Bastard! "I only need a rest. A few hours. And blood. I can make it across country if I get blood."

The old biddy stepped back. Seemed her commitment to the Third Reich didn't include her blood. "We certainly don't want you caught out in the open. I'll put the kettle on and find you a replacement shirt and jacket. Mr. Oak will explain about the blood."

She nipped out of the room at a speed impressive, given her age. Paul turned to Eiche. "Well then, Mr. Oak, would you kindly explain about the food supply."

Gerhardt grinned, showing his half-descended fangs, and let out a sharp harsh laugh. "My friend, there is a pig farm just outside the village. I had the benefit of it yesterday, be my guest tonight."

"I will. Should be fully dark soon. You'll direct me?"

Oak nodded. "By all means. And once you have rested, I will open the door for you."

Couldn't be more pointed. "I'll be gone before morning." High time he make his own contact after all.

Eiche inclined his head. Not a muscle in his face moved. So much for brotherly concern and native connection. Even for a vampire, his movements were slow and his mien threatening. How he planned on blending in with these yokels was beyond Paul. Not that that was any worry of his.

"Everything settled then?" Miss Waite bustled back, a dark shirt and knitted jacket over her left arm. "All sorted out? The kettle's on. I'll have us a nice cup of tea as soon as it boils and here"—she held out the clothes—"you can change in the downstairs cloakroom. I hope they fit. I knitted the cardigan myself. Try not to get any blood on the floor. I just polished it." She was like a damned caricature of an English spinster.

As he discarded his torn garments and washed in the minuscule hand basin, he couldn't help wonder how she came to be so committed to their side. Not that he really cared. She was good for a few hours' refuge and that was all that concerned him. That and how many cups of her infernal brew she expected him to digest. It was blood he craved. The dog had brought him back from semicomatose but he needed more. If Eiche hadn't been watching him like a hunter, he'd have had his teeth in her stringy neck. As it was . . .

Two weak cups of tea later, after full darkness fell, Miss Waite washed up the cups and pulled on a knitted jacket the color of sludge. "I'll leave you gentlemen to see to yourselves. There's a village whist drive to raise money for the French refugees."

Would be better to let them starve, but he supposed she had to blend in, as he would.

Once she was down the path, Eiche grudgingly led Schmidt over to Morgan's pig farm.

"Don't take more than you have to," the self-styled Gabriel Oak said. "I'll need to come here regularly. Better preserve the food supply."

Paul set his eyes on a fat sow. "Plenty of possible two-legged fodder in this village. I've seen a few myself."

"Yes," Eiche replied. "And weaken them too soon and some fool doctor will notice and start to investigate."

Since he already knew the local doctor's propensity to intervene and aid, and thanked Abel for it, Paul just grunted and laid a calming hand on the sow's neck, holding her upright as she leaned to one side, preparing to lie down. Getting his feet murky was quite enough; he was not about to kneel down in the mud and muck. He fastened his fangs into her ample neck and drew the warm blood. The old sow bled easily and amply. She wobbled a little on her fat little legs after he released her but otherwise seemed none the worst.

He hoped his contact had as ready and as convenient a supply laid on for him.

When he got there.

"I thank you," he said to Eiche as they returned to Miss Waite's abode. "Permit me a few hours and I will be gone."

He settled on the narrow bed in the little room overlooking the church. Already he felt restored. In a few hours he'd be himself again and ready for the long battle. What chance did these puny mortals have against a band of vampires?

"Eh! I forgot the dratted knave!" Howell Pendragon reluctantly played his last trump and lost the trick to Mother Longhurst. "Not bespelling those cards are you, Maggie?"

Margaret Longhurst shook her head, met his eyes, and shrugged. Her mouth was open to reply, and no doubt deny it, when her partner snapped. "Of course she isn't! Really! You'll be accusing her of cheating next. Men!"

Helen Burrows, Howell's partner, let out an exasperated hiss. "Honestly, Jane, he was just funning. It's your lead, get on with it."

Jane Waite led a low spade which Helen right away took with the king, and then took control of the game. Now Howell knew where all the spades were. His partner held them, and in five tricks won the game for them.

"No mention of bespelling now!" Jane said in a quiet, spiteful voice. Really, women could wear you down.

"That's because Helen can't do magic," Margaret replied in an obvious effort to dispel the tension with a bit of light-heartedness.

It didn't work. "Well, I'm off home! Need to see to my visitor. My nephew's come to recuperate," Jane said, standing and pushing the folding chair under the card table. Leaving it to be put away by someone else.

"Staying long is he?" Howell asked.

"Wounded?" Maggie added.

Jane nodded. "At Dunkirk. Come to visit and rest up for a few weeks."

"Bad injuries?" Howell asked.

She paused. "Exposure and pneumonia."

"Dear me, how dreadful for him," Maggie said, shaking head. "He'll need building up. You be sure to take his Army cards into Worleigh's store and you can register him for workman's rations."

Miss Waite gave a "humph." "I'll see about it later. I can't stand around here playing cards all evening. There's a war on, you know."

As if they hadn't noticed! Howell Pendragon shook his head. "Sharp and sour like acid drops," he muttered half to himself.

All three watched her go. "Proper misery guts if you ask me," Margaret Longhurst muttered. "Trust us to get stuck with Jane Waite. Why she picked Brytewood for her retirement, I'll never know."

"She's won't be going anywhere any time soon," he replied. More's the pity. It wasn't just because the woman was an outsider. He was one himself, so, come to that, was Helen but Jane Waite was a sour-tempered old biddy who spread ill will like dripping on toast.

"Her aura's gone even darker than usual," Helen said as she gathered up the discarded cards and shuffled them before sliding them back into the box.

"I noticed that, too," Mother Longhurst replied.

He shook his head. He often wondered about these two women. Maybe it was their oddness, the trace of Otherness that brought him back every fortnight to play whist with them. Maybe he imagined it. After all, who was he to talk? He longed to go up on Box Hill, race under the night sky, shift, and breathe a few gusts of dragonfire. But he didn't dare, not with the blackout. Hell, if the war went on much longer, he'd forget how to shift.

No point is worrying about that right now. "Well, ladies, may I get you each another cup of tea?"

"Yes, please, Howell," Helen replied. "Every cup we drink here saves the tea ration."

* * *

Jane Waite frowned as she strode home. Sometimes it was hard to put up with the insufferable English. So smug, so confident, and so ridiculously optimistic and cheerful. She let out a sharp dry laugh. Those inane smiles were due to fade and those stupid jokes shrivel on their lips under the might of the German Armed Forces. It wouldn't be long now, a few weeks or months at most. Her visitors were just a forerunner of the invasion.

But how different they were: Gordon Oak and that Smith creature. He was not what she'd call a chosen son of the Master Race. Arriving bedraggled, his clothes torn and blood-soaked. She'd done her bit for him. She just hoped he was gone and never coming back.

Her hopes were fulfilled. Eiche waited in the easy chair by the empty fireplace. Alone. Listening to Vera Lynn on the wireless.

"Our unexpected visitor is resting?" she asked. Just to be sure.

"Has rested and fed," he replied. "Mr. Paul Smith is off to make his own contact. He will not interfere with my plans for Brytewood."

She swore she saw fangs as he smiled. A cold tremor slid down her spine. She'd been trained to support a spy; having a vampire arrive had rather bowled her over. At least it was only one and he had no need of ration books. Workman's rations indeed! "I'll be making a cup of cocoa before bedtime— would you like one?"

He shook his head. "Thank you, but no. I will need to go out tonight."

"You have the spare key I gave you. And there's always the hidden one. Remember?"

"Under the pot of geraniums. Of course."

Leaving him to the wireless, she bustled in the kitchen.

Setting out the tray with cups for the morning, she tried to decide whether to have the egg she had left boiled or poached for breakfast, or whether to settle for toast. There was no shortage of bread after all.

As the cocoa came to the boil, she poured it into a mug and checked the back door was locked. She'd leave it unbolted. Gabriel could see to that when he got in.

Mug in hand, she poked her head round the sitting room door. He was engrossed in a Stanley Holloway monologue but he was gentleman enough to stand for her. "Mr. Oak, please be sure you shoot both bolts home when you get back in."

He gave her a little bow. So much nicer manners than these sloppy English. "I will. Good night, Miss Waite. Pleasant dreams."

He followed her to the bottom of the narrow stairs, and she felt him watch her as she climbed, mug in hand.

As she reached the top step, her foot slipped, her other leg wobbled, and she fell, head over heels backward to land in a crumpled heap. As she blinked and shook her head to clear it, she was vaguely aware of pain in the leg twisted impossibly under her and a burning in her arm. She must have spilled the cocoa. And she'd made it with real milk, too. Not the powdered sort. What a waste.

Eiche stepped close and bent over her. Her dazed eyes met his. Perfect. He'd been half afraid he'd killed her and that would have put a crimp in things but . . . "My Dear Miss Waite. You are injured. I must call the doctor."

If Jane Waite had been less dazed, she'd have noticed he knew the number, reciting it precisely to the operator.

"Doctor," he said after a few minutes. "I'm calling from Pear Tree Cottage. Miss Waite's house. I'm afraid Miss Waite has met with an accident."

* * *

Leaving Brytewood behind, and hoping he never had to return, Paul Schmidt ran through the night. He could have flown but decided to conserve his strength. The past twenty-four hours had taught him the wisdom of thrift and prudence. The image of his map in mind, he set off cross country on a roughly western direction. He took care leaping fences and gates—another injury was not part of his plans—and in twenty minutes of fast running reached the outskirts of Guildford.

Without vampire sight he'd never have found his way in the blackout. But since he wasn't hampered like puny mortals, it only took him ten minutes or so of running through near-deserted streets to find his contact.

In a narrow terrace house in a street just two steps up from a slum. Eiche ended up in rustic comfort with a view of a Saxon church while he, Paul Schmidt, ended up in a shabby back street. Just his luck.

Still, he was here. He made his way up the cracked path and rapped on the painted door.

"Who is it?" a male voice asked.

"Paul. Uncle Bob wrote to say I was coming."

The door opened a chink. "How's Auntie Violet?"

"Her rheumatism is getting worse but otherwise she's in good spirits." Whoever thought up these codes needed their brains examined, but it worked. The door opened halfway and a face peered at him in the dark.

"I was expecting you to arrive last night."

"So was I. Circumstances delayed me."

"Come on in then."

The door opened wide. Schmidt stepped in just as a voice down the street called, "Douse that light! Douse that light!"

"Crikey!" his contact muttered, pulling Paul inside and slamming the door shut. "Bloody air raid wardens. Think they run the flipping country. Come into the lounge and have a seat." He held out his hand. "I'm Stephen Thomas and honored to be part of the fight."

In the light of the room Paul got a good look at his contact and current host. He was as different from spinsterly Miss Waite as was possible given they were both mortals. Stephen Thomas was in his mid-twenties, tall, blonde with deep blue eyes and pale lashes and with an air about him that suggested back in Germany he'd be confined in a camp wearing a pink triangle. Not exactly the assistant Paul expected but . . .

"What delayed you?" Stephen asked.

Paul gave an expurgated version. No mention of the good samaritan doctor. Just his injury, hiding from daylight, finding Eiche and his contact, and then making his way across country.

"Rotten bad luck," Simon said. "Still, you're here now and they're expecting you to show up for work at the ambulance post the day after tomorrow. Will that be alright?"

"As a driver?"

"Night shift. Was easier than I thought. No one wants the night shifts and since one of the drivers was considerate enough to fall into the river and drown on his way back from the pub a couple of nights back, your arrival will be welcomed. Doubt anyone will question the dicey paperwork."

If they did they could meet an unfortunate end. Shocking things happened in wartime. "You live here alone?"

He shook his head. "No, my granny is upstairs. It's her house. She had a stroke last year and is bedridden. They were muttering about billeting evacuees here a while back, but your arrival should put paid to that."

And if it hadn't, regrettable things might happen to them. Still, seemed a snug enough base to operate from. He had a roof over his head, a good cover, and a job that would put him deep in the heart of the hurts and injuries and any time he hungered for fresh blood, there was a helpless old woman upstairs. "Does your grandmother know who you're working for?"

"Good God, no! She'd have a fit! She and my dear, departed grandfather were lifelong members of the Communist party."

High time the invasion got underway and these degenerates were disposed of. "Interesting," Paul replied with a smile. "Now, if you would be so good as to show me my resting quarters."

Chapter 4

"Is Miss Waite badly hurt?"

Alice looked up from her toast. "Could have been worse, Gran. Broken leg and wrist and a collection of colorful bruises. She was lucky it happened the night her nephew arrived. Alone, she'd have lain there until the milkman arrived this morning."

"Did you meet this nephew?"

Alice paused, toast halfway to her mouth. What exactly was Gran fishing for? "Of course. He was the one who called me after the accident and went with her in the ambulance."

She raised a gray eyebrow and Alice knew it wasn't over yet. "Arrived suddenly, didn't he? She never mentioned he was coming until he got here. Never heard her talk about him, or any family for that matter, in all the years she's been here. She sat at the same whist table as Howell and Maggie and me the other night and didn't say a word about his visit until she was leaving. Odd if you ask me."

Please! She had more to do than cope with village gossip. "Gran, is it really any of our business?"

"Maybe, maybe not, but I can't help wonder. Especially after what Mother Longhurst said."

The long pause demanded a response. A stronger woman

would have nodded and finished her toast. Alice caved. "What did the old witch say?"

"Don't mock her, Alice. She knows what she knows and your father wasn't too hidebound by science and qualifications to discount her lore." Rebuke noted. No sense in pointing out medical science had progressed a long way since the turn of the century when her father had trained at Barts. In Alice's silence, Gran went on. "She mentioned last night that Jane Waite's aura had blackened and it had. It's always been murky. Something sad in her past we always suspected but now it's darkened. She's been in contact with evil or bad trouble and odd it should so happen hours after her visitor arrives and just a short time before she has a serious fall."

Only true love and caring for her grandmother's feelings kept Alice's laughter contained. Gran believed this nonsense and so, it seemed, did half the village. "And talking about Miss Waite, they'll want her out of hospital as soon as possible. I'll ask Gloria to drop by and see what they'll need for her convalescence."

"You've got a good backup in Gloria Prewitt," Gran said, seeming to change the subject. "She's overworked, though, just as you are."

And would be even more so if she didn't get a move on. Alice drank down the last of her tea. "We've asked for help, even a part-time first aid worker would be a godsend." Especially with all the evacuees and now having to treat the workers up at the government plant on the heath.

Alice carried her dishes to the sink and kissed her grandmother. "I'll be back for lunch, all being well. I need to see how things are at the Watsons on top of all my other house calls. Bye, love."

Helen Burrows shook her head at Alice's departing form. The girl had a good heart but oh, if only she'd admit the truth right under her nose. Pixie blood flowed in her skeptical veins. Maybe someday soon she'd acknowledge what was hers by right.

No time to sigh and wish for "if only." Helen turned to the sink. She'd get the breakfast things done so when Doris came in, she could start on the floor. The young woman was a godsend. Evacuated to Brytewood with her infant, she soon tired of village gossip and the moans and complaints of the other evacuee mums and asked Alice if she knew anyone who needed a charlady. After Alice snagged her for once a week, Doris had no trouble finding other work in the village. She even confided to Helen one day that she was saving up all she could and planned on opening a "nice, little" tea shop after the war was over.

Meanwhile she "did" for the echelons of Brytewood who'd lost their housemaids and charladies to the war effort. Helen knew Doris wouldn't last. In a few months her toddler son would be old enough for a day nursery and no doubt Doris would be off for a better paid job up at the munitions camp on the heath or in one of the factories in Dorking or Leatherhead. But meanwhile, she came in every Friday morning and "did" for them.

"You know, mum," Doris said, as she paused for a morning cup of tea between vacuuming and starting on the bathroom. "Could you use me this afternoon? I could do out the office and surgery if you like."

"Aren't you going to Miss Waite's?" It was Doris's usual Friday afternoon.

"Should be, but I stopped there on my way up here this morning. Thought I'd ask if I could pick up anything for Miss Waite, seeing as she's in a bad way, and that nephew or whatever he is, rum lot he is, too, he said no need to come. He didn't need me and wasn't sure they'd need me next week. In fact he told me not to come back again until they called."

She paused to bite a corner off a chocolate digestive biscuit. "As good as fired me he did. Well, I told him I'd have

a word with Miss Waite when she got home. Seeing as she'd
hired me to do for her, it was her who'd tell me when I wasn't
needed. Proper shirty, he got. Nasty he was. I tell you, Mrs.
Burrows, if I didn't need the money, and didn't care to let
Miss Waite down, I'd never go back."

"Don't worry about it, Doris," Helen replied. "Men can
be abrupt. We can certainly use you here this afternoon. And
once the word gets out around the village that you have a free
afternoon, I don't doubt you'll be drowning under offers. I
know Mrs. Roundhill would grab you in a flash. She's up to
her ears with all those evacuees."

Doris finished her biscuit—one of the last of a prewar
cache Helen always offered her as a little luxury to supplement her modest wage. "Well, best get finished, and thanks
for mentioning Mrs. Roundhill. I'll stop off at the vicarage on
my way home. See what we can work out. Hope she won't
mind me bringing Joey."

"What would one more child be in that big house?"

Doris nodded. "Bet he'd like the company, too. He really
needs to be with other children. He spends all his days in a
playpen in other people's houses."

Helen drank her own tea down. Here she was wanting to
keep Doris as long as possible, when Doris had to think of
Joey first. "He's such a good boy." No lie. He really was a
most contented child, given he'd been whisked from his home.
Seemed babies settled more readily than some school-age
children. "How about I take him with me down to the village?
I need to pick up a few things in the shops."

"Fresh air would be good for him, wouldn't it? Sure it's
no bother?"

"Not a bit."

Sid Mosley's slap on the shoulder was just hard enough not
to be friendly. "Well then, boyo, sad times are upon us, seems

we have to lose you!" Peter might have suspected a mere trace of sincerity if Sid Mosley hadn't been grinning from ear to ear. After all, without him there, who'd clean the damn lavatories?

"Really?" He tried to sound bored. Wasn't as if he had any say in where he got sent.

"Yes, sonny boy conscie, really." Sid bent in so close Peter could have counted his nose hairs—if he'd cared to. "Got you a transfer we have. Don't need you here anymore. You're off on Monday morning to a new posting and they have the benefit of your yellow skin."

Peter stood. Sooner or later he'd learn where. He was not giving bloody Sid Mosley the satisfaction of asking. "Fine with me. Want me to finish my shift on Saturday?"

"Bloody fucking hell we do, don't we, Mike?"

Mike, the other driver sitting in the canteen, nodded. "Yeah, Sid." Mike wasn't too bad a sort, and if it weren't for Sid Mosley's constant baiting, he might just have left Peter alone.

"Fair enough then," Peter replied as he picked up his empty mug and plate. "I'll take my day off tomorrow." He couldn't but wonder if the next posting would be any better. Would be nice to actually use some of his training. He was probably being sent to dig potatoes somewhere.

Gerhardt Eiche swore slowly and thoroughly. No one, not a single person among his trainers and controllers, had ever mentioned the incessant traffic and activity in an English village. No fewer than six women of varying ages had trooped up the garden path and rung the bell to inquire after Jane Waite's health and, he suspected, to get an eyeful of yours truly. It had started with the damn servant. He'd put her off fast enough, but the baskets of apples and bowls of nuts, to say nothing of a knitted bed jacket, were impossible to reject without causing unwelcome gossip and comment.

If these damn thoughtful bitches came around like this

after Miss Waite got home he had no idea how he was going to cope.

Remote and rural were definitely not the same as quiet and undisturbed. He was just thankful the gardener had been called up or he'd be wanting access to the potting shed where Gerhardt had set up his radio until he found a safer place to hide it.

In the end, he left the house and decided to survey the village in daylight. It was going to be his little empire after the invasion. Might as well stake out his chosen abode and his possible servants: the favored few he would elect for transformation.

Did those foolish mortals tucked in their hideaway in the Black Forest really believe that vampires would work for them, whatever the threats and blusterings?

This was going to be an interesting few months.

He didn't take long to select his future residence: The large, Georgian rectory across from the church. It was shabby, but he'd soon have his minions take care of that. After he'd disposed of the current inhabitants, of course. The old Saxon church with its tower and muffled bells he'd leave for the peasants if they desired. He had no use for it, and they'd need some consolation in their short lives.

Strolling down toward the center of the village he had to admit he'd been given a very pleasant center of operations. A narrow stream ran beside the lane, a tributary of the Mole, the river that formed a gap in the Downs, as if designed to facilitate the coming invasion. To the east, the Downs rolled toward Box Hill—a place he had every intention of exploring as soon as it suited him. Might as well report to his petty masters about the supposed, and no doubt pathetic, defenses. To the west, and out of sight beyond the woods where Schmidt claimed to have been injured, was a broad heath and woods and the establishment that supposedly merited his investigation.

All in good time.

For now, he stood a few meters from the crossroads in the village center and surveyed.

Until a car had the effrontery to hoot at him to get out of the road. His error, yes, standing astride the white line, but how in heaven did anyone run a motor car if petrol was rationed?

Black market, he assumed.

Something else he need to investigate.

After jumping out of the way, in a manner he hoped was a reasonable imitation of a scared mortal, Gerhard turned and all but tripped over a baby pushchair.

He just managed to rein in the snarl as he met the mother's eyes. It was the servant who'd thumped on his door earlier.

She had short, curly dark hair, bright brown eyes, and skin that resembled rich cream. Just imagining the blood coursing through her veins had his gums tingling. He smiled, careful to keep his lips together. No point in terrifying mortals until it suited his purpose. "Sorry, wasn't looking where I was going."

"Good thing I was," she replied.

Eiche reminded himself she was no doubt disgruntled at being sacked and probably saw him as a human equal. He was going to have to get used to this. At least for now. "Yes, excuse me."

She had a child. He intended to keep all the children safe. They were his future servants after all. "The car coming so fast surprised me."

"That was Dr. Doyle. She's always in a hurry. She's probably been up to the Watsons' farm to check on the new twins."

Of course. The woman who'd arrived last night to attend to Miss Waite. There couldn't be two in a village this size. "You know the doctor well?"

"Of course! Everyone does. I clean for her."

"As you do for my aunt. I was perhaps curt this morning."

She gave a little shrug. "Never mind. I just wanted to check and see what Miss Waite needed."

"We might need your services later." Taking a little blood

wouldn't do her permanent harm and young blood was so much richer than old.

"I don't know if I can now. I just promised the vicarage an extra day." Without a word of apology or regret she marched on, pushing the carriage ahead of her.

Impudent peasant! If there were many more around like her, it was going to take some getting used to. He looked about him. A knot of women stood in front of the post office and an elderly but upright man walked out of the bank across the street. Between Miss Waite and the servant Doris, he'd had enough of mortal women for a while. He crossed the road toward the bank.

The man watched Eiche approach.

Eiche met his eyes and offered a slight smile.

"Afternoon," the man said. "You're new to Brytewood. Working up at the plant, are you?"

No, but any information about that establishment would keep his so-called masters happy. "Actually no. I'm visiting my aunt, Miss Waite."

"On leave are you?"

Impudent but not unexpected. "I was badly injured after Dunkirk. Took them a while to put me back together. I need a few more weeks before I have to report back." Long enough to serve his purposes anyway.

"Rotten luck." The man nodded as he offered his hand. "I'm Sergeant Pendragon. With the Home Guard. Any time you want to get back in the traces, we'd be honored to have you drill with us."

Might come in handy if he knew the exact extent of the local toy soldiers. "I'd be the one honored." His hand closed around Pendragon's and was met with almost equal strength. Odd. Impossible.

"What regiment were you with?"

Good thing he'd been well schooled. "The Hampshires." Nice losses they'd taken, too.

The old man let go of his hand and was eyeing him keenly. "Welcome to Brytewood. Things here aren't as they were before the war but we do our best for our visitors. You missed the whist drive yesterday afternoon. We have one every second Wednesday. But you might like to come along to the ARP planning meetings. We're always looking for more volunteers."

Any effort he put into Air Raid Precautions would be to direct the bombers to targets. "Let me think about it. I'd be delighted to help, but I'm afraid my aunt may need a lot of care when she gets back."

"Of course, of course." The old dodderer nodded and smiled. "I heard about her fall. Sad, but how fortunate you were there to give aid."

Fortunate indeed, Eiche agreed, and wished the aged yokel good-bye.

Now, should he try the post office, the butcher, the general store, or the baker? He had his own fake ration book in his jacket pocket and already knew Miss Waite was registered at the village store. Might as well see if his masters were right about food shortages.

Chapter 5

"Good heavens." Alice looked up from reading the afternoon mail. "Gran, you're not going to believe this. We're getting a first aid assistant." She went on, reading the typewritten page. "'In view of your increased workload with the influx of evacuees and the government security installation at Brytewood Heath, we are appointing an assistant with some medical training to oversee first aid at the installation and supplement civilian services in the Brytewood area.'

"Gran, it's a godsend. Gloria is stretched thin with the extra schoolchildren, and we're all doing double duty since Rob Abbot in Leatherhead was called up."

Her grandmother refilled her cup as Alice read on. "'It will be the responsibility of your local evacuee committee to find convenient accommodation for him, and to provide a bicycle.'"

"Why not see about billeting him with Howell Pendragon? He's alone in that cottage, too old to cope with children but I think he really misses his son. A young man would lift his spirits a bit."

"We don't know much about him, or even for that matter if he's young. I wonder what training he has, probably three weeks when he was thirteen in the Junior Red Cross." She looked back at the letter. "'Mr. Peter Watson will be arriving in Brytewood Sunday afternoon to assume duties 9 AM Monday morning . . .'"

She broke off at recognition of the name. Nonsense! Had to be a coincidence. Peter and Watson were common enough names. Heck, the village was full of Watsons. Had to be a cousin or someone posted near home.

"Peter Watson?" Gran asked, setting the topped-off cup in front of Alice. "Wasn't that the name of that young ambulance driver?"

Gran darn well knew it was. There was nothing wrong with her memory. "The CO. Yes."

"Didn't he say he'd started training as a vet?"

She couldn't hold back the laugh. "That will make him popular with the farmers." She stopped herself, smiling at the thought. She did not want to work with that coward.

Seemed Gran could read her thoughts. "You asked for help, Alice. You've been given it. Don't look a gift horse in the mouth. If it is the same man, he's intelligent and energetic and will be so relieved not to be working under that snirpy Sid Mosley he'll bend over backwards to oblige."

Gran had a point. "But he's a CO!"

"Yes, dear, and you're half Pixie—doesn't stop you doing a good job taking care of the sick of the parish."

Why, in the name of reason, was Gran forever harping on about that? Alice had long ago chosen science, reason, and the provable as her view on reality; Gran's talk of magic and power and auras just didn't add up to anything real or logical.

"Don't shake your head at me, my girl. Time will come you'll need what's tamped down inside you. You mark my words!"

"Yes, Gran." Alice stood and drank down the last of her tea. "And time has come for me to get to the surgery and take care of the piles, nits, and aches and pains of the parish." Feeling oddly guilty, not that she had any reason to, Alice crossed the kitchen and kissed her grandmother. "Shouldn't be too many this evening. They're showing *The Prisoner of Zenda* in the parish hall. Only the achiest and the sorest will forgo Ronald Colman for the tattered magazines in my waiting room."

The prospect of a closely packed crowd in a darkened room was too filled with opportunities to ignore. Gerhardt Eiche left Jane Waite's bedside in callous haste—she was mere mortal and eventually disposable after all—and ignoring the option of a crowded bus, set off cross country at vampire pace and arrived in Brytewood in plenty of time to detour to the wretched pig farm. The run had sapped his energy and he intended to be in prime fettle for the evening. First the parish village entertainment, then he intended a run in the opposite direction, toward Guildford, to sniff out Schmidt.

It was time the vamps set their own path.

But first a visit to the pigsties.

The sow squealed as Eiche dug his fangs into the fleshy neck. Straddling her to hold her still, he clamped her snout shut. She struggled and fought but soon collapsed in the mud as he sated his hunger. Standing, he looked in irritation at his now-soiled clothes. Damn! And with Jane Waite incapacitated and unable to see to his laundry. Maybe he'd call that servant back to take care of these matters or find some washerwoman to see to things.

That could wait.

"Hey! What you doing here?"

Eiche turned.

A short, shabby little mortal stood at the wall of the sty, righteous indignation oozing over his ruddy face.

Not what he'd planned on. At least not yet, but . . .

"Did you hear me?" the little pip-squeak demanded.

Eiche stood and bared his fangs.

The shock and horror in the man's face was quite satisfying. Eiche watched the peasant goggle and splutter for a few seconds, then leapt the wall toward him. The shriek of horror died in an instant as Eiche's fangs pierced his neck. He held tight, grasping the man's shoulders as he sucked. Little muffled gasps soon gave way to silence as the man fainted. Eiche held on, drinking fast. This was what he'd missed since his arrival—the last he'd fed from a sentient creature was that Fairy in the castle. She'd struggled and fought and sweetened the feed, but this creature's abject and petrified terror was even better.

The peasant was dead before Eiche realized. Unfortunate. Remembering the poster by the village hall exhorting the populace to "Waste Not, Want Not," Eiche drained him and left his limp and used-up body lying in the mud.

A fitting resting place for such a menial creature.

Eiche stood up, threw back his head, and howled at the moon before racing toward his safe house.

Fifteen minutes later he'd washed, changed into the interesting wardrobe supplied by Jane Waite, closed the door of the cottage behind him, and headed for the village entertainment.

Alice had guessed right. Only a few regular patients and a couple of perennial hypochondriacs skipped the adventure in Ruritania for her waiting room. She was writing out a prescription for stomach powder for old Mr. Harper when Gran put her head around the door.

"Sorry to interrupt dear, but when you finish, PC Parlett wants a word with you. He said it was urgent."

Alan Parlett had played cricket with her brothers on the village team. The ashen-faced policeman waiting in the front hall had little in common with the bright-eyed young man who'd bowled out the Bookham team captain back in the summer of 1939. A lifetime ago.

"What can I do for you, Constable?"

"Sergeant's compliments, Dr. Doyle, but would you please come up to Morgan's Farm? There's been an accident."

Alice grabbed her bag and asked Gran to warn the remaining

two patients it might be some time before she returned. With luck they'd leave and come back tomorrow. Taking her keys off the hall table, she led PC Parlett out of the front door.

He'd ridden his bicycle. "Why not toss it in the back and I'll drive you down there?"

"Righto!" he replied, settling his long legs into the passenger seat.

"What happened?" she asked as she headed toward the outskirts of the village and beyond.

"Don't rightly know. Mrs. Morgan called us. Fred had gone out as he'd heard a noise and then a little while later she heard a howl. Went out to investigate and found him lying in one of the pigsties. Sergeant thinks it might have been a heart attack. Fred Morgan was getting on, after all."

But otherwise hale and healthy. The only things she'd seen him for were chilblains every winter. "He's definitely dead then?"

"Not a doubt. I saw him."

So it was just a routine death certificate. They'd need to call in one of the doctors from Leatherhead since she hadn't seen Fred Morgan since the previous winter. "And poor old Muriel found him. Must have given her a nasty shock." No doubt she'd be needing professional services more than poor old Fred.

"Right upset she was on the phone. Can't blame her. Here she was all worried about her sister and the bombing in London and it's the old man cops it."

But he wasn't that old. Not compared to her gran, old Mother Longhurst, or Sergeant Pendragon. Heavens, Sir James was close to eighty. Fred Morgan wasn't much over fifty. Not that death was any respecter of age or youth.

They'd carried him into the farmhouse and now he lay stretched out on a sheet on the kitchen table. Muriel was sitting in the dim parlor, quietly sobbing with another woman.

Sergeant Jones gave Alice a worried nod. "Thought you'd best have a look at him, Doctor," he said. "Looks like just a heart attack or something, but Mrs. Morgan is certain she heard a loud scream. That was what brought her out to look for him."

He'd hardly have been screaming that loud if he was doubled over with a heart attack. "I'll have a look. Then see Mrs. Morgan."

Poor Fred Morgan showed no blueness around the mouth or fingertips, and his body seemed lighter and more shriveled than she remembered. But it had been months. She'd run into him a few times in the village but . . . something seemed wrong.

Picking up one of his hands, the fingers seemed just skin and bone. Certainly not the hands of a man who'd labored for pretty much all of his life. She couldn't throw off the sense of unease. "I think we need to call the coroner."

Sergeant Jones nodded. "I thought so, too. Something just not right about him. Don't rightly know how to tell poor Muriel." He looked Alice in the eye.

"I'll talk to her."

Alice regretted her hasty offer three minutes after she met Muriel Morgan's red-rimmed eyes.

"Doctor," the widow began, "what happened to my Fred?"

"Now, now Muriel," the woman with her said. "Don't get yourself upset."

Alice bit back the comment that a woman unexpectedly and suddenly widowed was entitled to be a bit upset. "Mrs. Morgan," she said, pulling up a chair and sitting next to her, "I've been talking to Sergeant Jones and we both want to call in the coroner."

"Why?" There was belligerence and fear in the swollen eyes.

"We're not sure of the cause of death. We'll need another opinion anyway since Mr. Morgan wasn't under my care."

"I thought he had a heart attack." She looked up at the other woman. "Didn't you say he had, Wendy?"

"I said it looked like one, Muriel."

Heaven save her from amateur diagnoses.

"Wasn't it then, Doctor?" Muriel Morgan asked. "Why the coroner? That means they're going to cut him up, doesn't it?"

"That depends." Scant comfort but . . .

"Doctor, I don't want him cut up. He'd hate that!" She broke down sobbing and Alice, loathing this part of the job like poison, handed over her own laundered handkerchief.

Muriel sobbed into it while Wendy muttered, "There, there, Muriel," and treated Alice to a definite scowl. "Is that really necessary?"

"We believe so."

Muriel looked up, her eyes redder than ever, and sniffed. "Your father would have known a heart attack when he saw one. If he were here . . ."

She refused to be hurt by the slight on her professional prowess. "I wish he were here, too, Mrs. Morgan. I can't sign the death certificate unless I'm completely certain. Your husband deserves better than that."

She nodded, her eyes blank with grief and shock. "I just know he'd hate to be cut up."

The poor man was long past being distressed by that. "I know the thought's upsetting, but once it's over and settled, it will be worth it." She hoped.

"I suppose the police will pester Muriel with more questions."

The woman was sharp-tongued. "No more than they feel necessary. I'm Dr. Doyle. I apologize for not introducing myself. I forget people outside Brytewood don't know me." She offered her had, which the woman took with an air of reluctance.

"I'm Wendy, I was helping Muriel with the pickles. We was busy in the kitchen when Fred went out."

"She's my sister. Visiting from London. I told her to come down here and get away from all those bombs," Muriel added.

"Welcome to Brytewood and I'm sorry this happened, but I am glad Mrs. Morgan has company. Can you stay a few days?"

"I was planning on it. My house in Clapham got a direct hit last week."

She was entitled to be a trifle acerbic. "How terrible for you." And thousands of others. "And now this on top of it, but I'm really glad Mrs. Morgan has company for a while. This will take a few days." Maybe longer given everyone was short-staffed.

"You've got more questions, I suppose."

"I'm afraid so." Wendy seemed to mellow a little so Alice pressed on. "What happened? You were both in the house?"

She nodded. "Bottling up a couple of recipes of piccalilli. We had plenty of vegetables and thought it might help brighten up a few meals now that rationing has started. We were all in the kitchen when Fred said he'd heard a noise outside. We've been bothered by a fox around the henhouse the last few nights so he went out to look."

"He took his gun?"

Wendy shook her head. "No, just a light. Said it would scare the blighter off."

Alice nodded, suspecting Farmer Morgan had used a saltier expression. "Was he out there long?"

"Long enough for us to fill seven or eight jars. First off we heard him shout, thought he was scaring off the fox. He didn't come back in, then we heard this awful scream, more like a howl than anything else. We both ran out and found him in Esmerelda's sty." It never ceased to amaze Alice the names given animals destined to be slaughtered. "The old sow was shivering in a corner, scared to bits to see her master drop dead in front of her."

"So he screamed before he died?"

"It wasn't just a scream," Muriel Morgan piped in. "It was

unearthly, like a sound from a nightmare." Even allowing the widow's grief, the description sent a shiver down Alice's back. "Was he in pain, d'you think, Doctor?"

Certainly sounded like it. "That's what the postmortem will establish."

Declining a belatedly offered cup of tea, Alice went back to the kitchen. Seemed somehow very sad that poor Fred Morgan was laid out on the very table where he'd no doubt tucked into Muriel's generous cooking.

"What d'you think, Doctor?" Sergeant Jones asked. "Call for them to come get him in the morning?"

They were asking her, and she had no idea. Brytewood residents tended to die peacefully in their beds, not like this.

"Think we should call the detectives in from Leather-head?" PC Parlett suggested.

The sergeant shook his head. "Not unless the doctor thinks so."

"Do we have any reason to suspect foul play?"

Both shook their heads. Alice tamped down the feeling of unease. "Let's see what the coroner has to say."

Gran was waiting when she finally got home. "You'll be needing a nice cup of cocoa. Have a seat, Alice, and I'll warm up the milk."

Alice hung up her coat, kicked off her shoes, and gladly accepted a couple of Osbourne biscuits and a mug of cocoa, which came, she noticed at the first sip, with a generous tot of rum. "Trying to knock me out, Gran?"

"No, love, but you looked so peaky when you came in, I decided you needed a little warm-up. Was it bad?"

Good question. "No death is easy, is it? But this was . . ." How the heck could she describe it? Gran waited as Alice took another drink and let her mind sort out the possible adjectives to describe the odd atmosphere up at Morgan farm. "It was . . . odd." Inadequate but . . .

"How did he die?"

"That was what was strange. We're calling in the coroner. Mrs. Morgan was upset about it, but I couldn't in all conscience sign the death certificate." She bit on one of the Osbourne biscuits and chewed, then dunked the other half and let it melt in her mouth. "Something wasn't right, Gran." She explained all she'd seen up at the farm and Mrs. Morgan's account of finding him. "It just seems wrong."

She half-expected another lecture about using her innate gifts but instead, Gran nodded. "Trust your instincts, Alice. They won't let you down. After all, it's not the first strange thing in the village this week."

"You mean the disappearing man?" Of course she did. "They could hardly be connected." Could they?

"Everything is connected, Alice. We can't always see how. Just remember to trust your instincts, and things turn out."

Maybe, but if she followed her instincts about her new assistant, she'd hand him the white feather.

Chapter 6

"One of them has killed," Bela told them when they returned in the early morning. They were not pleased. The anger came off them as cold waves despite their calm faces.

"Which one?" Zuerst asked.

"Eiche."

"You are certain of this?" Zweiten snapped.

"I sensed it. You told me to stay alert to them whenever I was awake."

"But you are sure he killed?"

She nodded at Zuerst. How many times did she have to speak to be believed? "He was feeding. At first it was an animal, a creature without a mind or thought, but then he was connected to a human. I felt his terror. I felt the life leave him." She would not add she also felt the victim's strength. Eiche must have absorbed some of it, but the rest flowed into her. After the shock and the pain of the death, she was stronger and *that* her captors would never know. If every time the vampires killed she strengthened; maybe one day she could cross the iron barriers that kept her imprisoned.

"Your attention, fräulein!"

She jumped at Zuerst's command. "Apologies. I am tired."

"You did not sleep?"

"It is hard to rest when they do not." Not completely true, but she did know when they were moving. And now, killing.

"Then rest while you can," Zweiten said. "In a few weeks you will need all your talents."

In a few weeks she hoped to be gone from here. Although where she could go that the dreaded Nazis would not find her was still an unanswered question.

But even a lone Fairy, once freed, was a force to be reckoned with.

Chapter 7

Peter Watson looked out of the window at the passing countryside and wondered what the heck he was doing riding a bus. If he had the sense he was born with he'd be spending his day off packing his few belongings or waiting for the pubs to open, but instead, after demanding the day off, he'd seen the bus waiting at the corner was going to Leatherhead via Brytewood. A roundabout route if ever there was one, and he'd taken it as sign from heaven and jumped on as it was moving off.

Now he had a good twenty minutes to consider the impulse.

He could see about a billet in Brytewood. He didn't have the billeting officer's name or phone number but how hard could it be to find out in a village?

While he was there, he might as well ask about work hours and duties. Even if it did entail meeting the scornful eyes of the downright beautiful doctor. Dash it all! Might as well admit he fancied her—snubs, sneering, and all. He had to be bonkers. And why on earth had he practically begged her not to judge him? Did it matter what she thought about him?

For some impossible-to-fathom reason, yes.

He spent the rest of the ride trying to sort that one out.

He got off the bus in the center of the village. Right across from the post office and general store and a few yards from the Pig and Whistle. Now that he was actually here, his impulse seemed stupid. Why meet trouble halfway? Monday would have been quite soon enough. But he was here and might as well look around.

He hadn't taken more than three steps from the bus stop when the grandmother, the woman from Devon, met his eyes with a broad smile. "You've come early. We were expecting you Monday."

"I had a day off due me and decided to have a look around."

"Wonderful!" She almost convinced him it was. "Do you have anywhere special to go then?"

"Just thought I'd have a look around and perhaps see the billeting officer." It struck him her eyes were just like the doctor's: a deep, clear blue.

"That's taken care of. You'll be staying with Sergeant Pendragon. His son's off in the Army and he'll be glad of the company."

That's what she thought! Blimey, was he getting back into the same situation? "Are you sure?" He hated sounding diffident but the last thing he wanted was an unwilling host. "Is he aware I'm a CO?"

"Of course. I told him." She patted his hand, and he couldn't miss how thin and delicate her skin was. She had to be older than she looked. "He understands you're fighting the war in your own way."

He'd never had another person put it quite like that. "I hope I'll be of use here. I've only the sketchiest idea of my assignment."

He wondered if the doctor laughed like her grandmother. "Oh, my love! Just you wait. You'll be stretched thin and overworked before the week is out." The prospect obviously delighted her. "You can't imagine how much we need you. When Alice's father ran the practice he had an assistant. Alice is now doing the work of two and has the evacuees in addition to the villagers and she's seeing the workers up at the government installation on the heath. Gloria—that's the district nurse—does more than her share and desperately needs another pair of hands." She gave him another pat. On his sleeve this time. "Trust me, you're going to be welcomed with open arms."

That he doubted. Open snarl from the good doctor was more likely. Pity that. He fancied she'd look smashing if she smiled.

". . . don't you think?"

He had been off in the outer reaches. "Beg your pardon, I was looking at the church. Interesting. Saxon is it?"

"Yes, or was until the Victorians started their improvements." She gave him an intent look. "Interested in ecclesiastical architecture?"

Was that a note of amusement or a tinge of sarcasm? "No more than the next person. Just something about a church and a duck pond and a village green reminds me of home."

"Life's different here, though," she replied, almost as if talking to herself. "Maybe it's the proximity to London. Maybe they are just all so English." She shook her head and gave a wry smile. "You'll understand, coming from the West Country."

She wasn't potty, that he was certain of. In fact, the way she spoke reminded him of his own grandmother. She'd died a few months before his father but he remembered her tales. "You mean the wild hunt? Pixies?"

She laughed. "The wild hunt is coming straight from Germany and falling from the skies these days. And as for the Good Folk, what does a young man know of them?"

"I know what my grandmother told me."

"And you believed her?"

"I was seven at the time." He believed everything back then. Even that grown-ups were invincible and indestructible.

"Don't tell Dr. Doyle you believe in the Good Folk." She gave a dry chuckle. "She'll think you as barmy as her old Gran."

It was hardly likely he'd end up discussing Devon folklore with the doctor. He'd be lucky to exchange two civil sentences.

"Don't you worry too much about Alice," she went on. Crikey, could she read his mind? "She's a good girl at heart and as good a doctor as her father was."

And she couldn't stand his guts.

Sergeant Pendragon proved as welcoming as Mrs. Burrows claimed. After the woman deposited Peter at the Pendragon front door and skeedadled off as fast as she could, even to the point of refusing a cup of tea, Peter and Howell Pendragon faced each other over the scrubbed kitchen table.

"Care for a bite of lunch?"

"No, thanks. Just tea would be splendid."

The old man shook his head. "Tell the truth, young man. Yer hungry, right? Never say 'no' to a chance to eat. I learned that in the last war."

Mention of the last war had to be a preamble to talk of the current one. "I hate to put you to the trouble."

"Think of it as giving me company. It's good to have a young man across the table and you might as well learn yer way around the kitchen. Bread's in the bread bin." He indicated a chipped enamel one by the back door. "And the board and knife over there." He nodded toward the edge of the draining board. "You cut us some bread. Don't have any butter left I'm afraid, but I've some cheese and pickled onions. I'll fetch them while the kettle boils."

They sat down to pint mugs of tea and doorsteps of bread with slices of delicious crumbly, white cheese and homemade pickled onions.

"Thank you," Peter said as Howell Pendragon refilled his mug. "I think that's the best meal I've had in weeks. Where did you get that cheese?" He hesitated—was that being rudely inquisitive?

"My old aunt back in Anglesey sends me a cheese every so often. She helps my cousins out on their farm. I don't ask how she has so much spare that the government don't grab. I just say 'thank you.'"

Peter couldn't hold back the smile and the thought of an old lady hiding cheese from the Ministry of Food inspectors. He raised his mug. "Good health and my thanks to your aunt in Anglesey!"

Howell Pendragon nodded and raised his own mug. "I think you'd get on with old Aunt Blod. She's always been one to face life her own way and damn what people say. And they've always said plenty about her. Some even say she's a witch."

The last statement contained a loaded question. And demanded a response. "Doesn't every village claim a witch or two? Where I grew up there was an old lady lived down by the old millpond. Old Mother Hastings was her name. She scared the willies out of us children, but women in the village went to her for herbal remedies and all sorts of things. I can remember even my mother going to her when she had a skin rash that nothing the doctor prescribed could cure."

Howell Pendragon smiled. "Don't say things like that within earshot of the doctor—she'd brush it off as superstition."

"And you don't?" Peter held little faith in all that superstition himself.

"I'd say go for whatever works. No one knows everything."

Heavens was that true! "You're right there."

"Mind if I smoke?"

In his own kitchen? "Go ahead."

He spent a few minutes cleaning the dottle out of his pipe, refilling carefully, and puffing on it as he lit the tobacco. All set, he took the pipe out of his mouth and exhaled toward the window. "Nothing like a good pipe after a meal. I think we'll deal well together, young man. Just one thing I have to know, seeing as how we're going to be sitting across the table from each other for the next heaven knows how long: What made you stand up as a CO?"

Talk about hitting a man between the metaphorical eyes! Peter stared, stunned for several seconds, then took a breath. He'd faced the question before and evaded the sticky issue of personal details, but Howell Pendragon offered friendship and courtesy and he had a point. If Peter was going to be living in the man's house, he was entitled to ask. Another deep breath. "Can I have your word this stays between us?"

He nodded, putting the stem on the pipe between his teeth. "You have it. I'm not one to gossip at any time. This is between the two of us and the kitchen table, if that's what you want."

Fair enough. Better make it a precise as possible. "My father always promised me that when I turned ten, he'd teach me to shoot. I was a demanding and impatient little bugger and couldn't wait. I was forbidden to touch his guns. I disobeyed. Went into his gun room one afternoon, took down his Rigby, and ignoring any rules I'd ever had pounded into my thick skull, loaded it, and practiced sighting.

"Dad walked in on me and demanded to know what I was doing. I was so startled, as I turned around, my fingers closed on the trigger. I got him in the chest at about four feet."

The memory still seared his mind like acid. Peter paused and picked up his mug and drained it, leaves and all.

His head was still buzzing when he set the mug down with a thud.

"Crikey, lad!"

"He died, there on the floor. Looking back I was lucky not to end up in Borstal or an Approved School, but it was ruled an accident. My mother made me promise, hand on the family Bible, to never touch a gun again and I haven't. I told the tribunal that. They accepted it. I told them I'd do anything, as long as it didn't violate that promise. Aside from that, just thinking about picking up a gun turns my stomach into knots.

I'll never forget how Dad's warm blood felt on my hands and the smell of cordite in the gunroom."

That Howell had no trouble believing. The lad had gone so pale he looked green. "What were you doing before the war?"

"I was training to be a vet."

Howell almost managed to stifle the wry laugh. "So they sent you off to patch up people."

"And now I'm here."

"You'll do, lad. You'll do. Those two women will like as work you to death, like they do themselves." He stood. "Tell you what, you go fill up the coke"—he nodded at the battered enamel hod by the kitchen stove—"while I clear the table, and then I'll take you round the village and introduce you to Nurse Prewitt. I'd take you along to the doctor's, but she's off talking to the coroner. We had someone die here last night and dunno when she'll be back."

The lad seemed almost relieved as he hefted the empty coal hod and went out the door.

Nice boy, Howell decided. A bit nervous, but wasn't everyone these days? And what a hell of thing to have to live with. He, for one, would never forget the look in the face of the Jerry he'd gutted with his bayonet back at Verdun. It had given him nightmares and that had been a total stranger. But for a kid to kill his da? He shook his head. It wasn't just wars that ripped lives apart.

Peter scooped the coke into the hod. Some stray nuts fell to the ground, so he bent and picked them up, dropped them back in the hod, and brushed his fingers together. He looked toward the back door and smiled. Had he ended up lucky here! Howell Pendragon was a good man. At least to all appearances so far. If he had harsh judgments, he kept them to himself. Maybe the tart doctor would mellow. Maybe not.

He hefted the now heavy hod with both hands. Whatever happened, he'd cope.

"The wc's down the hall if you want to wash off the coal dust," Howell Pendragon said as Peter put the hod down beside the boiler.

"Want me to make the boiler up first?"

"Thanks, lad."

Boiler topped up, Peter nipped out the door. On the right was a closed door, presumably the parlor kept for high days and holidays, and on the left, under the stairs, was a small and chilly wc. But the water was warm. He washed his face and looked at himself in the narrow mirror. No smuts on his face. Hands clean.

He really should thank the old man and continue his tour of the village. He couldn't impose on his day much longer.

Howell Pendragon had other ideas.

"Best we nip along and meet Nurse Prewitt before you go. She'll be wanting to talk to you. You can put money on it that Helen Burrows told her you're in the village. Now you don't want her to feel slighted after you've spent half the day nattering with me."

A bit of an exaggeration, but Sergeant Pendragon had a point. "Alright then, but I don't want to impose."

The old man smiled and reached for his jacket and cap.

As they walked through the village, Peter began to suspect the doctor's grandmother and the sergeant had concocted a scheme to introduce him to half the village population. Would have been smashing if he had an earthly chance of remembering their names, but whatever the plans, he had sense enough to be grateful.

The nurse lived in a small flint cottage at the far end of the village. A well used, but very well maintained, Hercules bicycle stood propped by the back door. He'd need to get himself one Peter thought—or perhaps one came as part of the job. He was about to ask when Howell Pendragon announced, "Best we go in," and opened the gate and made for the back door, which he opened without knocking.

"Nurse Prewitt?" he called and a young, female voice answered, "Come in. I just made some tea."

He opened the door wide and stepped in. "Brought someone for you to meet: Peter Watson, your new assistant."

"Wonderful! Come in." She was medium height and slim with short red hair and dark, intelligent eyes, and she held out her hand in welcome. "I can't tell you how thrilled we are to have help. Between the evacuees and the workers up at the big hush-hush plant on the heath, we're up to our necks." As she smiled her eyes crinkled at the corners. She was a nice-looking woman with an open, honest face and strong, hard-working hands. "It's wonderful to meet you. Take off your coat and sit down." She moved aside as they both stepped into the kitchen. "Look who's here, Alice."

"We've met."

Dr. Alice Doyle sat at the end of the table, clutching the handle of a pink-flowered china teacup. Her eyes were as blue as ever, but held not one iota of welcome.

Chapter 8

Alice couldn't believe her eyes. He was here. Standing in the doorway of Gloria's kitchen. His hair as dark as ever, his brown eyes clear and penetrating, and the same air of quiet confidence. He should be skulking in, tail between his legs, instead of smiling. And darn Howell Pendragon was grinning as if he'd won the pools.

"Ladies," he said, "we just dropped in to see Nurse Prewitt and I find you both here. Couldn't be better. Wanted to introduce you to your new assistant." He turned and smiled at the man. "Peter Watson. First aid specialist."

Gloria grinned. "Good heavens! I never really thought it would happen. You are real, aren't you?" she asked, putting down the teapot on the draining board and crossing the kitchen. "We really need another pair of hands."

"I hope I'll be useful."

"It used to be even busier. Quite a few evacuees went home over the summer, but I think they might trickle back now the bombing has started." She smiled at Sergeant Pendragon. "Can you both stop for a cup of tea?"

The sergeant accepted for both of them, then turned to her. "And this," he said, "is Dr. Doyle. You'll be working with her most, I imagine."

Peter Watson met her eyes and smiled. Well, almost smiled. Before he could come close enough to offer his hand, Alice said, "We've met."

She should have kept quiet.

"Well I never," the sergeant said, looking from her to Watson and back again.

"And you never told me," Gloria said, sounding a trifle peeved. "Kept the good news to yourself, did you?"

"Mr. Watson was part of an ambulance crew when we met."

"When?" Gloria asked.

"I was called out to Brytewood earlier in the week to pick up an injured man," Watson said.

"Who was that?"

Gloria would not let go.

"An injured man who disappeared on us." Having said that, she had to go on and explain the whole ridiculous incident.

"Which day was that?" the sergeant asked.

"Monday. I was on my way back from delivering Melanie's twins."

"Odd," Gloria said, then turned to pick up the teapot again. "Hang your coats up and have a seat. I'll have this ready in a jiffy."

They peeled off their jackets and hung them on the pegs by the door. Peter Watson, either by design or chance, took the chair directly opposite Alice. Oh well, dammit, she was going to have to work with him, but she didn't have to like him, did she? But why, oh why, did a measly conscie have to come in such an attractive package?

"When do you start?" Gloria asked.

"Monday. I was due a day off so I took a bus in to look around. Then I ran into Mrs. Burrows, who took me down and introduced me to Sergeant Pendragon. He, very kindly, brought me down here to meet you."

"Good of him."

"Yes."

"Tell me, Doctor," Sergeant Pendragon said. "Wasn't it Monday night you found your dog dead?"

"Yes." Trust Gran to tell the world. "That was strange. She'd slowed down a bit but wasn't ill. Or so I thought. Must have been her heart gave out. I'll miss her. Daddy gave her to me." She shook her head to chase away the thought. "Mustn't get maudlin. She was good dog and had a darn good innings and heck, I can't get upset over a dog when people are dying."

"Doesn't stop you missing her, though, does it?" Watson asked.

Darn, how dare he be so understanding? "No. When I went downstairs this morning, I found myself listening for the sound of her claws on the kitchen floor." Why the blazes was she agreeing with him? Accepting his sympathy? Yes, he was right on the nail but . . .

"Here you are." Gloria handed around cups. "Sorry I don't have any biscuits to offer. I meant to get down to Worleigh's but things got so busy."

"Don't worry about it, dear. Besides, if you had, odds are he'd have not had any. Not this late in the week."

Sergeant Pendragon left unsaid that Samuel Whorleigh had plenty of everything, off the ration and under the counter.

"Never mind, Gloria. As long as we have a nice cup of tea." Heaven help her, she was sounding like Gran but, as Alice sipped the still-too-hot drink, she decided it was pretty much the truth. Of course while the caffeine perked you up, the tannin was mucking up your stomach, but these days, that was hardly what you'd call a worry.

"Are you staying the weekend?" Gloria asked Peter Watson.

He shook his head. "Have to get back. Got to work my last day tomorrow. Just came to have a look-see. Now I know where I've a billet." He gave Sergeant Pendragon a nod and a smile. "I'll bring my bags back Sunday evening. If that's convenient," he added, turning to the sergeant.

"Any time, son. Any time."

"Don't leave it too late," Gloria said. "The buses are dreadful on a Sunday."

That was putting it mildly. Half the time they never ran at all. Lack of fuel was the excuse. And it might possibly be true.

"That's right," the sergeant agreed, "and you'll have bags with you. Listen, lad, if the conductor gives you any guff, you tell him that you've been assigned here and you need to report."

Fat lot of difference that would make. Last week one of them refused to let Doris on with her toddler's pushchair.

"Don't worry. I'll give you a lift." Alice all but christened herself with tea. What in the name of heaven made her say that? She remembered to close her gaping mouth but the look on his face showed he was as thunderstruck as she was. He managed to close his mouth pretty fast, too.

"Are you sure?"

Not in the least. Or rather she was definitely sure she didn't mean the offer.

"It's awfully nice of you, but what about the petrol?"

He was giving her the perfect grounds to withdraw her idiotic offer. "That's alright. I've a patient to check up on in the hospital in Dorking and I need to go over to the Watson farm and see how Melanie and her twins are doing."

Gloria had good reason to stare. Not five minutes before Peter and Sergeant Pendragon arrived, she'd told Alice about her own visit there that morning. Twins seemed to be doing well; the rest of the household was permanently bleary-eyed from lack of sleep.

Oh well! She'd offered. She was committed. She'd make the best of it. "Can't guarantee the exact time. Depends on how long my calls take and if there's an emergency." Heaven help her it was impossible! "Do you have a phone number?" She could call and cancel, couldn't she? As long as she gave him time to get a bus.

He shook his head. "Not in my billet. There's the phone at the ambulance depot of course." He sounded as thrilled at the idea of using that as anyone would be at the prospect of that weasly Sid Mosely censoring phone calls.

"Never mind. I might be late but I'll be there." Like the soft-headed twerp she obviously was. "I'll need directions."

"Tell you what, why not meet me at the bus station? If you're held up, I can sit and read. And if you really get late, I can always try my luck with the buses."

If she let him down, he meant. "I'll try to get there by five. Before dark."

That seemed to be it. They both declined Gloria's offer of a second cup—Peter Watson to catch the bus, and Sergeant Pendragon to "take a stroll." On a Friday night there was only one possible direction for that stroll: the Pig and Whistle.

"You don't like him, do you?" Gloria said after both men were safely down the path and out in the lane.

"Who?" Playing thick was useless with Gloria. They'd known each other too long for that.

"I wasn't talking about Howell Pendragon."

No. Alice shrugged. "I don't know. Just something about him." It was on the tip of her tongue to spill all Peter Watson's unsavory past and perfidious present but . . .

"Well, if you don't fancy him, why offer to drive over and pick him up? But if you really don't, I do. I think he's dishy. Those gorgeous dark eyes and that smile." She let out a little sigh. And Alice stifled the utterly irrational spike of . . . definitely not jealousy.

"I don't know what you see in him, Gloria, honestly."

"Alice, he's smashing looking, he's going to make our lives easier, and . . ." She paused. "He looks like the sort of man who can always find a taxi when it's raining."

Was she laughing because she agreed or because Gloria's claims were so preposterous? Peter Watson did have an air of competence. Picked up at Blundells no doubt. Just as her brothers had acquired their polish at Epsom College. Mind you, that was where the resemblance ended. Simon and Alan were doing their bit for King and Country.

"Something wrong?" Gloria asked. "You're scowling. Got a headache?"

Only a big one called Peter Watson. "Just tired. I need an early night."

"You'd be better off coming into Leatherhead to the dance hall with June Groves and me. Why don't you?"

Now that was a thought. "No. Thank you for asking. I need to do paperwork and really should work out some sort of rota for next week and talk to Mr. Barron up at the plant and decide how to split this Peter Watson between us."

Gloria chuckled as she gathered up the cups and plates and piled them in the sink. "Don't dismember him completely, Alice. We need his body in one piece!"

Driving the short distance up the hill home, Gloria's words echoed in Alice's mind. Half of her would love to dismember Peter Watson limb from limb to let him pay for his refusal to join up, but Gloria was right: He was good looking. Pleasant, intelligent, and yes, his skills as an assistant were welcome as the proverbial flowers in the spring, but that was it. She had far, far better things to do with her time than dwell on the man's smile and the shameless "come hither" glint of his eyes.

And she, senseless twit that she was, had freely volunteered to drive over to Dorking and give him a lift. She needed her brains examining.

Chapter 9

Gerhardt Eiche strolled down the village street in the gathering dusk. Watching humans was an intriguing spectator sport. Not as satisfying as enjoying their life blood, but enough was enough and leaving multiple corpses dotted around the village would bring on unwelcome attention.

He was satisfied for now. For an old man that farmer last night had been rich in blood.

So fortifying, in fact, Eiche had skipped the doubtful cultural advantages of the film night in the village hall and taken himself to the heath to fly, run, and indulge in his über strength, and, while he was enjoying himself, spend a little time reconnoitering the encampment on the heath.

He had been sent to sabotage it after all.

He hadn't learned much—even a vampire had difficulty scaling eight foot high electrified barbed wire. And after the nasty injury Schmidt incurred, Eiche avoided climbing trees.

But his scouting confirmed that whatever was going on there, it needed to be neutralized well before the invasion. Of course, if they'd given a date for the invasion it might help, but it was coming soon. Hell, even the pathetic Britishers were on edge and anxious. Eiche smiled. He'd give them anxious. With screams and agony. Give him time.

Meanwhile, it was not easy maintaining the facade of concerned mortal visiting a much respected and cherished aunt. Too many more weeks and he'd end up ripping open the old bag's throat.

He'd visited her that afternoon and since the strength from the farmer hadn't lasted as he'd expected (maybe that hack Stoker was right about the native earth business), he'd taken a little sustenance when he was embracing her good-bye. It had just been the top up he needed. She might come in handy. Keeping her weak wouldn't be any trouble once he had her back in the house.

And meanwhile, given his current vigor and energy, he'd visit the Pig and Whistle and mingle with the populace. Someone there had to know what was going on up on the heath. A few rounds of substandard English beer would surely loosen tongues. If it didn't, he'd follow some drunken fool home and compel the information.

Eiche wasn't the only one headed for the pub.

Ahead of him, a knot of three men fumbled their way down the street, feeling for fences and gates in the dark. One of then stumbled into the gutter and was hauled up by his companions.

My, my the blackout was a handicap to anyone without vampire sight. He'd have to remember to pretend to stumble a bit. Might as well make the effort to pass for human.

Timing things so he arrived just after the group, Eiche paused, hand on the door. The place was crowded. He sensed the press of human bodies and the scent of their blood. Odd that he still hungered. A feeding to the death such as he'd enjoyed from that farmer should have lasted him a week or two.

He opened the door and stepped into the warm, close atmosphere of the public bar and immediately wished he'd settled for the lounge next door. But his sources insisted the public bar was where working men gathered.

Only the British could divide up a beer house into social strata and here he was, Gerhardt Eiche, in the bottom of the pile. And it was busy. As he closed the door behind him and looked around an elderly man in a group of four of five nodded and said, "Evening."

Eiche nodded back, aware of the scrutiny as he crossed to the bar. The mortals were curious. He chuckled. How they'd gape in shock and drool their tepid beer down their wagging chins if they knew what walked in their midst. Smiling, Eiche strolled over to the bar and ordered—as his trainers had taught—a half pint of bitter.

That drew attention.

"Cautious drinker, are you then?" the publican asked with an impudent grin on his fat red face. "Just a half?"

"Thank you, yes."

"Right you are." He picked up a heavy dimpled mug, smaller, Eiche noticed, than those everyone around seemed to hold, and nudging it under the tap, slowly pulled the wooden lever and filled the mug with dark, amber liquid. "Here you are," he said, dabbing the bottom of the mug on a spread towel before setting it in front of Eiche.

Eiche nodded and picked it up. Might as well have a taste. It wasn't quite as bad as he expected. "Good health," he said, raising his mug to the publican and taking another taste.

"And to you, sir," the man replied. "Now, would you be paying, or d'you want me to set up a tab for you, Mr. Oak?"

A mortal would have choked on his beer. Eiche swallowed and looked up. "A tab? You give strangers credit?" No wonder the country was ripe for invasion. And come to that, how in Hades did the man know his name?"

"Good heavens no, sir. Wouldn't stay in business if I did that now, would I? No, but we all know you're poor Miss Waite's nephew. Right lucky she was that you happened to be here when she needs you. Not what you'd planned on when you came down here, though, is it?"

The man had no idea. "I'm very glad I'm here right now."

No lie that. "But if you'd be so obliging as to set me up a tab, I'd be most grateful." And would never need to settle up.

"Put it on mine, Fred."

Eiche stared at the gray-haired and upright man and remembered to smile through his surprise. Mortals! Sometimes you just couldn't predict them! "Well, thank you. To whom do I owe my thanks?"

"I'm Howell Pendragon, and you're very welcome. We met in the village a couple of days back." Yes, Eiche remembered the invitation to drill with the Home Guard. "On recuperation leave if I remember rightly?"

The man didn't offer his hand, just a smile and a very pointed question. Eiche's answer came as learned. "Yes." He lowered his voice. "I was supposed to report in a couple of days, but now Aunt Jane is laid up, I'll putting things off if I can. War or no war, she can't be left alone."

"Don't worry about that, young man. Between the doctor and Nurse Prewitt, they'll take care of things. You just go ahead and do your bit."

He intended to, just not quite in the way this old geezer meant.

And besides, Eiche decided to take a risk in a crowded place and sent a mind probe his way and found a wall. The old man shrugged and shook his head as if shaking off flies, but that was all. His mind was impenetrable. What in the name of Hades was he? A fellow vampire? He'd been warned he might encounter one. But no. This man smelled of the living. So what was he? He'd find out. In time the entire village would be his.

All he had to do was accomplish his mission.

"That's grand," he replied, putting on the concerned but relieved nephew act. "I've been so worried about her. She's so frail and at her age . . ."

The old man laughed. "She's not so old. And don't you let her hear you call her frail. She'd like as not thump you one with her crutches if you try suggesting she's old and helpless. Your aunt dug out for her Anderson shelter all by herself. Accepted help to assemble it, she did, then covered it over all on her own. Even went out to the woods and dug up some wild blackberry canes and planted on top of it."

Not what Eiche really wanted to hear. He gave a laugh. "Sounds like Aunt Jane. Ever the tartar. I bet she was one strict teacher."

"A teacher, was she?" The landlord intruded in the conversation. "Not around here, though. Where did she teach?"

Damn! Not a detail he'd memorized. "Up North." Shit! As a loving nephew he was supposed to know these things. "A village out on the moors." There were moors up in the North of England, weren't there? How dare these mortals be so inquisitive!

"Yorkshire?" Howell Pendragon asked.

"Yes, Yorkshire." It was the biggest county in England so should be the safest bet.

"To hear her speak, you'd never guess she was from Yorkshire," the landlord said, reaching for a glass from the overhead rack.

"True," intruded another man standing on Eiche's left. "I always thought Miss Waite was from Kent. Don't you remember how she got all het up with the vicar's wife over the 'Men of Kent' and 'Kentish Men' business?"

For appearance's sake, Eiche joined in the general laughter. Although what was so hilarious was quite beyond him.

"Something to do with the Medway, wasn't it?" Fred the landlord said and took down another glass. "All due respect to Miss Waite," he added. "She's a nice lady, but you can tell she was a schoolmistress."

In the ensuing chatter, Eiche drank his beer.

"Staying long?" the second man asked.

Questions, endless questions! Like all peasants they were

curious about newcomers. This he'd been briefed for. "Originally just a couple of weeks, but now my aunt is laid up . . ."

Howell Pendragon said, "Now the doctor and Nurse Prewitt have a new assistant there will be plenty of people to keep an eye on her."

"A new assistant?" The man from the left intruded again. "First I've heard of that."

"Oh, he's coming alright. Starting Monday. Just met him myself. He's being billeted on me. Nice, quiet chap," the old man replied.

"Must be the same one Barron was on about. Said we were going to have a part-time first aid chap." The speaker had a narrow face, pointed chin, and sharp nose. He reminded Eiche of a rat. "We'll need more than first aid unless we're lucky." He paused and took a swig of his beer. "I caught another damn girl today wearing her engagement ring around her neck. Docked her pay for it, I did. Honest, this job."

Pendragon gave a noncommittal grunt. Eiche held back the smile. So, it was a munitions plant. Had to be. Where else would wearing metal be a safety hazard? "Some workers never learn, do they?"

"My lot don't. Bunch of useless giggling girls. I tell Barron he's far too soft with them. If he docked their pay and cut their leave a bit more often they'd shape up right enough." He took another drink while leaning on the bar for support. "But I don't run the plant. Would be damn sight different it I did."

"Let me buy you a drink."

"Don't mind if I do." He drained his mug and set it down on the polished counter with a thump. "Thanks."

Eiche turned to his right. "Sergeant Pendragon, may I get you one?"

Pendragon shook his head. "Another time, thank you. I must be off." With a nod to the landlord, he left.

"Standoffish lot these villagers. Bunch of proper snobs if you ask me." The man seemed oblivious to the dozen or so villagers within earshot. Or maybe he was so drunk he didn't care. "I'm Jeff Williams. Stuck here in the back of beyond and delighted to make your acquaintance." The slurred speak was unmistakable.

"Gabriel Oak. Visiting my aunt who had the misfortune to break her leg."

Williams scowled. "What's a man your age doing out of uniform? You're not one of those bloody conscies, are you?"

That was easy to deny. "Wounded at Dunkirk. I'm here on leave to recuperate."

Another scowl. Thinking was obviously quite an effort for this specimen of humanity. "Wounded, eh? Which of the forces?"

"Army. Hampshire Regiment."

"Rotten luck getting shot up, if you ask me."

Eiche had no intention of asking his opinion, just of using him. "Sounds as though you have a rough job."

"It's hell! Nothing but stupid women jabbering on and crying when you tell them to take their earrings off. Then they all get to carrying-on together and fussing and wiping each other's tears. Proper argey bargey." He paused to down a good quarter of the pint. "Still beats shoving bayonets in people's guts."

"Been here long?" As he asked, Eiche sensed the landlord seemed unduly interested in the conversation.

"Too bloody long. Arrived just before last Christmas. Mucked up the holiday something proper it did."

"I bet it did." Yes, the damn landlord was far too interested. "Tell you what. I've been on my feet all day, let's go and sit in that corner." Far enough and out of the way enough to pump this foolish mortal in private until he spilled the beans and more.

It only took two more beers.

The man was scarcely able to stand but Eiche knew for certain the establishment he'd been sent to investigate, and destroy, was a munitions manufactory with a staff that worked three shifts around the clock producing for the war effort. Rendering it inoperative would be a pleasure and the loquacious, disgruntled assistant supervisor would be the perfect tool.

Eiche needed to know more about the running of the place and who worked where and when. Not that he had any qualms about killing the workers. The fewer inhabitants left in the way of invasion, the better.

"It's been grand meeting someone from outside Brytewood," Eiche said as he stood. "Hate to go, but I've got an old aunt to visit in hospital."

For some reason the fool mortal thought that amusing. Would he laugh at fangs in his neck? Later. For now, he did have an old aunt to take care of and the old cow still had a role to play in service to the Reich.

"See you around," the man said, or rather slurred.

"Oh, yes." Eiche would make sure of it.

"Sorry to bother you so late," Howell said as Helen Burrows opened the back door to him. "Alright if I come in a minute?"

"Of course." She opened the door wide and he stepped into the warm kitchen. "Something wrong?" She was canny. Probably smelled it on him. "You need to see Alice? She's doing paperwork."

"No, don't bother her. I came to see you."

Chapter 10

"Come on in then." She shut the door behind him. "Give me your coat and have a seat. I'd just finished the dishes and was about to sit down with a cup of tea but would you rather have a beer or coffee?"

"I've just come from the Pig," he said as he took off his coat. "Coffee would be perfect. If you can spare it."

She chuckled. "I've a secret bottle of Camp coffee. Alice goes on so if I get things under the counter but once in a while, I treat myself."

He took an easy chair by the fire, stretched his feet out in front of him, and leaned back against the pillows. Now he was actually here, his idea of confiding his concerns to Helen Burrows seemed utterly loony. But who else could he tell? If he shared his suspicions with anyone else in the village, he'd be carted off in a padded van.

Would Helen Burrows have the same reaction? He sensed not. There was an Otherness about her that led him to believe she wouldn't scoff when he started talking about a dead man walking the village streets. Howell watched as she put cups in saucers, measured out the thick dark coffee, and poured on water from the kettle. "Milk and sugar?" she asked.

"No sugar. I gave it up when they started rationing." Not

quite true—he still had it at home, but wasn't about to deplete anyone else's ration.

"So did Alice. I still indulge," she replied with a smile in his direction. "Sure you won't?"

"No, thank you. Just milk."

He took a sip after she handed it to him. "Delicious." He watched as she settled herself in the chair opposite and tasted her coffee.

"Mmm," she said looking up at him over the rim of the cup. "What a treat. Everyone needs a little indulgence once in a while." She put her cup back in the saucer. "How did you get on with our new young man? Everything alright?"

"Oh, yes, fine. I'll enjoy his company. I miss Gryffyth. Not that I saw him that often, but he would always call me. All I get now are letters written on those army forms."

"Same with Simon and Allan. Worse with Simon really, just those Red Cross forms and he can't go a word over the limit. Still, one has to hope, doesn't one?"

"It's already been more than a year. So much for 'All be over by Christmas.'"

She gave a tight dry laugh. "They said that the last time. Look how long it went on." She took another sip of coffee. "Well, Howell, you didn't come here to complain about the government and your young billet is not a problem. So is something wrong?"

Might as well jump in and get on with it. "Maybe. Could just be an old man's imagination."

"That I doubt! You wouldn't leave the Pig early and ride your bicycle up this hill for something you imagined."

She was right there. "Bear with me. Hear me out." He took a long drink to fortify himself. "What would you say to a man who tries to invade people's minds?" It was out.

"Here in Brytewood?"

He nodded. Heart racing and mind soaring. She didn't think him utterly moonstruck. Or did she and she was humoring him? He nodded. "That new chap who claims to be Miss Waite's nephew."

"You say claims? You think he isn't?"

She had to be humoring him but what matter? He'd gone this far. "He said she was from Yorkshire. She told me she'd taught in a girl's school in Faversham."

She nodded. "I'd heard that, too."

So far so good. He'd plow on. "She has this fall right after this nephew arrives. Alright, people do fall down stairs, but Miss Waite is neither frail nor doddery. Perhaps he just made a mistake over where she lived. But I tell you, Helen—" He permitted himself the familiarity. He was making a fool of himself after all. "I bought him a beer and while we stood there talking, he tried to pry into my mind."

Now was her turn to scoff, ask him how the heck he knew. Tell him he was blabbering.

She did none of them.

Little tight creases appeared between her brows as she shook her head. "I haven't seen him. Tell me what he looks like."

Not what he'd expected but . . . "Tall, looks about thirty or so, waffled a bit over what he was doing for the war, dark eyes and hair, pale skin."

"Dark hair you say? Black? Brown?"

"Dark brown. Much like Gryffyth's to be told."

She shook her head. "It's not him," she said half to herself. "There must be two of them."

"Two?"

She nodded. "Yes, whatever they are. Remember the man Alice found up in Fletcher's Woods? The one you helped us get into the surgery? He had no aura. No life force. Alice said his heartbeat was slow. Very slow. That was what had her worried. And a few hours later, he disappeared. Had to have walked out under his own steam."

"But it's not the same man. The injured one was fair, and

younger than this so-called nephew." He only half-credited they were having this conversation. She not only believed him, she acted as if this conversation was perfectly normal.

"Then there are two of them. One appears to be hiding or has left the neighborhood. The other seems to be digging in. I wonder what they're up to?"

"Or what they really are?"

A coal shifted in the grate, and a sudden squall sent rain against the window as they both thought on that one.

"We can't tell Jones or anyone, I don't think. Not yet at any rate. They'll think we're a pair of senile old fools."

She was right but . . . "We've got to do something. What if they are some sort of spies? Or at the very least this Oak chap means harm to Miss Waite?"

"You're right, but we have to be sure what we're dealing with. If they're something more than normal, what can the law or even the Army do against them?"

"Come to that, what can we do?"

"More than anyone will ever guess. What are you, Howell?"

"I'm your friend, Helen."

She snorted. "You're Other. I've know it for years. That you can sense a mind probe proves it. If we're going to sort this odd business out together, I need to know what you are."

His chest clenched. He'd never, ever admitted this to another living soul—except Gryffyth when the lad was approaching puberty and about to enter his own powers. This would get him laughed at. Or would it? She'd accepted everything so far and she was no mere human either. "I'm a Dragon."

She stared, lips parted, eyes wide as she gasped. "A true Welsh Dragon of the hills." It was not a question. "I heard speak of them but never thought I'd live to make one a cup of coffee."

"I never thought to sit here and admit it aloud."

"Not the sort of thing ones brings up at a parish whist drive is it?"

Hardly. "And you?" Might as well ask and satisfy his curiosity. "What are you?"

"Nothing so impressive as a Dragon, I'm afraid, but we have our uses and strengths. I'm a Devon Pixie. Full-blooded. My parents were, so was my husband, Jonathan. Alice's mother inherited all our strengths. But she married a garden human."

"And the doctor?" This he had to know.

Helen shook her head, frown lines creasing her forehead. "She's strong but refuses to believe it. Thinks it's all a bunch of superstition and old tales."

"What a pity. We could use another. I think our intruder will take some besting."

"I've tried. Maybe between us we can convince Alice."

"What do I need convincing of, Gran?"

The door opened, bringing a draft of cool air, and Alice Doyle walked in. "Good evening, Sergeant Pendragon. Keeping Gran company? I've been poring over books and government forms all evening. Seems they don't ever expect evacuees to need medical attention and some of these poor children!" She shook her head.

She looked all done in. Howell stood. "Have a seat, Doctor, you look as if you need to put your feet up."

"No, thanks." She shook her head. "Sit back down, I prefer an upright chair." She pulled over one of the Windsor chairs from the kitchen table. "Well," she went on, as she sat down. "What do I need convincing of, Gran?"

He had to hand it to Helen Burrows. She was a fast thinker. "Just something Howell mentioned, dear. He wondered if you'd keep an eye on something."

"What's the matter? Not evacuees scrumping again?"

That was always a problem but Sergeant Jones and his

cohorts could deal with minor thefts from orchards. "Not that." How in Hades was she going to explain this?"

"It's Miss Waite," Helen continued. "When she gets home you will keep an eye on things, won't you, dear? It's that nephew."

"Oh, him!" She rolled her eyes. "What a specimen. I ran into him this afternoon when I dropped by the hospital to see how she was doing. He went on and on about when she was coming home and couldn't we keep her longer. I told him there was a war on and air raid victims got priority. By the time I finished with him I had a blazing headache."

So he'd tried a mind probe on her, had he? And no doubt she resisted instinctively. He had to talk to Helen more. Find out what exactly a Pixie could do. "Might be nothing," he said, although she'd pretty much convinced him his hunch was dead on. "But please keep an eye on things."

"I will."

"So will I, Howell. I'll pop in whenever I can just to see how things are. Between us we'll make sure nothing untoward happens."

And just to be sure, he'd have a look around on his way home. Maybe the dubious nephew was still down at the Pig.

As the drunken Williams wended his inebriated way homeward, Eiche set off in the opposite direction: toward the munitions manufactory on the heath. A few extra beers had loosened the man's tongue to a most gratifying degree. And now, with the supervisor apparently up in London and the assistant supervisor sleeping off more beers than his body could metabolize in an evening, it seemed the perfect time for a little soul-satisfying mayhem.

Tonight was for chaos and confusion. A measure of the effectiveness of their defenses. He'd save the real destruction for later. Perhaps when he had aerial support. Nothing like a few bombs dropping to let the Inselaffen, the cursed Island Monkeys, know who really was fit to rule the world.

Taking advantage of the night, Eiche ran across the village green into the woods that fringed the common. He crossed the onetime open land that was now divided into allotments and sported a boring assortment of vegetables, stopping just long enough to break open the padlock on a small tool shed and steal a couple of hoes and a spade before heading for the higher ground of Brytewood Heath.

Watching from the shadows of a cluster of trees, Eiche confirmed what he'd learned from Williams. They did work around the clock, but at night things were relaxed. A little group of women stood gossiping outside one of the huts. With his vampire hearing, Eiche didn't miss a word and smiled, knowing their idle chatter was about to be rudely interrupted.

Would be interesting to see how they handled attack.

He had two hoes and the spade. Metal against the electrified wire would create interesting effects. He tossed the first hoe. Aiming carefully, his vampire strength sent it flying across the fifteen or so meters in a graceful arc. It came down right where he'd aimed, the curved metal head snagging the topmost wire with a loud pop and a satisfying display of sparks and flashes.

The shouts and shocked noises from the crowd of chattering females was equally gratifying.

He ran fast to his right and tossed the second hoe onto a stretch of wire almost directly across the area from the first. Not quite as pretty fireworks but hearing the shouts and confusion made up for that. Seemed this one was near a sleeping hut and the occupants came pouring out in various stages of undress. His final missile, a straightedged spade, he sent flying at what looked like a utility pole. Would have been nice to take out electricity to the entire encampment, but it was not to be.

This time.

With the shouts of consternation fading in the distance, Eiche ran back down to the village, skirting the green this time to follow the lane around the church and toward Pear Tree Cottage.

Once inside he was not pleased to see the mud on his shoes and trouser legs. Really, this rustic living was not to be endured for very much longer. Heading upstairs to make free of Jane Waite's hot water and bath towels, he noticed the afternoon post on the mat.

He tossed Jane Waite's aside. Nothing to her could surely merit his attention, but the square white envelope addressed to him caught his eye. He ripped it open and frowned at the square of white card and the blocky handwriting. He was invited to a musical soiree in aid of the war effort. That was code for an emergency meeting of the vampire cell. Fair enough, one or two were to be expected and endured, but what made him curse aloud was the date of the summons: Sunday evening. Just about the time he'd been planning on settling his dear, invalid aunt back home.

How annoying.

Chapter 11

Today was not the day to have to stand by her offer to drive into Dorking and give Peter Watson a lift. Too much was happening close to home. Sleepy little Brytewood that didn't even show up on some maps, was crawling with police from Leatherhead, half the homeguard of the county, and even a couple of Jeeps full of army types, all in a frightful tizz wazz over the sudden power outage up on the heath, and the village was boiling over with rumors of sabotage, death, and murder.

The last she'd squashed the instant she heard it. Apart from a few scratches and bruises where a section of fence had fallen on a couple enjoying a few passionate moments behind the main storeroom, no one was hurt, although production pretty much ceased for the night. With the Army crawling all over the place, and the buzz about Farmer Morgan's unexpected death (her decision to call in the coroner had fueled all manner of speculation), the gossips were having a field day.

But worst of all was the barely voiced suspicion that it was some sort of enemy action sabotage and if that idea persisted, everyone would end up looking sideways at each other.

Not that she could do much about that worry. Better get her mind around how she was going to work with her new assistant. Gran's parting comment—that she was glad Alice was warming up toward the "nice young man"—did nothing to help. Alice knew exactly what Gran had in mind about the "nice, young man" and wasn't interested.

She couldn't be, could she?

She wasn't, and she never would be.

The man she definitely would never fancy was waiting for her by the bus station. In the twilight he looked like a tall shadow. A tall shadow surrounded by luggage. He'd never have been able to get away with all that on the bus.

"Let me give you a hand," she said, getting out of the car.

"I hope it's not too much."

"No. There's lots of space in the back. This was my father's jalopy. It's carried everything, even a sick foal once." And the weird disappearing patient. She opened the back door. "Let's load up and get back before it's pitch dark. There's no moon tonight."

He hefted up a suitcase, then another, a large zip bag, and what looked like his old tuck box from school. "I was worried it wouldn't all go in," he said as he balanced the zip bag on top of the box. "This is some vehicle."

"My mother used to call it the pantechnicon. It burns petrol at a horrid rate; the rationing people had a fit over it. But since there are only half a dozen cars in the village and my patients are scattered in all directions, I get what I need in the wat of petrol coupons." Most of the time at least.

He got in the passenger seat and balanced his gasmask on his knees as she started the engine. "Want to toss that on the back seat?" she asked.

"Why not? Doubt I'll need it in the next half hour."

"At least you carry yours. I noticed on Friday. I'm afraid we've got very slack in the village. I carried it religiously the first few months, but now I forget it more than remember. The teachers get on at the children to carry them to and from school but the grown-ups give a rotten example."

"Brytewood is rather out of the way of things, isn't it? Would be different if you were right in the middle of London."

True. But she ought to make a point of carrying hers. If she could find it. "Hope you weren't waiting long," she said as she pulled away from the curb. "We had a bit of a panic in the village last night."

"Nothing wrong?"

"Depends on how you define 'wrong'," she replied, changing gear as she turned the corner. "No one hurt, but power went out up at the camp on the heath and they're trying to decide if it's the fault of the generating board, the Germans, or some likely lads from the village whose hijinks got out of hand."

"Not trouble, you don't think?"

How did you define "trouble" these days? She shrugged. "If it is, would they tell us?"

He smiled, and really, his eyes did crinkle up nicely in the gloom. "I bet your grandmother would magic the truth out of them."

Alice almost swerved. "What makes you say that?"

"Just the way she is. She reminds me of Granny Weatherby in our village when I was a boy. There were all sorts of tales about her: that she'd been struck by lightning as a girl, that she was touched, even that she had Pixie blood in her." He gave a little laugh. "You wouldn't believe half the stories." She would, actually. "But she knew things and people listened. If she said there was a bad storm coming, people got on ladders to check the roof."

"Do you believe the stories about Pixies?" Why was she asking that?

He was silent a moment or two, as if considering his reply. "I'm not sure. Logically one says 'no.' It has to be just myth and legend, but my grandmother believed, as did a lot of her generation. My old nanny did. Heck, she once took me down to a stream that the villagers claimed was magical and dunked me in. My mother had a fit. I was only four or five at the time, but I remember her practically going into orbit over it."

"And did it imbue you with magic powers?"

His chuckle echoed in the dark confines of the car. "If it did, I haven't noticed."

At least he didn't believe all that nonsense. A definite point in his favor.

They rode on in silence a few minutes.

"You'll need a bicycle to get around on. Sergeant Pendragon has promised to find one."

"He seems a very nice chap."

"Yes. Not local, but I imagine you guessed that hearing him speak."

"Are most people in the village local?"

"Before the war, yes, but now, with the evacuees and the workers that moved in, the whole place has changed. The population doubled at one point. It's a little less now. Quite a few people left." A thought struck her. "You think they'll be suspicious of an outsider? Don't worry. You'll stop being an outsider once someone's child falls out of a tree and needs stitches. It's a village, yes, odd in some ways. I can see that and I grew up here, but like everywhere else these days, we've changed." But maybe not enough to welcome a CO with open arms.

"I'd rather live in a village than a town any day."

So would she but she wasn't quite up to agreeing. Not with him. Not yet.

Not ever.

The drive seemed interminable. Peter Watson was not a chatty sort, thank heaven, but somehow the silences seemed to wrap them both in a closeness she did not care for.

"I'm most obliged to you for coming over to pick me up," Peter said as they came down the hill toward the darkened village. "I know it had to have been a bother. It was good of you."

Seemed rude to agree, even though she did, wholeheartedly. "I wanted to be sure my new assistant was here and ready first thing Monday." Darn, that sounded curt.

"I will be, don't worry. What time do I come up to the surgery?"

She wasn't sure she wanted him up in her house, her territory. Not that she could avoid it—he would be there eventually. "Let's meet at Gloria's at nine. Mondays she goes down to the school and we thought that might be a good way for you to start."

"Throw me to the wolves from the start, eh?"

"That's right, and it's a big pack. Some of those evacuee infants are wild things and our locally bred ones aren't exactly sweet little angels either."

"So Brytewood breeds rapscallions and roisterers. Has anyone warned the War Office?"

Alice chuckled. He might just last here after all. "I don't think they could cope." She paused as she changed gear to go down the hill. "Seriously, though. They're good children on the whole. It's just so many are on edge. I don't think there's a household in the village that hasn't experience some sort of upheaval. Brother, sons, and fathers gone, strangers deposited on their doorsteps, extra family members moved in, and people living in close quarters. We might be in the back of beyond, but everyone, children included, knows about the bombing. We even had a stray one dropped out in the middle of a cornfield a couple of weeks back. No one hurt but it brought the war very close. Grown-ups are tense; it can't help but rub off on the children."

"And having pillboxes and those massive concrete Dragons' teeth all over the countryside can't help either."

No. Frankly the lines of great concrete obelisks gave her the willies and caused nightmares about German tanks coming across the Downs. "They don't. So we just keep going and do the best we can."

"How many evacuees do we have in Brytewood?"

She couldn't miss the "we." Did she like that or not? "About a fifth of the school population, and a half dozen under school age, and a few mothers. Many went back to London. Village life didn't suit them. Parents hated to be parted. Some stayed. Our charlady, Doris, is one. Her husband's away, she found work here, and seems to like the change. Others couldn't stand it. One came to me for sleeping pills because the quiet kept her awake.

"We had a teacher evacuated too and that's helped. The school was close to bursting at the seams. It was due to get an addition built on last year, but war broke out and we'll never see it now, but they took over the parish hall and people manage."

And so, she thought to herself, as she pulled up in front of Sergeant Pendragon's cottage, would she.

"Thanks again for the lift," Peter said as Sergeant Pendragon came out with a hurricane lamp and helped carry the boxes and suitcases into the house. "It was smashing of you." Why, oh why, did he have such a wonderfully sincere and open smile?

Maybe that last bit was a trick of the dark.

"We need you here, Mr. Watson. See you in the morning at Gloria's. Remember the way?"

"I'll see he gets there, don't you worry," Sergeant Pendragon said. "Will you stay and have a cup of tea, Doctor?"

She declined as graciously as she could. She'd seen quite enough of her new assistant for one day, and it was entirely true that Gran was alone and Alice did want to get back to her.

But when she walked into the house, she realized she'd lied. Gran was not alone, the sitting room fire was burning, and the room was full of villagers knitting. She'd forgotten the Sunday evening sessions Gran was organizing to knit "comforts for the troops." The quiet clicking and buzz of conversation stopped as Alice walked in.

"Everything alright, my love?" Gran asked.

"Oh, yes." A lie, but worth the risk to her immortal soul.

She was not telling the worst gossips in the village that her new assistant was causing imprudent and foolish fancies. "Just let me hang up my coat and I'll be with you."

After she hung up her coat she poured herself a cup of rather stewed tea from the pot on the table and took a seat next to June Groves, who was busy knitting away at something roughly round and khaki. "Not socks?" she asked, wondering what it was.

June shook her head. "No, a balaclava helmet for a radio operator." She reached into her knitting bag and pulled out the pattern.

Yes, definitely a balaclava, but with little ear flaps that lifted up. Reminded Alice of the gunner's gloves with peelback fingertips on the thumb and forefinger. Interesting how anything could be adapted for war. Needed to be. "Someone will be glad of that this winter."

"I need to get it finished first. I'm not a fast knitter."

"Is your hand healed enough to knit?" She did sound like a doctor but it had been nasty only days ago.

"Oh, yes! That poultice did the trick and I'm going to be more careful opening tins in future."

"Well, Doctor." It was Mrs. Willows, who lived down by the school. "I hear you've been over to Dorking to pick up the new young man."

She should have expected that. The arrival of any single male under ninety was a matter of prime interest. "Yes. Our new first aid assistant. He had his luggage to move and you know what the bus conductors are like when anyone wants to bring suitcases on."

For a little while the sad failings of London Transport employees occupied the company, but Mrs. Willows was not to be put off for long. "It'll be good to have a young man around for a change. Think he'd suit June? I've been telling her she needs to find herself a young man."

No, he would not suit June!

And why did that matter? Better not even think that one out. Not right now. "Better leave that up to June. Of course he might be engaged or even married." Not that he'd said anything either way but . . .

"Now, that would be a shame." That was Mother Longhurst, reputed witch and village herbalist. She hadn't yet poisoned anyone to Alice's knowledge, but her potions and mixtures were decidedly suspect.

"You seem to have plenty of wool," Alice said. Better to discuss knitting than Peter Watson. "Weren't you running short last week?"

June chuckled. "Mrs. Burrows took care of that. Seems that they had a supply down at Worleigh's but it never got onto the shelves until your grandmother had a word with them."

"I bet she did." Alice had to smile. Sam Whorleigh was notorious for keeping choice stock under the counter and charging exorbitant prices. Gran must have shamed him into selling the wool at a fair price. He was probably still writhing over the loss of revenue. Really! Profiteering over wool for the troops was beyond the pale.

"He said there was a lot of demand for it," Gran said. "I agreed. After all, the troops need socks and gloves and what else can it be used for?"

Alice had seen more than one baby tucked under a khaki blanket or wearing a knitted jacket of Air Force blue.

"About that young man." Mrs. Willows would not give up. "I wonder why he's not been called up." None of her business. Although why Alice felt so protective of him, heaven alone knew. The man was a CO after all. "You'd think he'd be off doing his bit somewhere."

"Instead, he's doing his bit right here where we need him. Alice and Gloria are stretched thin what with all the newcomers and the plant up on the heath." Bless Gran and what's more, it was true.

"What about the trouble up there last night? Did they ever

find out what caused it?" Miss Downs, who lived next door to Miss Waite, set off a good five minutes of speculation.

Speculation that led nowhere and stirred a good deal of invasion fever.

"How are your charges doing, June?" Alice asked. It made a change from the "Huns among us" tempo of the current conversation.

"Not too badly, really. A lot went home, parents missed them, and some of the children were miserable. When you're used to London, Brytewood is a big change."

"A lot safer, if you ask me," added Miss Downs.

"To be honest, I'm not sure we're safe anywhere," June replied.

Alice didn't blame her caution. After the retreat from France, and the Germans had taking the Channel Islands, who didn't wonder if the mainland was next? Alice shook that thought away.

"You're as safe here as anywhere," Gran said. "And we're glad you're here. Mrs. Roundhill was just saying the other day what a help you were with the children at the vicarage."

"She's so nice," June said. "Never minds if I go out, but I hate to leave her with four children, plus the two older boys who can be a handful. She insisted I come here this evening. Said I needed to come and knit for her."

That stirred a few laughs. Eleanor Roundhill, the vicar's wife, was a lovely woman and good at organizing the parish, but her sewing and knitting skills were notoriously lacking.

"We're glad you came, my love," Gran said. "You're welcome here any day you feel like riding your bike up the hill to The Gallop."

"Talking about riding bikes, I'd best be getting home," said Miss Downs, and everyone took up the idea, leaving in pairs or riding bicycles with shaded lights.

As Gran closed the door behind the last ones, she turned to Alice. "Everything go alright with young Mr. Watson, dear?"

Alice took a deep breath. "Perfectly. He was waiting for me. We got back to Brytewood without mishap and Sergeant Pendragon was home and ready for him."

"That's good to hear. You know, Alice, something tells me, before long we'll all be very glad that young man came to Brytewood." She shook her head as Alice was about to speak. "I know how you feel about him."

Alice forbore interrupting and telling Gran that if she knew exactly how Alice felt about Peter Watson, then Gran was one step ahead of her.

"He's a good man and with the trouble brewing we'll need him."

Did Gran mean invasion? Or what? Did she want to ask? No doubt Gran had a "feeling" of impending disaster. Trouble was, Gran's vague and often unspecified "feelings" of trouble on the horizon had a singularly amazing habit of coming true. But there was more than that—her grandmother looked really worn tonight.

"What's worrying you, Gran?"

"Come and help me clear up the teacups, please, dear. I'm feeling tired. I hope that nice Miss Groves gets back safely."

"Gran, she has as much chance as anyone of getting home in one piece." Brytewood was safer than many places these days.

"I know that." It was almost an irritated snap. "She just seems so young and so lonely. She spends day and night with those children. I wish we could have put her in another billet away from them. Never mind that, just give me a hand with the washing up. I'm feeling a little weary."

Small wonder. Gran had been awake most of the night while Alice was up at the camp taking care of minor injuries and, she had to admit, wishing she already had her assistant. Well, she had him now. Trouble now was, she wasn't sure what she was going to do about that. "Why don't you go up to bed and I'll see to the washing up?"

"I may go up and have a bath, but dear, I don't think we should sleep upstairs tonight. Something's in the air."

German planes headed for London, no doubt. "You want to sleep out in the air raid shelter, Gran?" They'd done that a few times early in the war. Alice felt it was like being shut in a tin can.

"You need to be close to the phone, dear. How about we take pillows and things down to the cellar? We still have the old mattress down there."

"Alright, Gran."

Alice half pooh-poohed Gran's "feelings," but they'd been right often enough that she kept her skepticism to herself. "Go and have your bath and I'll be up in a while. I'll make us both a cup of cocoa."

"And I'll be sure to save the hot water for you, dear."

Alice sighed. Once the war was over, she'd never share bath water again but now, it beat a cold bath.

The milk—alright, dried milk reconstituted—was simmering when Gran came down wrapped in a thick toweling dressing gown. "I'll finish drying the dishes, dear, you nip upstairs and I'll see to the cocoa."

Alice soaked until the water went cold, got out, and glanced at her watch as she toweled off. Eleven-thirty, later than she'd thought. She hoped Gran was wrong about the air raid.

Chapter 12

Bela stood by the window. Closer than she'd ever been able to stand. She felt a slight tingling from the iron frame and bars but that was all. No stab of pain. Tentatively, she reached out and touched the iron band with the tip of a finger. No burning, no sizzling agony lancing her body, just a minor itch. Why?

Was this a result of the strength that poured into her when Eiche killed the mortal? She backed away from the window, her stomach twisting. Was she becoming vampire? Had the bites infected her and turned her? Was it even possible? Almost all she knew about vampirekind she'd learned from her captors, and she had no reason to think they'd told her all, or even any, of the truth.

But whatever they had or had not told her, she was changing, and by all the woodland gods and sprites, Zweiten and Zuerst were never ever to know. There had to be a way she could use this to help her family. Could she mind meld with them despite the iron perimeter? If they too were imprisoned in forged iron, could she penetrate that, too?

There was only one way to find out. Tonight, when all was dark, she would test herself by passing her arms through the bars. Then she would attempt a mind meld.

She sat on the floor a while, looking out of the window at

the autumn sky and the changing colors of the trees on the distant hills. It had been spring when they brought her here. Five months, nearly six, ago. Where was her family now? Were they being used, too?

In a shivering flash of horror, Bela imagined them all imprisoned in iron girt cells and like her, bound to vampires spread all over the German dominions. What if they weren't just linked to vampires? What if they'd been bitten by worse—werewolves or other vicious shifters? Bela shuddered at the thought. Were they all being used to further Nazi power?

Zuerst and Zweiten threatened to kill her family if she refused to cooperate. Had her parents and sisters been coerced the same way?

Her brain ached from worry.

They were coming.

She rose from the floor and turned to face them as the door opened, schooling her face to hide her turmoil and worry.

"Sit down," Zweiten said. "Focus and connect. We need to know what's happening?"

Why the sudden urgency? They'd answer that and tell her what was going on, wouldn't they? She held back the smile. "Which one?"

That gave him a second's pause. "Weiss," Zuerst answered. "Connect with him first. Then the others. What is each doing and where are they?"

Something was definitely up. Bela walked over to the straight-backed chair by the bed and sat down. She'd invented this ritual for their benefit and drew a few meager beads of useless pleasure from watching their rapt fascination overcome their assumed indifference. She placed her hands palm to palm and rested them against her forehead, breathing slowly and shutting her eyes. She didn't need to look at her captors to know they were fascinated, despite their air of superiority over a despised "Other."

Quietly, she whispered a few words in the ancient tongue

of the Fairies. Zuerst and Zweiten no doubt imagined it to be a magic charm or spell. In fact, it was a plea to the wood sprites to lure them into the depths of the forest and let them wander lost forever.

Unfortunately, with neither turned earth nor blood to offer, her plea would never be heard, but the simple act of defiance gave her a wisp of satisfaction before she opened her mind and the pain of linking with the bloodsuckers ripped through her.

Letting the pain flow over her like an infection, Bela focused, blinked in shock, and refocussed, reaching out with her mind in surprise to confirm her first impression. She jerked as each vampire in turn felt her connection, let her in momentarily, then blocked her. Except Schmidt. He left her hovering on the rim of his consciousness, and through him, she heard everything that was said.

She'd thought herself beyond shock.

She had been gravely mistaken.

Seemed the vampires were not entirely dedicated to the Third Reich but despised the Inselaffen even more. If this group had their way, the invasion forces had a few surprises in store for them.

If . . .

Did four people, even four vampires, think they could take on the power of the German war machine? They'd be crushed just as the foolish British were destined to be flattened into their fertile soil.

Fascinated, she listened on. Seemed all the horror tales she'd heard about the walking dead were true, if not understatements.

Pain ripped though her as Schmidt forced her out, then the others opened and she connected as they discussed problems with late buses and disruptions in telephone service due to bombing, and Eiche got a severe scolding for killing the pig farmer.

Meanwhile Zweiten and Zuerst waited, their cruel eyes

gleaming with excitement. They sensed something different had occurred. She had to play this to her advantage.

She took several deep breaths, almost gasps. She needed to cleanse her mind. She yearned to swim in the clear waters of a mountain lake and wash the taint of vampire from her body. She contented herself with struggling to her feet, grabbing the end of the bed, and adding a theatrical wobble or two. Standing several feet from the window—better keep up the appearances of being repelled by the iron—she breathed slowly and deeply. Zuerst spoke and she shook her head and waved both hands, palm out, as if to beg a moment's respite.

To think fast and select the information to pass on. Her big question: Why had Schmidt let her listen in? Did the rest of them know? Or was he the rogue in the quartet. If so, why?

"Well?" Zuerst demanded and Bela knew she could delay no longer.

She turned to them, letting herself appear as confused and shocked as she felt. "Something has happened."

"What!"

"Schieße!" She'd never heard Zweiten swear before. They'd sensed something was different. Hardly surprising. She was still shaking and it wasn't acting.

She took another deep breath and focused the thoughts. If she told them the vamps were plotting mutiny, she'd be disposed of without delay.

"It's about the farmer Eiche killed. He was called to Weiss to explain himself. The others are worried he will draw attention and expose them all."

That last her captors could have deduced for themselves, but it never paid to appear too clever. A simple Wood Fairy was what they thought her and a simple Wood Fairy would deliver the news. "Seems he also injured his host. The spy in Brytewood."

"What!" they both snapped, almost in unison.

"You did not hear that!" Zweiten said.

"He cannot have!" Zuerst was as wrong as his partner.

"He admitted it to the others. I heard clearly. He believes she is more use to him incapacitated. Seems he intends to use her as fodder." That was the very word he'd used. Vampires sickened her.

"That would explain why she failed to report in yesterday," Zuerst said.

Zweiten nodded in agreement, then they both scowled at her.

"What else did you hear?"

She looked Zuerst in the eyes. They would not know she was lying by omission, if she could help it. "That was most of it. They talked back and forth, they're worried and all of them annoyed with Eiche and the attention his killing will draw.

Zuerst laughed. "That the Inselaffen care about one dead peasant, while we rain bombs and kill them by the hundreds? They worry like old women."

And plot mutiny like vampires.

Bela waited until the day faded and they'd taken away the tray from her supper. She would be alone until morning. As darkness fell over the hills and forest outside, she opened the windows wide and breathed in the clear night air. She yearned to run in it, to let the night breeze caress her and ease the torment inside.

Now was not the time for ease of any sort.

There was a war on.

Several of them it seemed.

The vamps could plot and scheme. She had a family to take care of. She couldn't cross the iron bars but she could, miraculously, reach her arms between then, with only a shimmer of an itch over her skin. She pressed her forehead against the cold iron and opened her mind.

Nothing.

Was the distance too far? The lack of barrier in the iron an illusion? Her hope unjustified? There was nothing there, no connection, no flicker of existence. Hope faded. Maybe they were imprisoned in iron and her new strength inadequate to pass it, but she caught something.

She focused all of her being of the faint senses of . . . Gela. Her sister. Unmistakable. As birth twins they were more strongly linked than even to their parents.

"Bela!" It was so faint. Like a rustle of leaves in a gentle breeze, but it was her sister.

"Gela! Yes, it's me. Where are you?"

"They told us you were dead!"

"They lied." She could say so much more but sensed Gela's weakness. "What happened to you? Mamma and Papa? Dana, Jakub, and Jiri?

She felt the pain in Gela's soul. "They took Papa and the boys away when they brought us here. A week or so later, Mama said they were dead."

And Mama would know. Bela fought back the tears. So much for their promises. She'd agreed to work for them to save her family. "What about Mama?"

Gela's hesitation told everything. "She expired, Bela. A few weeks back. They told her you were dead and she gave up."

Revenge burned in Bela's soul. One day these accused *schwein* would feel the full fury of Fairy wrath but for that she and Gela had to survive, regain their strength, and gather power. How? That mattered little. "And you, Gela? Are you sick?"

"I was. I believed you dead. Alone I could not go on, but now you live."

"You will live. We both will. We will live and avenge our family."

"Yes!" In that single word, Bela felt her sister's growing resolve. "Where are you?" Gela asked.

"I'm not sure exactly. In a *schloss* up in the hills beyond Munich. They drove me here in a car and I recognized the outskirts of the town as we drove through." She wasn't about to let her thoughts stray to that carefree time in Munich, just before the war, when she and Bela thought to spend time among humans. "Where are you?"

"In hell! We are in a prison near Flossenburgh. You cannot believe this place, Bela."

With all she'd heard and overheard, Bela could, but didn't want to. She couldn't bear the thought of her sister—laughing, lighthearted Gela—in such a pit of misery. "Whatever horror is around you, Gela, you must survive, as I will."

"Why did they take you away, Bela?"

"They are making me work for them." She would not admit exactly how. "Gela. You must live and I will live, and when we can we will escape." How, she had no idea, but will produced means. "Listen, we must connect, but not too often. It will weaken us and we may be discovered."

"At each full moon," Gela said. "Once it rises, we will connect."

"As long as it's dark." She could not risk being discovered and Gela certainly couldn't. "If the moon rises in the day, we wait until nightfall."

"Yes." She felt her sister's weakness. "Now I know you live. I will, sister mine."

"We will."

How could they escape and get together? Bela had no idea. but she had hope and the cold desire for revenge burning in her veins.

Chapter 13

Alice heard a few planes pass overhead. Headed for London no doubt. Poor, old London, but was Gran really serious about sleeping downstairs?

Yes. Alice pulled on her nightgown and went down to her room for warm woollies. It was darn cold in the cellar.

She was reaching in the drawer for a pair of thick socks when she heard the explosion.

Running down the stairs, she met Gran coming up from the cellar.

"Alice? You heard that? It was close!"

Too damn close. That wasn't a stray bomb falling out in a field somewhere.

The phone rang and for a few seconds Alice stared at it, then snatched the receiver off the cradle. "Doctor?" It was one of the air raid wardens, calling no doubt from the post in the village hall. "The vicarage got a hit."

"I'm on my way." The vicarage with all those children! Alice shuddered. "Better send some with a message to my assistant. He's billeted with Sergeant Pendragon." If only the sergeant had a phone!

"We will. After I call Nurse Prewitt."

"I'm on my way!"

There was nothing else to say. Alice ran back upstairs, pulled a pair of winter woollies under her nightgown and put a thick skirt and sweater on top. She grabbed a coat and her bag and was heading for the door.

"Want me to come down, my love?"

It was a cold night and Gran looked so worn. "Why not stay here? Stoke up the fire and we can bring people up here if we need to."

"I'll put on the kettle."

Tea, the secret weapon against all trouble and disaster.

Alice headed across the damp grass to the garage. She could probably ride Gran's bicycle down there in the time it took to start the engine, but she might well be glad of the car later.

She grabbed the crank handle and turned. Seemed the engine gods smiled—it started on the first go and in minutes she was heading down the hill toward the vicarage.

As, it seemed, was half the population.

Peter had been dozing off to sleep when the blast hit. Memories rushed back of his first few weeks in jail: locked in his cell as bombs fell outside. He overcame the terror by schooling himself with the belief that there was nothing he could do. He'd be hit or he wouldn't and he'd survived. Helped, he was convinced, by a lot of desperate prayers.

There would be no all clear. Howell had told him Brytewood was still waiting to receive air raid sirens. There was just a blast and some poor beggar got his.

Damn! He sat up in bed. This wasn't his cell in Pentonville. This was Howell Pendragon's spare bedroom, and he, Peter Watson, was the doctor's assistant. He was out of bed and reaching for his trousers when the sergeant put his head round the door.

"Lad, you're up. Good for you. Get dressed. You've got a job to do. See you downstairs.

Peter pulled on his sweater as he ran downstairs. Howell Pendragon was ahead of him, a hefty leather bag in his hand. "Best take this with us. The doctor will bring her supplies and the post has a store, but you can never have too many bandages."

Ominous, but true, though. "Know where we're headed?"

"Somewhere at the bottom of the village, I think."

As they stepped outside, a figure came running up the path. "Sergeant, got a message for the new doctor!"

Now was not the time to point out he wasn't any sort of doctor. "Yes?"

"We need you. The vicarage got a hit."

"A direct hit?" If they had, there wasn't much he or anyone could do.

"Landed on the vicar's tennis court. Took out half the vicarage, though, and did some damage to the cottages down the lane."

"Miss Waite's place? Pear Tree Cottage?" the Sergeant asked as he wheeled two bicycles from the shed.

"Yes, and the one next door, but no one seems hurt. It's the children and Reverend and Mrs. Roundhill we're worried about."

"We're on our way."

They left the breathless lad behind. They had to make haste if there were children trapped in the rubble. Peter shuddered. They must be petrified.

He decided to follow Howell rather than ride abreast. He knew his way, and negotiating the twisting lanes with a shaded headlight, no street lights, and enthusiastically blacked out houses was no picnic. That was on top of a long, uphill pull. Not that the sergeant seemed to have any trouble. *Dash it all, he really had got out of condition those months in prison.* Cycling around here on a regular basis would soon fix that.

They rounded the corner and headed for the church. It was still standing, but as they came closer, Peter couldn't miss the broken windows in one of the cottages, and the vast crater beside the vicarage. The house hadn't taken a direct hit, but the tennis court wouldn't ever see play again, and a great oak that probably saw the coming of the Normans, or at the very least sheltered someone during the Civil War, had taken off the back of the house.

"Looks nasty," Howell Pendragon said as he hopped off his bicycle with an energy Peter envied and propped it up against the hedge.

Looked more like a disaster to Peter. "Have they got somewhere set up?"

"If they haven't they will soon. Follow me."

Brytewood ARP was set up in the church hall, the open door sending a forbidden beam of light across the road.

"Shut the bleedin' door!" a voice called.

"Why worry now?" Another voice came clear in the night. "Jerry's been and gone and done it!"

"He's halfway to Berlin by now!"

As if to make a liar out of the last speaker, another plane, no, several, approached. The door slammed shut, cutting of a distinctly saltier expletive, and Peter and Howell hit the ground just as the planes passed overhead and a car came around the bend and stopped, extinguishing the lone, shuttered headlight.

Peter heard the car door open and Sergeant Pendragon called, "Is that you, Doctor?"

"It's me." Alice's voice came though the dark. "Think there's any more coming?"

"I hope not! We need to see what's going on across the road."

After the noise, lights, and blazes of London bombing, this dark quiet was eerie and terrifying. "We're going to need lights," Peter said. "Or we'll end up breaking our legs tripping over the mess."

"I've a torch," Alice said. Damn, he shouldn't be thinking of her as Alice. She was the doctor. "They've several hurricane lamps in the post. At least they did last week, and paraffin for them. I'll check." She looked toward the damaged vicarage. "Is anyone still in there?"

"I'm afraid so," Howell replied.

The emergency post was definitely equipped with hurricane lamps. No wonder the light from the open door had lit up the surrounding area. Eight or ten lamps burned on the cluttered table, or suspended from the roof, casting light on the two ancient villagers who appeared to be manning the place.

"Good to see you, Doctor," the younger one, who looked about eighty, said. "And you too, Sergeant," he added with a nod and then gave Peter a curious stare.

"My new assistant, Peter Watson," the doctor supplied. "Arrived today. He's supposed to start duties tomorrow but we're breaking him in early. This is Mr. Black and Mr. Baines."

"Hope I can help." Peter offered his hand.

It was taken in a strong, meaty one.

"Glad to have you." It was a better welcome than he'd received other places.

"Anyone get out yet?" Alice asked.

"Just me, I come over with Ming Li the instant I saw someone here." The speaker was a middle-aged woman clutching a Pekingese to her chest. She wore knitted gloves, and a good foot or so of pale flannel nightgown showed under the coat. "We were so scared, I tell you. I told Ming Li we were coming over here where we were safe from having the house topple over on us."

"It's not your house we've got to worry about, Mrs. Chivers. The vicarage and Miss Waite's took the worst of it."

The look she gave Black would have felled a lesser man. "You'd worry if you heard your chimney go and the tiles fall off your roof."

"Of course we would, Mrs. Chivers," Alice jumped right in. "But right now, getting everyone out of the vicarage is our priority. Tell you what, I bet Mr. Black and Mr. Baines would be relieved to have someone take care of making the tea." She looked in their direction. "How about it?"

"Yes, please," Baines replied. "You'll have to use the gas ring in the back since that hit took down the electricity pole, but that would be grand."

Alice set two bags on a table. "Let's see what's going on then."

As she spoke, the door pushed open and June Groves entered carrying a child. "Thank God you're so close!" she said. "We're going to need help. The back part of the house is ruined and I've got to go back and get the others, and Mrs. Roundhill is unconscious."

"June, how many are hurt?" Alice asked. "And what about you?"

Good question—the woman was bleeding from a gash in her head and she was covered in what Peter guessed was plaster dust.

"I'll be alright, honest. I got Sammy out as he was nearest the door. I'm worried about Mrs. Roundhill and the two older boys are trapped down in the cellar."

"What about the vicar?"

"He went up to London and was staying the night. Poor Mrs. Roundhill was so worried about him being up there with the bombing, and look where they land."

Baines took the whimpering child from her arms. The child cried out; his head was matted with blood and the way he cradled his arm pretty much suggested it was broken. If that was all the little blighter's injuries he'd come off lightly by the sound of things.

"I'll have a look at him," the doctor said, pulling off her coat to reveal a pullover and tweed skirt and a frill of night-gown underneath.

Peter told himself to get his thoughts right back on the wounded.

"Let's see what's happened to you then, Sammy," Alice

said, reaching for one of the lamps. "Mr. Baines will put you down here on the blanket, and we'll have a look."

"Come on, lad. Best get the others. We'll need a stretcher for Mrs. Roundhill by the sound of things."

"Are the phone lines still up?" the doctor asked. "We'd better call the ambulances in."

"Do I have to go to hospital?" the pitiful little voice asked from the table.

"I'm afraid so, Sammy. I can stitch you up, but I think your arm's broken. You'll be fine, though, not much else hurt that I can see." She looked right at Peter, her blue eyes tired but bright. "Better go and see what else is needed, and someone call those ambulances."

"Thank heaven for the field phone," Baines said. "I think Jerry took out our phone line along with the electricity."

"How are the other children?" Alice asked.

"Scared witless," June replied. She looked in much the same condition. "I told them to stay put and get their shoes on and I'd be right back. Two are just scared and shaken up but Celia looks as if her leg's broken. I was scared to move her."

"How many little 'uns are there?" Howell asked as they stood in the lane by the hedge, or rather what was left of it.

"Six, counting Sammy. We rather took over the vicarage. Lord knows where we'll end up now."

The last wasn't a moan or gripe, just tired resignation.

Close up, Peter understood her worry. "We'd better look at Miss Waite's cottage later," Baines said, glancing down the lane. At this distance it appeared worse damage than Mrs. Chivers's several doors away.

"She's lucky she was in hospital," Howell muttered half to himself.

"Wonder where that visitor of hers is," Baines said and shrugged. "I'll send someone to check." He looked around at the cluster of villagers slowly gathering. One Peter noticed

was Gloria, the nurse, on a bicycle with a roll of blankets tied
to the carrier.

"Want me to check?" she asked as she dismounted and
wheeled her bike to the side and propped it near theirs.

"We'll need you here, Gloria. Let someone else go,"
Alice said.

"Right!" Baines looked around the crowd and met a tall
heavyset man's eyes. "Fred, do us a favor, go and look over
Miss Waite's house, see if everyone's alright."

Fred set off down the lane. Howell opened the vicarage
front gate. The hedge was twisted and uprooted, but the
wooden gate swung easily on the gateposts.

"Now you lot wait back here," Baines said to the crowd.
"We'll see if it's safe. We'll need stretcher bearers once we see
where everyone is."

Between the lanterns and electric torches the group made
a fine beacon for another attack, but skies appeared empty.
Thank the Lord.

Peter followed the others into the house.

A woman Peter presumed was Mrs. Roundhill lay unconscious on the dining room floor, dried blood on her face and
arms. Beside her sat two children, ash pale and shivering. The
blanket covering the vicar's wife might have been better
around them.

"Good, children," Gloria said. "You put your shoes on and
found something warm. Now we're going to take Mrs. Roundhill over to the doctor."

A sad, scared voice called from the bottom of the stairs.
"Don't forget me."

"We won't," June replied. "We're coming."

"That's Celia," she explained. "She fell coming down the
stairs. I think, no, I'm pretty sure her leg's broken. It looks all
wrong."

She turned back to the two still huddled together by the

unconscious Mrs. Roundhill. "You get up and hold my hand. We're getting out of here."

"Tell you what," Baines interrupted. "How about we carry them? I'll get some of that lot hanging about outside to help. They look all done in."

June didn't argue, being, Peter guessed, pretty much done in herself.

Didn't take long to get two stretchers in. With luck the ambulances would arrive soon. As long as it had been a quiet night in Dorking.

"What happened to Mrs. Roundhill?" the sergeant asked.

"I'm not sure. We'd all gone to bed. She often stays up late when the vicar's away. Can't sleep. When I came down with the younger children, I found her on the floor. I think the blast threw her against the fender," June replied. "I moved her off it. I know you're not supposed to move people but she looked so uncomfortable."

"Don't worry." Gloria had her arm around her shoulders. "I'd have done the same. We'll see how she is once we get her in the light."

The woman didn't stir as they lifted her onto the stretcher. A bad sign, Peter thought, but he'd seen people in worse states, and they often survived.

"That's the lot then," Baines said as the last child was handed to a pair of willing arms.

"Yes, oh God! No!" June as good as shrieked. "How could I? I forgot Sidney and Dave!"

"Eh?" Baines said.

"The two older boys. The brothers?" Gloria asked.

"Yes! Oh, dear heaven! How could I? I was so wrapped up worrying about Mrs. Roundhill and the younger ones. I forgot they were down there. How could I?" She burst into tears and was approaching hysterics.

Gloria slapped her on the face. The sound cut off her wails, which subsided to a few sniffs and gulps. "Calm down," Gloria told her. "Tell us where they are."

"Down in the cellar. They didn't like sleeping upstairs, got scared every time a plane went over, and used to get the little ones all het up, so we set up a room for them there with beds and an electric fire and now . . ."

They all looked toward the kitchen, or what was left of it.

"Looks like we'll need to call out the entire squad to dig them out," Baines said.

June gave a loud sob. "The poor things must be terrified."

"You need to sit down," Gloria said. "I'm going to take you over to the hut. You need to be with the other children. They'll be getting anxious without you. Shock does a lot to children."

And adults, Peter could have added, but why state what everyone already knew?

With Gloria and June gone, Black, Peter, and the sergeant stared at each other. "Best see what's going on," Black said and led the way over the rubble.

The house was in a bad state. By daylight it would look worse. Peter held his lamp low to light the floor and followed the others.

The back corner and the kitchen seemed to have taken the worst of the damage, the floor above had caved in, and the night breeze blew though the gaping gap in the wall.

"Where the blazes is the cellar?" Black asked, looking around the mess.

"The door's over there," Howell said. "I remember carrying some potatoes down there for Mrs. Roundhill a few weeks back."

"Over there" was a heap of wall and a pile of splintered wood that had once been the back stairs.

"Damn! We'll have to dig them out," Black muttered as he stepped back to avoid a chunk of falling masonry.

Chapter 14

"Crikey! It's about to go!"

Peter wasn't about to argue. The entire back stairs, what was still left of them, rocked precariously.

"We've got to get them out," Pendragon said. "Can't leave them there."

"They could be goners," Black said.

"No, they're alive." The Sergeant spoke with such conviction, it never occurred to Peter to doubt him.

"We'll need a winch and crane and crew to clear that lot," Sam said, shaking his head.

Howell hesitated a few seconds. "The lad and I can do it," he said. "I see a gap, you make sure we have stretchers waiting for them, and leave your torch and give the lad your tin hat."

"You're certain about this?" Black asked. "Maybe we should get help for this."

"I don't think so." As Pendragon spoke, another chunk of wall settled on the stairway. "Too many won't help at all. Our weight is making it less stable. Go carefully and get those stretchers."

As he left Howell asked, "Want to go too, lad? This is risky."

So was spending nights locked in a cell on the second tier. "Sergeant, if you think it can be done, let's have a bash at it."

"Put on that damn tin pot, first!"

It was warm from the other man's head as Peter buckled it on. "What now?"

"You're going to have to go in and see what's happening. Are you game?"

"Yes." He could hardly say "no" at this point.

As if in reply a faint, half-broken voice called, "Is someone there? Please help us!"

"Coming, lad." As if in reply to Howell's assurance, the stairs rocked and another chunk of wall fell to the floor.

"How are we going to do this?" Peter hoped the sergeant had a brilliant idea as he was devoid of anything but numb fear.

"First thing, lad, you won't be seeing what I'm about to do, but I'm going to lift the back stairs, or what's left of them, and you're going to crawl in under, get through the broken door, and go down into the cellar."

Either the man was demented, or he possessed supernatural strength. Peter opted for demented and he half-choked on out, "Alright."

Howell replied, "Right you are then, here we go." And pressing his back and shoulders under the remains of the back stairs, and bracing one hand against the wobbling wall, lifted the stairway enough for Peter to crawl under. "I'm going to let it down," he said once Peter was through and crouching at the top of the cellar stairs. "Call when you're ready and I'll pick it up again. You'd best see how those boys are doing."

The boys were huddled sobbing in a corner, covered with brick dust and plaster and surrounded by the ruins of the vicar's study floor. They stared like frightened rabbits, mesmerized by a car's high beams, when the lamp shone in their direction.

"We're rescued, Sid," one said to the other, patting him on the shoulder. "We're bloody rescued. Sorry, sir," he added.

"Don't apologize, you're entitled to swear." Heck, quite a few oaths hovered on the tip of Peter's tongue, not the least how the fucking hell that old man held up half a wall and the back stairs. "Are you hurt?"

"My shoulder hurts," the other one, who had to be Dave, said. "Something fell on it."

"Think you can walk?"

"To get out of here, I'd friggin' fly!"

Seemed he was taking Peter's assurances about swearing to heart. "Alright then. One at a time. I'll get you first as you're hurt."

"No! I ain't leaving Sid, we go together. I promised my dad."

"That's right," Sid corroborated. "He said to stick together, whatever happens."

Peter wasn't too sure their absent parent had actually meant whilst trapped in the cellar of a bombed building prone to collapse any minute. "Right-o, you stick together and then stick to me, but we have to go one at a time up the stairs. The whole wall above is flimsy." If indeed the sergeant could manage a repeat miracle.

From the foot of the stairs Peter called, "Sergeant, they're both alive and only one is hurt. Can you lift again?"

He could. A gap of eighteen inches or so appeared in the the dim light. "You go first, Sid. Keep on your belly."

Sid got through. Dave had a harder time of it, obviously gritting his teeth against the pain. It took him ages to belly crawl up the stairs. Surely Howell couldn't take that weight all this time? Peter stifled the panicky prospect that he'd be the one trapped.

Darn, if the sergeant could do the impossible, he could do it five minutes longer.

He did. Peter wiggled his way through the gap to see Sid helping Dave down the hallway. "Keep going," Howell told them. "Head for the front door. We'll be after you in a jiffy."

"Didn't want them to see what I was really doing," he

added in a low voice to Peter. "Now lad, grab both lanterns. This wall really is about to go. Step away and get clear."

"What about you?"

"I can move fast. You get going after those young 'uns."

This wasn't real. Couldn't be. But Peter knew he wasn't hallucinating. Or was he? He stepped back, the sergeant moved from under the shattered staircase, and yes, even in poor light, Peter saw the damaged stairway sag and the wall rock.

"Move!"

No one hesitated at the sergeant's order. Even Dave sprinted toward the wide open front door and all four of them dashed though just as the wall and back stairs gave way, pulling half the house with them.

Outside on the now trampled vicarage lawn Black, Baines, and a couple of others waited with the stretchers.

"Hell! You got them out!"

"Wasn't as bad as it looked at first," Sergeant Pendragon lied. "We just shifted a few bits of broken stairs and Peter got down and fished them out. What it is to be young, eh?"

Just then, with a loud roar, the house shifted and the roof on one side fell in, taking most of the upper floor with it.

Everyone darted back toward the road, watching with nervous horror as dust rose from the ruins.

"Blimey!" someone muttered. "Good thing you got out when you did."

Not a statement Peter was about to argue with. Cold washed over him like an icy rush as the realization hit just how close they'd all been to finding themselves buried under that mess.

Took all he had not to start shaking.

"You should be proud of yourself, young man," a tall, mustachioed man said as he held out his hand to Peter. "I'm Sir James Gregory, commander of the Home Guard. I live just up the road and came down to see if we could help. I heard you've just arrived. Welcome to Brytewood, young man, and may I say, on behalf of the entire village, we're thankful to God you came. As I bet those two boys are."

Peter wasn't quite ready to be the hero of the hour but seemed no one cared about his consent. The aftermath was downright embarrassing. Besides feeling an utter fraud, he darn well wanted to know how an old man like Sergeant Pendragon could hold up an entire wall and half a staircase.

Not that he was likely to find out tonight.

Too much work to do.

The hall was a buzz of activity. The doctor and Gloria and a couple of other women were busy ministering to the still shaken and sobbing children.

Peter walked over to Alice. "Need another pair of hands?"

She looked up, brushing her hair off her forehead. "Yes, but you look as if you need first aid yourself."

"What?" Not the most polite thing to say. "I'm alright."

"You might be, but your forehead isn't."

"What?" Yes, his vocabulary was sadly lacking, but it had been a tough evening.

"You must have hit it at some point," she said, stepping close. Damn, he could smell the fresh sweat on her, and something underneath like floral soap. She touched his forehead and as he gulped, praying to not shame himself in front of half the village, she brushed his forehead with her fingertip. "You're bleeding."

She met his eyes a second, then turned abruptly and swiveled back, handing him a pad of gauze. "Mop it up. If you hadn't noticed, it probably isn't too bad."

Except now that she'd mentioned it, and he saw the stain of blood on the gauze, it throbbed and hurt like hell.

A scream from the half open doorway distracted him for the growing ache in his head—and other places. Getting close to Dr. Doyle was not a good idea.

"No, you won't!" a young voice shouted. "Damn and blast you! I'm coming and don't you try . . ."

It was young Sid. Peter strode back to the doorway; Sergeant Pendragon was ahead of him. They were trying to load Dave's stretcher into the ambulance and Sid was resisting attempts to hold him back. The child was kicking and screeching manfully but his strength was no match for the burly man holding him: Mosley.

"Let him go," Peter said. "It's his brother that's hurt."

Mosley's ratlike eyes peered out of his fleshy face and met Peter's. "You! Would be you, wouldn't it? Handing round orders. Well, this little scrubber isn't going anywhere in my ambulance and that's final!"

"Why not?" Somehow Sergeant Pendragon's voice got attention. "That's his brother in the ambulance. All they have here is each other. They're evacuees. Won't do any harm to let him ride along. Better not to separate them."

A glimmer of hope lit the boy's eyes and soon faded.

"Oh! yes! Clever idea that! Who's going to watch this little so-and-so when we get there? I'm not."

"I'll come and take care of him. He shouldn't be left alone anyway and he was trapped too. Wouldn't hurt to get him checked as well."

Before Mosley could come back with any objection, Howell had wrested the child from his grasp, picked the boy up in his arms, and hopped up into the open door of the ambulance. "Lad!" he called down to Peter. "See my bicycle gets home alright, will you, please?"

"With pleasure, Sergeant!"

Mosley gave what could only be described as a derisive sneer. He didn't exactly spit in Peter's direction, but he got the message.

"Hoped I'd never see you again, you lousy conscie. They're welcome to you." Saying that, he turned to shut the ambulance door.

"Now, look here, my good man!" It was Sir James Gregory,

his voice carrying all the authority of his position and station. "That is no way to speak!"

Mosley had little respect for rank or station. "Oh, no? Well, I don't pal up with bloody conscies!"

A leaden lump formed in Peter's gut. Yes, he expected the news to get out, but in this fashion?

"Mind your language, there are ladies and children here. Those two boys in the ambulance owe their lives to this young man." He clapped Peter on the shoulder. "I think I speak for all of Brytewood when I say we are delighted to have him in our midst."

"You're welcome to him then!"

The doors slammed and with another scowl, Mosley turned to his assistant. "Let's get the hell out of here."

"Is that true, young man?" Sir Gregory asked, his voice quiet but brooking no evasion.

He wouldn't have bothered anyway. "That I'm a CO? Yes, sir."

The man pondered that a second or two, then held out his hand. "Seems the Army's loss is our gain. No doubt you had your reasons."

"Yes, sir, I did."

"And you need fixing up, too. That knock on your head could be nasty."

He'd forgotten all about it, but now it was throbbing again. "The doctor mentioned it." And now he was going to have to go back there. What the hell! He'd have to learn to work with her. At close quarters. Might as well start now but he was rather embarrassed at the cheers that greeted him when he reentered the parish hall.

"We need to get you a bleeding medal," Mr. Black said.

"It wasn't me, it was Sergeant Pendragon."

"Not what he says," Baines replied, "but no point in arguing about it now. We've got all this lot to sort out."

Two women, Voluntary Service ladies no doubt, were

taking names and pondering where to house the six children and the teacher.

"Trouble is, we're pretty much full to the seams as it is," one said.

"We'll take them," the doctor said, "at least for tonight. We'll need extra blankets. And they'll need clothes come morning, but we can manage."

"I've got Maggie here to stitch up. Celia is on her way to the hospital with Mrs. Roundhill and the two older boys. Can someone drive them up to The Gallop and bring the car back?"

"I can," Peter said.

"You need to stay and get stitched yourself," Alice said.

"I can be back by the time you're done with the child."

"I think we've had enough heroics from you for one night," Gloria piped in. "Have a seat. Let someone else drive."

"I will," said Mr. Black. "I'll take them up to the doctor's house and be back in no time at all."

"Take June Groves with you; she can help Gran."

At least the crowds had dispersed. The children, poor little blighters in every stage of disheveled undress, were herded together by the teacher, who looked dead on her feet herself. Sam Black covered them all with an armful of blankets he fetched from the back of the hall, and off they went.

Peter returned to the church hall and gratefully sank into the first chair he reached.

He was lightheaded and giddy. Shock? Probably. He still hadn't quite grasped what had happened back there in the vicarage.

Someone handed him a cup of tea. It was too sweet, but the warmth was welcome. He sagged against the back of the chair and watched the activity around him. Baines was tidying up, hoping for a quiet rest of the night no doubt. Gloria was gathering up bloody swabs and used kidney dishes. And beautiful, sexy, desirable, unreachable Dr. Doyle (he was punch-drunk but enjoying the view) was stitching up the last child and telling her she was going to be alright and that she was coming home with her in a little while.

The child was offered a mug of tea and the good doctor turned her attention to Peter.

"Come on over here then. Let's have a look."

He declined to stretch out on one on the trestle tables, so he carried his chair over with him and sat down far too close to her for comfort.

"You shouldn't have been running around with a cut like this."

"The ambulance driver was giving Sid what for. The boy's had enough for one night without that man adding to his misery."

"Mr. Mosley? He's not the most affable man around, is he?" He'd have agreed but she'd just swabbed his forehead with ice cold Dettol. Talk about stinging! Maybe the shock was catching upon him. "Doesn't look too bad, really," she said, "but since you're here we might as well stitch it up." He felt the sting of the local anesthetic, then the gentle tug as she put in the stitches.

Dear heaven! Just feeling her fingers against his skin sent a warm rush of sensation right down to where he didn't want it. At least not now, in this makeshift first aid station, with an audience.

"Better take your shirt off," she said as she taped a pad of gauze over his stitches. "If you got that and didn't notice, who knows if you have other abrasions."

"That's all, honest." And about all he could take right now.

"Mr. Watson, you're not being coy, are you?" Nurse Gloria asked.

He laughed. He could do that much anyway. "No, just want to keep warm. It's like a tomb in here. I'll give myself the once-over when I get home. Might have a few bruises but I can put Arnica on them."

The doctor didn't press the point. Just nodded. "Let's clean up here then, and I'll take Maggie home with me. You rode down did you, Gloria?"

The nurse nodded. "You go ahead. I'll clean up."

"Can't go anywhere until Mr. Black gets back with my car."

"I'll help," Peter offered. Might as well do something as sit around.

"Listen," Baines said. "We can clean up after you go. We've got all night. Let's all have another cuppa."

Seemed the war was going to be won on pints of Darjeeling.

Sitting in the gloom with the lamps turned down to save the oil was like a surreal party: the child in nightgown and slippers, a blanket over her shoulders, the doctor and Gloria, both worn and tired, the two WVS ladies cheerfully chatty, Baines handing around the sugar and a teaspoon, and Peter Watson tired and aching in body but every nerve and cell alert to the woman sitting opposite him.

This was not going to be an easy job. He might just be better off back on Sid Mosley's ambulance. At least he was utterly devoid of sex appeal!

Chapter 15

Eiche perched on the church tower and scowled. Enough was enough and this was, to purloin a phrase from the accursed Inselaffen, the giddy limit. First, he'd endured a summons by Weiss, only to be chided, in front of the others, if you please, as if he were a recalcitrant mortal child. Now he returned to find his nest damaged by a bomb attack, although he was delighted to see the vicarage a shattered shell. There'd be no more annoying singing and playing, and the next door house had a ruined chimney and roof. Maybe that old biddy would be forced to move out with her yappy hound. Both those thoughts were sheer pleasure to his immortal heart. After all, human misery was not to be missed. Seemed there were injured enough to be carted off to the mortuary—he hoped. And that boy's distress was quite restorative.

But much as the damage by the Luffwaffe was a joy to behold, why did they also have to render his current lodgings temporarily uninhabitable?

He'd had a good look while the yokels were running around like ants, fussing over whining children and wringing their work-worn hands. Broken windows, a damaged roof, and a chimney pot sitting in shards on the back lawn were trivial to a vampire, but would present difficulties with Miss

Waite supposedly returning home soon. If she caught pneumonia and died he would be severely inconvenienced. He needed her for nourishment.

And nourishment itself was presenting a conundrum. He wanted to ask the others if they'd noticed less than usual strength after feeding, but after Weiss's totally unjustified rebuke over killing that peasant (and how had he known about that anyway?), Eiche was not about to admit to anything that could be twisted into weakness.

Still, it bothered him. A full deep feeding that ended in death should have sustained him for days—maybe a week to two—but after running back from Guildford, he was spent. He should have paused on the way to feed. He wasn't risking another mysterious death in his territory. Not this week anyway. Common sense dictated that caution, not Weiss's pedantic chastisement.

Dammit! It would have to be one of the farm animals tonight. There was a barn full of cows half a mile away.

He'd content himself with bovine blood, and then see just how habitable dear Aunt Jane's cottage was.

He couldn't help wondering if the mortals who considered themselves his masters had foreseen this little snag in their master plan.

Maybe he should send them a message.

Chapter 16

Peter hadn't meant to accept a lift home, but by the time he'd settled the drowsy child on a nest of blankets on the back seat, Black had swung both bicycles up in the back of the shooting brake.

Seemed downright churlish to yank them out again, so Peter hopped into the passenger seat, reminding himself he was quite possibly going to be working with this woman for the duration of the war and lust was out of the question.

Even if it had taken possession of his brain.

Sitting this close in the dark was nothing short of painful. At least it was dark. It was only five minutes back to Sergeant Pendragon's cottage. And there was a child on the back seat. Who was right now snoring. No doubt needed her adenoids out.

"It never ceases to amaze me," Alice—Dr. Doyle, he reminded himself—said, "how a child can sleep like that after a night of trauma. But she's been taken care of, rescued, stitched up, and tucked up. The grown-ups are looking after her." She sighed and Peter was about to comment that things weren't that secure for many children when Alice went on. "She'll not worry until she wakes up, and wonders where she'll end up living now, if she'll be with her friends, and if she'll be late for school tomorrow."

"Or if you're going to get bombed again tomorrow night."

"Or the Germans march up the gap in the Downs. They haven't put up all those pillboxes and Dragons' teeth barriers all over the place just to complicate the harvest."

"They've got to get here first." He hadn't expected to be talking about the war and invasion, but it was safer than saying what really was on his mind. Nothing like a bit of worry to take care of his urges. "Although I suppose nights like tonight are meant to soften us up so we just roll over when they tramp up from the beaches and head for London."

"Judging by the mood in London, they're more likely to be met with carving knives and knitting needles."

"And pitchforks and scythes in these parts."

She glanced at him in the night, then set her gaze back on the road. One blinkered headlight was not enough to see well in the twisting lane. "You'd take up a pitchforks or a scythe, Mr. Watson? How does that reconcile with your CO stance? Sorry!" She glanced his way again and shook her head. "I had no right to ask that."

"You put it a lot more tactfully than most people do. 'You'd sit by and watch your sister get raped by a German, would you?' is one of the favorite lines." Why was he telling her this? Had to be a combination of tiredness and the odd isolation of the dark.

"Do you even have a sister?"

"Actually, no. I've two little half brothers, and if anyone laid a hand on them I'd plant him a facer and then attack below the waist." He sensed her smile in the dark. "It's a long story, but I cannot, will not, pick up a gun. The board accepted that." And he hoped to hell she did.

She'd stopped the car.

They were back at his cottage.

Just as well. Another half mile he'd no doubt have spilled his whole hideous past. "Er . . . thanks."

He hopped out of the car and went around the back to retrieve the bicycles.

She was there with him, turned the handle, and opened the back. "Try to get a few hours' sleep, Mr. Watson. And this is a doctor talking. We still need to start at nine in the morning. Gloria will need help with the home visits and we need to find out what to do with all the children, to say nothing of the Arckle boys."

The Arckle boys? "You mean Dave and Sid."

"Yes. The billeting committee is going to have its hands full. I can't keep them all in my place indefinitely."

He reached for the sergeant's bicycle at precisely the same moment she did and their hands closed on the handlebars together. And just about undid all his brilliant efforts at self control.

Her hands were warm, smooth, and darn strong as she grasped the handlebars, and his hand, for a split second before drawing back. "Sorry. You want to get that one?"

He did, and the other actually, but she swung his down with little effort and wheeled it beside him up the path. But forget the blackout, their exhaustion, and the injured child sleeping in the car, and they might have been returning after an afternoon spin across the Surrey Hills, stopping off for a picnic by some river, and now he'd be getting ready to ask her in for coffee.

He almost laughed out loud.

Seemed stress and fatigue made his imagination run riot.

"Er . . . excuse me . . ."

She'd been talking to him, or trying to, while he was verging on impure thoughts. "Sorry."

"That's alright. I'm the one needs to apologize." She leaned the bicycle against the side of the house and looked up at him. Her face was a pale shape in the darkness. "I'm not good at apologizing. Never have been. But I owe you one. That first afternoon I made some very rude, unjustified comments. I'm sorry." She paused as if to catch her breath. "You're not a coward. Tonight proved it and I had no business to make such a sweeping judgment without knowing a thing about you."

He shrugged, unsure how to reply. "Tonight I just did my job." With a lot of help.

"Without you, those two brothers would have been buried alive and no doubt dead the time they dug them out. You saved their lives."

"I didn't do it alone. Sergeant Pendragon . . ."

"Is an old man. You went down into the cellar—he told me that. You went looking for them, not knowing if you'd be able to get out again. That, Mr. Watson, is courage in my book." He ought to tell the truth, but she'd think he was out of his mind. Perhaps he was. "Thank you," she went on, "and I look forward to working with you."

She offered her hand.

He took it.

His earlier impression had been dead on. Her skin was still warm, even in the chilly night, her grasp strong, and he might sense rather than see her smile, but he just knew it crinkled the corners of her blue eyes. Which must sparkle with life and beauty and . . .

Oh, dash it all!

Holding hands was nowhere near enough. Why waste the night and the moment?

He put his arm on her shoulders, drawing her closer. To his utter amazement and delight, she stepped into him, looking up at him. This close he could almost see the soft curve of her lips. He felt the warmth of her breath as he lowered his mouth and brushed her lips with his.

That was all he intended: a reckless, stolen kiss that they could both forget in daylight.

If they had any sense.

Which they obviously didn't.

Instead of stepping back, she leaned into him, warm and

soft against him; and, tilting her neck, opened her mouth and wrapped her arms around him.

His lips pressed hers and dash it, she was kissing him back. Hard. With a little sigh she came even closer, pressing herself into him and reaching up to pull his head down. His tongue touched hers. Just a cautious, gentle caress of tip to tip. But not for long. High explosive wasn't the word for what happened between them. His mind went up in a blaze of need, possessiveness, and passion as he deepened the kiss.

She let him. Damn! She was leading now, holding him, letting her tongue curl and caress over his as he basked in her warmth and breathed her scent in the night.

He pulled her even closer, holding her tighter in his embrace, never wanting this to end, wishing to stay here forever, lost in the dream and the sheer and utter wonder of Alice Doyle's kiss.

His hands slid up and down her back, making him suddenly aware of her skirt and sweater pulled on over her night clothes. He was only too aware of no brassiere under her clothes and maybe no . . .

Holy smoke! He had to stop. Didn't want to. Couldn't. Wanted to stand here, on the garden path, for eternity, their mouths pressed and bodies warm against each other.

At last she drew away to pause for breath.

"Dr. Doyle, I . . ." Damn! He was not apologizing. Or should he? Christ, what was . . .

"Good night, Mr. Watson. Good night." She stepped back before giving him a quick peck on the cheek. "Don't be late in the morning. Gloria will need you."

And she didn't?

He hadn't dreamt it. Had he?

He stood like a blamed fool in the dark, listening to the sound of her engine fade in the distance.

Hell! What next?

He was too elated to worry and too flat out exhausted to

think. Making sure the cycles were propped up inside the shed, he closed the door on them and went into the house.

He undressed. He really needed a good bath after clambering over the walls and rubble but the stove had gone out in their absence and a quick wash in cold water was all he bothered with. He lay in bed for some time thinking over the evening, and in particular, the last few minutes of it.

He'd witnessed the impossible, managed the unthinkable, and stolen a kiss, no, a KISS, from a woman who would perhaps revile him in the morning.

And if she did, blow it. It had been worth it, even if he couldn't roll over on his stomach right now.

It took all Alice had to keep her hands from shaking on the steering wheel. She had to get Maggie back safely and herself under control. Whatever Gran and June Groves had managed, there was still a long night ahead of them getting children to sleep; even finding spots for all of them to stretch out was going to be a challenge.

And, as if she didn't have more than enough on her plate, she only had to throw herself at her new assistant!

He'd not exactly repulsed her, but what man ever said "no" to a free kiss? What maggot had seized her brain? Apologizing was one thing. She owed him that. Gran had been right: There were many sorts of courage and she, Alice Doyle, had witnessed one of the finest tonight. Peter Watson has risked his life to save two boys he'd never met. He was incredible, honorable, and wonderful.

And she was a total fool.

How in the name of heaven had a handshake become an out-and-out, tongue-down-the-throat kiss with her loving it all and wanting more?

How had she let herself get so . . .

A whimper from the back seat brought Alice back to her

responsibilities. "Won't be long now, Maggie. Just up the hill and we'll be home. My gran will fix you a nice cup of cocoa and we'll find you somewhere to sleep."

She might as well give up her bed to one of the others who needed it. Alice doubted she'd sleep much tonight. It would take all the time she had until dawn and more to work out how she was going to face her new assistant in the morning.

Chapter 17

What Alice needed was a long, quiet evening with a soak in a hot bath and a glass of wine. She might as well yearn to fly. It was about as likely.

As she walked into the kitchen, Gran looked up from washing a little girl's hair in the sink. "Hello, dear," Gran said. "A long night?"

And it wasn't over yet. June, looking as weary as Alice felt, was drying the boy's hair with a towel. She was still in her torn and dusty clothes; the children were wearing an odd assortment of clean garments Gran had obviously scrounged up. Alice recognized one of her own shortie nightgowns, Alan's rolled up pajama bottoms, and the old shawl her grandmother wore to read in bed.

As expected, her grandmother had managed.

"How's Maggie and Celia and the boys?" June asked.

"Maggie's asleep on my back seat. I came in to ask someone to hold open the doors when I carry her in. Celia went off in the ambulance with Mrs. Roundhill. Dave has a broken arm at least, maybe his collarbone, and I think you were right about Celia's leg. Sid went along with Dave with Sergeant Pendragon as chaperone. Where should I take Maggie? I don't want to wake her if I can help."

"Take her up to Simon's room," Gran replied. "Two can sleep there. We've taken the mattress off the box springs."

With June's help, they got the child upstairs. She woke briefly but settled under the covers. Alice rather envied her.

"Mrs. Burrows," June said when they stood outside the door, "is incredible. She found clean night things for all of us, she had beds set up and blankets airing for us, and I can't thank her enough. Splitting the children up right now would have been upsetting."

"Gran knew the vicarage had been hit and guessed you'd need a place for the night."

"For more than a night, but we can't impose on her for long."

"Things will work out. Everyone can camp out here until something permanent can get arranged."

It took almost another hour to get everyone settled and asleep. Everyone under the age of ten that was. June gladly stretched out on the mattress in Simon's room in case Maggie woke up scared, and Alice prepared to follow suit, grateful Gran hadn't put any of the children in her room. She tried to shove that selfish thought away but she longed for solitude. And a few hours' sleep. Actually, she yearned for a good eight hours, but she'd told Peter not to be late, so she had to be on time.

Peter, yes! She needed more that eight hours' sleep to get that sorted out. He'd kissed her but it hadn't stopped there. She'd kissed him back with all her might and main and would still be doing so if she hadn't fortuitously paused for breath, and the influx of oxygen to her brain had yanked her back to her senses.

"Let me bring you a cup of mint and lavender tea," Gran said. "It'll help you relax."

Gran and her potions and tisanes. Alice wanted to shake her head, but it was too much effort, and when Gran did bring it up a few minutes later, the scent of it put Alice in mind of a summer day in the garden in far less frantic times. She sniffed back a tear.

"Weary and worn, my love?"

That was putting it mildly. "Just tired, Gran. To think that people in London put up with this every night. Poor Mrs. Roundhill is in sorry shape, and it was only touch-and-go that we got the two older boys out."

"Yes, June told me about that."

There was a long, pregnant pause. Her grandmother waited. "You were right, Gran. I made a hasty and unjustified judgment. I apologized to him." And just about swallowed his tonsils in the process. That she was not sharing with Gran.

"I think he'll be a great support and help to you, my love. He's what you need."

"Another pair of hands will be a godsend." And what hands! She could still feel the warmth of them on her back.

"He'll be an asset to the village, Alice, but he's what *you* need. You'll suit each other well."

Gran had never been eager to pair her off. Why now? "Gran, he's my assistant."

"And a very good looking, intelligent young man. Don't be obtuse, my love. You've eyes in your head and a brain between your ears. He's exactly what you need; don't deny the obvious."

"What's so obvious?"

All she got was a rather smug smile.

"Gran, I've know him barely a week and thoroughly insulted him the first time we met."

"He'll get over that. Has already, I don't doubt. Alice, trust me. I know these things." Like she knew the planes weren't just passing over tonight.

"Gran, you put too much stock in feelings and guesses."

"Child, they're not guesses, nor are they wild, senile imaginings. That young man is here for you, a fact you'd recognize if you'd just harness the powers you possess instead of denying them. Now good night, sleep well."

Surprisingly, she did.

Thank heaven for alarm clocks. As Peter rolled over and tapped off the ringer, he forced himself to sitting. He was bone tired, his stitches ached and pulled, and he was most definitely not rested.

But he had, last night, kissed the most beautiful and sexiest woman in the world. Even if hell did break loose this morning, it was worth it.

Pulling on his dressing gown he noticed a note pinned on the inside of his door.

Lad, I stoked up the boiler so there's plenty of hot water. I'll bet you're needing it as much as I did. Be as quiet as you can going downstairs; the boy is sleeping on the sofa in the front room.

H. Pendragon

P.S. His brother has a broken arm and collarbone and several broken ribs and needed some stitches but is otherwise in fine shape, thanks to you.

Peter shook his head. He and Sergeant Pendragon were going to have to have a talk and soon. After he had a nice, hot bath.

The Pendragon bathroom was a lean-to built off the kitchen, the floor stone and cold, and the hip bath a trifle snug, but Sergeant Pendragon hadn't lied about the hot water. Peter scrubbed himself twice, letting out the water and refilling the bath between times—in the dark he hadn't realized exactly how filthy he'd been—and then shampooed his hair, combing it smooth so it would dry while he shaved.

Of course that little indulgence took time. He'd have to scramble if he was going to be on time. But he wasn't arriving unshaven.

He emerged to the aroma of frying. Pendragon stood at the stove, frying pan in hand. "Morning, lad. I thought we both deserve a good fry up after our efforts last night."

And a good talk. "I'm supposed to meet Nurse Prewitt at nine."

"After last night, no one in this village is going to look askance if you're fifteen minutes late. Nip upstairs lad, and by the time you're dressed, I'll have us a pot of tea and a plate of fried bread and tomatoes. Do you like your eggs fried hard or runny?"

With fried bread? Only one way. "Runny, please. I'll be back down in half a mo."

He was going to be late, dammit, but he wasn't churl enough to refuse a cooked meal, which reminded him, he needed to hand over his ration book, and above all else he needed a talk with the sergeant.

It wasn't going to be easy. How exactly do you ask your host, who's just put in front of you the best breakfast you've seen in months, if he possessed supernatural strength, or if you'd been hallucinating on overly strong tea the night before? What was Sherlock Holmes's line about if one eliminated the impossible the improbable had to be true? Or was it the other way round?

Either way . . .

"Eat up, lad," the sergeant said as he put a mug of tea on the table in front of Peter. "I can make you toast if you want. No marmalade, but I've some dripping to spread on it."

Peter eyed the two thick doorsteps of fried bread, what

looked like three or four tomatoes, and the promised egg. "I think this will be plenty. Save the toast for tomorrow. Oh! I need to give you my ration book, and we ought to talk about board and . . ."

"Time enough later, lad. I've got a nice, tidy vegetable patch and I swap with Mother Longhurst for eggs, so we'll do alright. I will need your ration book, but right now"—he paused to take a long swig of his tea—"we need to talk about last night."

"Yes." Although what exactly was he going to say?

That was done for him. "What happened last night happened. You didn't imagine anything. But I'll ask you to keep it to yourself."

"Yes." Downright loquacious that was. "I meant, of course, it's good to know I wasn't hallucinating."

"You weren't, but there are some things I prefer to keep to myself. Last night those boys needed rescuing, and you trusted me with what you don't tell others, so I decided I could do the same."

Fair enough. Perhaps. "But how could you do that? You as good as held the house up. That was a supporting wall and when you moved away . . ."

"I'm stronger than anyone imagines. Including you. I was born in North Wales. They say we have the stone of the mountains in our blood."

There was more. Much more. Had to be. But for the life of him, Peter couldn't imagine what it was and he wasn't about to ask. "I won't tell, but you deserve some of the credit. I couldn't have done it alone."

"They got out, that's all that matters."

"And Sid is still asleep on the parlor sofa?" He hoped to high heaven he hadn't overheard that last little bit.

"I checked on him while you were dressing. He'll be out a while, yet. I made him a cup of cocoa when we got back and slipped in half of a sleeping pill I had left over from when my wife was ill. The boy needed it. Rest's the best thing at his age and missing a day of school won't make much difference to him. He's not the scholarly sort."

"Where will they go?" Sleeping on the sofa couldn't be permanent, even with a war on.

"The ladies on the evacuee committee will find somewhere. They're not bad boys. Rough. What would you expect from the East End? They've had a bit of trouble at school, but Mrs. Roundhill knew how to handle them. Taught in London herself before she married. And now . . ." He shook his head. "She's in a bad way, poor lady, and with the vicar due home this morning."

Coming home to bad news. How many other people in the country woke up to bad news or had no roof over their heads this morning?

If he started on that line he'd end up in the doldrums. "Someone's meeting him?"

"Aye. Jimmy Black will, they're friends. Eat up, lad. Want another mug of tea?"

He skipped the tea, but made short work of the breakfast. Something told Peter it was going to be a long day.

Chapter 18

"You've survived two days," Gloria said to Peter as they rode their bicycles down into the village. "Think you can cope with the school visit on your own tomorrow?"

"Checking for head lice?"

"Should have been done the first week after the holidays, but as you've seen, we're spread a bit thin."

"If I can't deal with head lice, I'm not going to be much use to you, am I? It'll be a first for me, but they can't be that different from sheep lice, can they?"

After she regained control of her bike, Gloria gave him a scowl. Hard to do when she was still chuckling. "I'd keep that thought to myself, if I were you. Mothers get very touchy over head lice. Tend to blame it all on the evacuees, which isn't at all fair. But suggest their little cherubs have been rubbing heads with sheep . . ."

"I get the message. Forget sheep. School is one place where my veterinarian skills will not be highly esteemed."

"I think you have it. It's not that tricky, really. Just do a class at a time. It'll be easier than slogging across a muddy field to look at sick cows."

"Dying cows," Peter added. "At least I convinced him to

keep them indoors, but I doubt they'll make it. I've never seen anything like it. They should call in a qualified vet."

"You're pretty well all they've got. The vet in Leatherhead who used to come out here is in the Army now. There's a vet in Dorking, but he's about a hundred years old and prefers dealing with lap dogs and old ladies' budgies. I think you've found yourself an unofficial job on the side. Won't take long for the news to get out that you're a vet."

"Gloria, I had three years in veterinarian college and that was before the war."

"That's three more years than anyone else hereabouts."

Maybe, but he did rather worry about the ethics of setting up an unofficial practice, and besides, he was still mystified over those two cows.

"Peter," Gloria went on—they'd come to first names easily. "Would you mind taking the eggs up to Alice? Would save me the pull up the hill and I need to stop in the village and see how Mrs. Brown is doing."

"Not at all." Would give him a chance to say a few words to her alone. High time he did. "I'll drop them off. What about this afternoon? You need me for anything?"

"You're on duty tonight at the first aid post. Take the afternoon off. Read up about head lice."

Halfway up the hill toward Alice's house, Peter almost turned back, but darn it, he did have the eggs to deliver and he wanted to see her again. Hell, he wanted to do more than see her, and if she was upset with him, best to find out. Perhaps.

She'd been civil enough yesterday when he'd seen her for maximum two minutes, but dash it all, a woman didn't kiss as if it were going to be illegal tomorrow unless she was at least a teeny bit interested, did she?

He was about to find out.

If she gave him what for and turfed him out by his ear, at least he'd know where he stood.

In the doghouse.

And with that sobering thought in mind, he opened the gate and wheeled his bicycle up the path toward The Gallop. Now which door to head for? That was decided for him when the back door opened and Alice walked out, a laundry basket in her arms.

"Dr. Doyle?"

She turned as he approached. "Hello, Mr. Watson."

That was better than "Go away!" He propped his cycle against the side of the house and took the eggs out of the basket, hoping to heaven they weren't already scrambled. "Mother Longhurst asked me to bring you up some eggs. She said you'd need them with the house full."

"We certainly could. Ours went off laying after the bombing." She balanced the laundry basket on one hip and reached for the eggs.

"Let me hold that for you."

She gave an odd little smile but handed the basket over and took the string bag with the box of eggs. "I'll just be a jiffy." She was back right away and handed him the string bag. "Better be sure she gets this back, or she'll put the hex on us both."

"Eh?"

She smiled and the sun on her hair made little bright spots of shine. "Surely Nurse Prewitt filled you in about Mother Longhurst's reputation."

Oh, that. "You mean that she's the village witch? You believe that?"

"No." God, her smile was lovely and crinkled up the corners of her eyes. "But my grandmother does, along with half the village. They'll often go to her before they come to me. I think her 'cures' are more in the mind than anything else. Mind you, her hens lay better than anyone else's in the village, and I bet hers aren't pitching a snit because we had a bomb two nights ago."

"Could I help you with this?" He indicated the basket of laundry he'd kept ahold of.

"You want to hang up the washing?"

"No. I want to talk to you, but thought offering to help might be a good way to get you to listen."

She looked a lot more than doubtful, but nodded. "I'd be a fool to turn down an offer to help peg it out, wouldn't I?"

Was he being the fool? The next half hour would settle it one way or the other. He hoped.

Actually, standing in the sun and hanging out sheets wasn't a bad way to spend an afternoon in her company.

"Well, Mr. Watson, how's the job so far?"

"So far, so good but I'm not too thrilled about checking for head lice tomorrow."

She had a wonderful laugh, too, like bottled sunshine poured over warm skin. Oops! Thinking about warm skin might not be the best line of thought.

"Gloria foisted that one on you, did she?"

"Is it some sort of initiation rite?"

This time it was a chuckle, sexy and alluring. "You could call it that. Really, it's a job we all hate. The children get upset and embarrassed, the parents mortified. The locals blame it on the evacuees bringing the evil lice into the pristine village and the poor old evacuees swear blue murder they never, ever had them in their sweet lives until they ended up in louse-infested Surrey."

She slung a sheet over the line and handed him a couple of pegs. He'd done this before. When he was about seven helping his grandmother. "So it's a sticky situation."

"You could say that. Not that these days aren't laden with sticky situations."

He wasn't missing this chance. "Yes, about Sunday night."

"What about it?"

"Something you want to apologize for?" There was a definite edge in that.

"I was asking you."

She flipped another sheet on the line. He took the cue and dug into the peg bag for a handful.

"Let's put it this way: If, by some chance, you gave me a lift home on another occasion, and the same thing happened, would you object?" That was a damn wordy way of asking, "May I kiss you again."

She apparently thought so, too. Not that he could read her expression as she hung the final sheet up and almost stabbed the line with the clothes pegs.

"Mr. Watson," she said after what seemed like ten hours but was really that many seconds. "Do you think for one minute I'd have let you kiss me if I objected? I have two brothers; I learned early how to fight. If I'd not been willing, you'd have ended up bent double on Howell Pendragon's front lawn clutching your family jewels."

Put that way . . . "I see."

"I'm not sure you do, Mr. Watson."

"Then try to explain so that I do understand."

She picked up the now empty basket. "Have you had lunch? Gloria tends to skip it, I know."

"Er . . . er no. As a matter of fact, I haven't."

"Gran put a pot of stew on for tonight. She won't miss a couple of servings. Come in"—she turned toward the door, hesitated a moment, and looked back at him—"Peter."

Deep breath. Dash it all, two deep breaths. If that last wasn't an invitation, he'd never received one, but an invitation to what? Lunch?

Right!

Peter followed her into the large kitchen. A vast enamel pot simmered on the stove, and a pile of clean dishes was stacked on the draining board. Alice reached for two bowls. "There's a toilet down the hall on the right if you want to wash up."

She lifted the lid on the pot and a wonderful savory aroma wafted up in the steam. "The meat might still be chewy, but the veggies should be ready."

"Don't worry, I've got good teeth." Yes, he loved her chuckle. "I'll be back in a tick!"

After spending the time it took to lather up his hands, worrying that his teeth comment might be misconstrued, Peter emerged. Nervous wasn't the word. He had a chance, he wasn't sure what of, but Alice Doyle was inviting his company.

Now it was up to him.

"Did you find a towel? Soap? With our surprise visitors, things seem to go missing."

"No, I mean, yes. Everything was fine." He'd taken longer than he'd thought. While he was soaping and worrying away, she'd laid the table, served two bowls of stew, sliced bread, and put the kettle on. "Smells wonderful."

"I'm never quite sure what Gran puts in her stews, but they always turn out well."

"A bit of Devon magic?" Now, what was that look for? "The stew looks marvelous. Hadn't realized how hungry I was."

"You need to watch out for meals when you're with Gloria. Be sure to pack a sandwich or something. She never seems to eat much—must be why she stays so thin."

He took the seat she indicated. She sat directly opposite. Gave him a perfect view. Pity it was rude to stare.

The aroma hadn't misled—the stew was delicious, and once he started eating, Peter realized just how hungry he was; the bowl of porridge for breakfast had been hours earlier. "This is delicious; your grandmother's a super cook. I remember those custard tarts."

"Good thing she is, too, or I'd eat as little as Gloria does."

"I like her." That got him a sharp look. "She's a good nurse. Listens to everyone."

Alice relaxed. Just a wee bit. "She is. She's been here about five years or so. At first people thought she was standoffish because she keeps to herself a lot, lives alone, and has so far avoided getting any evacuees. Mind you, she's on call as much as I am, and being in the village sees people who can't or don't want to bike up here."

"Talking of evacuees, what about your surprise visitors?"

"That's where Gran is, off to harass Lady Gregory and the billeting board to find somewhere for them that doesn't entail putting them out one by one. We can't keep them here and houses are full to the seams. What about Sid Arckle?"

"He's still sleeping on the sofa in the parlor, but seems there's a farmer offered to take him and Dave. Said he'd take on Dave when he gets well as paid help."

"A bit irregular, but Dave's almost fourteen; plenty leave school before then. Remember who it was?"

"A Tom Longhurst."

She nodded. "His farm's up on Cherry Hill. He'll be a fair employer, I think. Keeps his farm and animals well, and he lost a bunch of his laborers. They signed up right at the beginning of the war. His farm is up a bit beyond the heath where the encampment is that no one's supposed to know makes munitions. Beats me how Sid will get to school."

The kettle whistled on the oven top and she got up to fill the pot. "Want some more stew? We've got heaps."

"Thanks, but this is enough." She had a houseful to feed tonight after all.

"Milk and sugar."

"Just milk."

She went into the pantry for the milk. "So," she said, coming out with the bottle, "the Arckle boys set for a farmer's life? Odd end for a pair from Shoreditch."

"Their father's coming down in a day or two. To see Dave most of all, but also I think to talk things over with Tom Longhurst."

"Must be awful sending your children off into the unknown. But . . ." She shrugged. "A bit like going off to boarding school but much worse. Plus the worry of not knowing what's happening and if you'll ever see your parents again. Small wonder half of them are bed-wetting. Oh well. That's a minor detail really. Here . . ." She handed him a cup. "Want a more comfortable seat? Let's sit in the lounge."

She let the way to a sofa by a bay window that overlooked the front garden. The sofa was large and soft and he resisted the temptation to sit right next to her.

Later. If he was extraordinarily lucky.

She put her cup and saucer down on the round coffee table. "Tell me something about yourself," she said.

"You know a good bit already. I'm from Devon, went to Blundells, started training as a vet and ended up a CO and working here as a first aid assistant." He didn't want to go any deeper, not now. "Tell me about yourself. Your father was the doctor before you, and you have brothers."

"Two. Simon was taken prisoner after Dunkirk, and Alan is in the Navy. Dad really wanted one of them to become a doctor, but the mantle fell on me."

"Not an easy job."

"Inheriting Dad's mantle or being a country doctor?"

"Both, perhaps. It's not an easy job in peacetime but now . . ." Why elaborate? They both knew, only too recently, what it entailed.

"I do what I have to. Dad used to have an assistant, but he joined up very early on in the war. I was working with Dad before he was killed so I just took over."

"He died in the blitz?"

"No, that was the irony of it. We were crossing the road in Dorking after going to the cinema and got run over by a bus in the blackout. I ended up with a scrapes and bruises, but the bus went over Dad. Killed him instantly."

What a lousy thing to happen. "And your mother?"

"She died when I was ten. Pneumonia." She went quiet. Just for a few moments. "What about your parents?"

He should have expected this. "My father's dead, too. Died when I was nine. My mother's remarried. Nice chap, and I have two little half brothers: nine and twelve. Don't get to see them much. Just hope this war's over before they get old enough to be conscripted."

"It can't last that long, surely!"

"Who's to tell? And if the Jerries get here, as everyone seems to expect . . ."

"It could be over fast." She shuddered. "The idea's horrific, but it happened to the French, the Belgians, the Dutch, the Norwegians. It surely can't happen here."

But they both feared it could. "The Channel stopped Bonaparte."

She nodded. "Gran keeps saying that. I hope she's right. The way they're dropping bombs, they might not need to use boats. Just parachutes." She drained her cup and put it down. "Let's get off that, or I'll end up maudlin. I didn't invite you in to hash over the war and invasion."

Why had she asked him in? Was he supposed to take his cue from her comments regarding their kiss two night ago? Hell, it hadn't been a kiss, it was a KISS, and he would all but kill for another.

"How did your father die? An accident?"

He went cold, then the heat of a flush raced up his neck, and his throat went tight. It would be so easy to say, "Yes, an accident," but he couldn't lie to her, not even with part truths. He told her.

"Oh, dear heaven!" She reached out with both arms and somehow they connected, only it was his head on her shoulder and her strong arms enfolding him. "Sweet Jesus, Peter, and I said all those awful things. Gran was so right. I make far too hasty judgments. I'm sorry. How absolutely hideous and then I did my nasty little extra."

He lifted his head a little. "You weren't to know, and given your brother is a POW, I can understand."

"You're a lot more gracious than I was." Her kiss was soft and gentle, a brush of her lips on his cheek, a friendly kiss such as she'd give to comfort a child, or greet a friend or her brothers. Only it wasn't the least fraternal.

He lifted his face.

Their mouths were mere inches apart.

This was insane. She smiled and he moved those last few inches and her comforting smile became raw heat and their lips joined.

They both shifted, pulling each other closer and kissing in a wild rush of need and sheer, wondrous desire.

For a few moments, they drew apart to catch their breaths. She was flushed, her eyes bright, and her chest heaving with her ragged breathing. "Peter, this is nuts. It's . . ."

"What I want."

"Me, too."

She didn't give his much chance to discuss it. Just plastered her mouth on his and kissed him.

Again.

And again.

He was no doubt hallucinating or dreaming but just in case this was real, he gently opened her mouth with his lips and caressed the tip of her tongue. She responded by stroking his tongue with hers and curling her body into his. Putting her soft breasts against his chest.

He couldn't refuse; his hand cupped her breast, every sense, every ounce of his being alert to the sweet feminine heat beneath her sweater.

Damn, it was in the way.

His hand was under her sweater.

He hesitated a few heartbeats, waiting for her protest, objection, or affronted complaint. All he heard was a gloriously sexy sigh as skin touched skin and a sweet, little grunt as she renewed the kiss. Deeper and hotter and . . . His mind was about to short out. Everything above and below the waist was tuned into her breathing, her heat, and the wonder of her desire.

She pulled away a little to catch her breath again and smile at him. Her eyes were bright with desire and her face flushed with pleasure. "Peter, you're incredible."

"My pleasure, Dr. Doyle."

Her laugh set her breast jiggling against his hand. "Alice, given we've come this far." And how far was that?

"Alice," he repeated, letting her name roll on his tongue and seep into his mind. "You are wonderful!"

Her smile was an invitation no gentleman would refuse.

"This really is . . ." he began, but gave up on any attempts at conversation when she slid her hand under his shirt and brought her sweet lips back to his. It was nothing but need, hunger, and a wild, almost magical melding of their desire. His hand caressed both breasts. The darn brassiere was in the way, so he slid his hand behind her back and flicked the hooks. Better. Much better. Now he could feel her luscious breasts and the tight nipples that hardened even more under his touch.

She pulled away a little, not to break the kiss but to get both hands inside his shirt, popping buttons in her haste and running the flats of her hands over his chest.

He almost groaned. Would have if he had any spare breath, but why waste energy? Her hands were like a warm tide caressing his skin, pinching his nipple so he did groan, and then paid her back by pulling up her blouse and fastening his mouth on her nipple. She grasped his head and held him closer. At least one hand grasped his head, the other yanked his shirt out from his trousers before she gently raked her fingernails over his bare back.

It was more. It was wonderful. It was too much and nowhere near enough.

She apparently felt the same way. If her hands fumbling with his belt buckle was anything to go by.

"Peter. Peter," she muttered as she yanked and tugged and he gave off licking her nipple to give her a hand.

Somehow her skirt ended up on the floor in a tangle with his trousers and her hand was inside his Y fronts and he almost lost it there and then.

"I want you," he managed to say, or rather the insane creature that had invaded his brain did.

"Me too!" It came as a wild little gasp. "Do you have a rubber raincoat?"

"What?" He was lost, unable to make the leap from crazed need to wet weather garb.

"Sorry. My brothers called them that. A French letter?"

"No." He wanted to scream. "I don't!"

"Damn! Neither do I." She pulled away and sagged against the back of the chintz-covered sofa. "We can't, you know. Not without one."

He knew only too well. "I'm going to get some."

"I will too." She shook her head and leaned into him. "Oh, Peter, this is insane but I want you so much. Have from the moment I first saw you. I couldn't get over it when that snirpy Sid Mosely told me you were a CO."

"You got over it now."

"I know you now."

"Not yet, in the biblical sense, but you will."

"I know. I'm sorry we couldn't."

"No, this is fine. It will be better. But I tell you, I've never felt this way, this in need."

"And we need to get dressed."

Didn't take long. She gave a most regretful glance at his only too apparent erection and gently stroked him as she tucked him back into his Y fronts. It was when she blew him a kiss that he almost lost everything. She was so delicious, and decidedly rumpled.

"I went insane for a minute," she said once they were more or less put back together.

"I know I did, but I don't regret it."

Her smile pretty much indicated she didn't either. "It could be tricky."

"We're in the middle of a war, with bombs dropping around us. Living is tricky. Come for a spin when I'm next off. You have a bicycle?"

"Gran does, but I have a car." She paused, no doubt remembering strictures about using petrol for essential journeys only. "Thursday I'm making a call up at the Watson farm. I need to check on Melanie and her twins. I think you, as my assistant, should drive up with me and meet them. After all, they might be some distant relation."

"Yes, doctor."

"You know," she went on. "You're right. This is insane, but it feels so right and wonderful I don't much care for sanity. This is like magic."

"Maybe it was something in your grandmother's stew." Why that odd, searching look? But it didn't last long; the scowl melted into a smile.

The phone ringing cut off that line of conversation. While Alice answered the phone Peter went back into the kitchen and cleared and scraped the bowls and put them in the sink.

"Peter." Alice walked back in. "That was the coroner in Epsom. The oddest thing. Seems when Fred Morgan died, a couple of nights before you came, he had almost no blood in his body. Some sort of bizarre bleeding disease. Makes you wonder if they haven't dropped some new, invisible gas, but he's just an isolated case."

Not completely. "I got a message to please come by the Abbotts' farm. Seems the news I've had three years of vet school preceded me. He had a problem with two of his cows. They were wasted, feeble, and when I tried to take a blood sample, thinking maybe somewhere there was a lab that might look at it, it was almost impossible to find a vein—they'd all collapsed. The animals had very little blood in them. Odd to have two strange happenings on top of the bombing."

"Three strange things," she replied. "Don't forget the disappearing injured man."

How could he? That was the reason they met.

Chapter 19

Eiche looked the old woman in the eyes and resisted the urge to rip her throat out. Time enough for that. Right now, he needed a new base of operations and these blasted mortals were obstructive in the extreme.

"I'm really sorry, Mr. Oak," the bitch announced in tones that suggested her sympathy was as false as her teeth. "But you're not a resident and not working here. Your aunt we can rehouse. In fact, we're working on finding her somewhere so we can have her discharged from hospital, but in your case, you'd do best to return home. Yorkshire, wasn't it?"

Would have been fun to say, "Bavaria" and watch her reaction, but he had more pressing things on his mind than taunting old biddies. "I considered that, but I don't feel I can abandon Aunt Jane right now."

"We'll take good care of her."

And he'll take care of this old bat. He caught her eyes and held them with his. She spluttered and whined as he imposed his mind on hers. Silly woman. She really thought her WVS uniform gave her authority to defy him? Women's Voluntary Service indeed! He'd give her service, Involuntary Service to the Third Reich at that. "You will find me a billet," he willed at her as she shuddered but was unable to break the contact.

"In the village and with no one else in the house but my host." Preferably a stout, healthy young person, but no point in overloading a mortal mind. After all, even the elderly had plenty of blood in them. Trouble was their minds were often harder to compel.

He let her go with a sharp and abrupt break in the connection. She slumped back in her chair and, for a minute, he thought he'd have the pleasure of watching her crumple on the dingy linoleum, but she stayed in her seat, just wobbled a bit. "Yes, Mr. Oak, we need to find a place for you." She shuffled cards, frowning and shaking her head, and she took so long he half expected to have to repeat the compulsion, but eventually she looked up at him as she reached for the phone.

"We can put you up with Mr. Williams. He has a second bedroom in that cottage and no one else there. Perfect for you."

"Would that be the Jeff Williams who works up at the plant on the heath?"

She peered at the card again. "It would be."

Praise Father Abel and all his minions. Fortune was on his side. "I've met him. Pleasant chap."

Her startled expression suggested she did not share his opinion. The old bitch had deliberately picked someone she considered inhospitable or unpleasant. Little would her puny mortal mind ever guess. "It's only temporary. For a few weeks at most."

He only needed it until the victorious German army marched up the Mole Gap. "Will be perfect, thank you so much, and where will dear Aunt Jane be?"

"We're working on getting her house habitable as soon as possible, but until then, we're putting her with Nurse Prewitt. That way she'll have someone handy if she needs care. It's only a short walk from Mr. Williams when you want to pop in and see her."

He'd do more than pop in.

But this was only a minor crimp in his plans, and as Weiss had reminded him so forcefully yesterday, it was time to get on with his mission of destroying the munitions plant. He'd even loaded him down with supplies of explosives and fuses. Seems their masters wanted a fireworks display.

By nine the temporary visitors—at least the ones under twenty-one—were fast asleep. Fifteen minutes later, June decided to follow suit. Understandably, she looked in need of an undisturbed night's rest.

Alice was tempted to follow her, but first . . . "Want a last cup of tea, Gran?"

"You'd be better off with Horlicks, Alice, my dear. There's a jar in the larder."

There was and a brand new one. "Get this today, Gran?"

"Yes, dear, when I dropped by Whorleigh's. I thought maybe the children would like it, but they didn't seem to need anything to help them sleep. Make us both a nice cup, please, dear. Then you can tell me what's bothering you."

She knew better than deny the bothering bit. Gran had always been able to read her. Made it impossible to lie when she was a child, and that hadn't changed one iota. At least Gran hadn't twigged about Peter. That was a tricky situation, but darn it, she'd learned the hard way in the past year that life was too short and too uncertain to waste. Was love too strong a word for what she felt? Neither of them had mentioned it.

"Well, dear." Gran took a slow sip of her Horlicks and licked the froth off her lips before putting the cup down. "You're not happy about the new arrangements?"

Quick jump back to bedrooms and evacuees. "No, Gran. Not that. They can't all stay here indefinitely, and your idea of putting June with Gloria was inspired—they'll get on well. It will be a bit cramped with Miss Waite there as well, but that's only temporary. I'm worried about Mrs. Roundhill, she's still unconscious, and by all accounts the vicar isn't coping too well."

"She did hold him and the parish together, but he's going to have to manage for himself. Lots of people do." Gran looked at her. "Nice to have those eggs. We can give everyone a boiled egg for breakfast. Give them a proper treat."

"How Mother Longhurst keeps her hens laying through war and disaster beats me."

"She has her ways." Gran paused to take another sip. "Nice of that Mr. Watson to bring them by."

She was blushing. Drat! "Yes, it was. He should do well. Seems to get on well with people."

"So, my love, you've changed your mind about him?"

Her face was downright burning but she was not about to share with Gran the details of the afternoon. "Yes. But that's not what I want to talk about." Until she decided exactly how she felt about Mr. Peter Watson, she was keeping her thoughts to herself. "Just two odd things, three if you count that disappearing patient last week." Why she was burdening Gran with all this when she had more than enough on her plate? But she trusted Gran's insight on odd things. "Remember the postmortem on Farmer Morgan, how he had very little blood in him, and the conclusion was he'd bled much more than we first thought?" Gran nodded. She'd always been a good listener. "Well, Peter, Mr. Watson, told me he'd seen two wasted cows out on one of the farms. He offered to take blood but the cows seemed to be drastically short of blood."

Gran went silent, creased her brows the way she did when pondering tricky problems, and finally said, "What do you make of it?"

"I've no idea. It just feels wrong." Very scientific that, but how else could she put it?

"Look at the facts, Alice. Remember how our disappearing patient tried to bite you. Had you forgotten?"

"Yes, I had."

"Don't scoff, dear, but add he had no aura. Not even a darkened or faded one. All living things have an aura, even the plants in the garden."

She'd dismissed that as more of her Pixies talk but . . . "Gran, that makes no sense. If he weren't alive, how could he speak, crawl along the ground, grab me, and later pick up his proverbial bed and walk?"

"Don't forget that was the evening we found Susie dead." What was Gran getting to? "Think about it, my love." She counted the points off on her fingers. "A creature who has no aura, so must, by rights, be dead, you find injured, in a state of collapse, but who gets up and walks away and is never seen again, animals and one man found either dead or weak and lacking blood."

"Gran, that's preposterous." But it was exactly how it happened. "What are you getting at?"

"You tell me, my love. Dead who walk and take blood."

And just when she thought Gran was going to make sense! "A vampire! Honestly, Gran!"

"You have a better, more logical idea?"

"Vampires are fiction, Gran, they're in stories, Hollywood horror films, they don't really exist. Besides, for all your talk of no aura, that one had a heartbeat."

"Maybe the walking dead have heartbeats. Didn't you say his was abnormally slow? Wasn't that one of your concerns?"

Yes, but . . . "I don't care, Gran. Vampires don't really exist!"

"Some people would say Pixies don't really exist, but you and I are sitting here drinking Horlicks."

"Gran . . ."

"Don't deny what you are, Alice. Besides, you claim to be a scientist, look at the facts."

She pondered them for as long as it took her to drain her mug. "Gran, if you're right, and only *if,* mind you, and if he is lurking around here and emerging at intervals to ravage the population, why here and why now?"

"Maybe war and disaster bring them out. I don't know that for a fact, my love. I know very little about them, but we do know what this one looks like, and we know he was injured by that tree."

"So we stock up on stakes?"

"Why not, dear? If we don't need them, they'll come in handy this winter for firewood."

Gran was taking this so seriously it was impossible to scoff. "If it is a vampire, what do we do?" Sweet heaven! She's actually admitting to the possibility of vampires.

"Keep our eyes peeled and our ears flapping. I'll increase my time with the WVS—everything that happens in the village gets filtered through them—and you have an entrée in everyone's house. Listen and use your powers, Alice. It's time to toss off your skepticism and accept what you are."

"Gran . . ."

She went on, determined to have her say. "Alice, science is all very well, but when it denies the truth, it isn't your servant. You're half Pixie, your hearing and sight are better than any human's, and you know that as well as I do. You can move fast. Wasn't for nothing you won those cups and ribbons at school, and to get them required no effort. If you exerted yourself, you could move as fast as I can when I choose. How much you're able to influence mortals' minds, I don't know, but I've seen you calm frightened children and soothe anxious patients.

"Think of this evening. You read those children one story, then you tell them it's time to go to bed and sleep, and look what happens. Even June toddled off to dreamland."

"Gran, that's ridiculous. I just read to them, and they were worn out. I didn't do that!"

Gran smiled.

It was utterly preposterous, but so was the walking dead,

or comatose patients who got up and strolled off. "Gran, what does it mean?"

"I don't know, dear. We must be very vigilant. I'm inclined to think it can't mean anything good for any of us. I know very little about vampires, mostly the stories my grandmother told me." Alice waited. "When we fled from the Romans to the west country, they fled to the Northlands. I've heard tell they survived. But I always heard they kept to themselves. One hears stories . . ." Gran went very quiet and very thoughtful. "Let's go to bed, Alice. Nothing we can do tonight, or in the morning, come to that, but keep alert, and I'm going to talk to Howell about this."

"You're going to tell him there's a vampire in Brytewood?"

"I'm going to tell him we suspect one." Alice wasn't too sure about that "we." "He'll listen, Alice. He understands there's more to the world that humans."

"He's Pixie, too?" Heavyset, six-foot Sergeant Pendragon!

"No, dear, he isn't Pixie, but he's Other."

"What does that mean, Gran?"

"He's more than he looks, Alice. How much more."

"Other?"

"A little more than mere human, child. There's more than Pixies in the world, my love."

"Not here in Brytewood?"

Gran sighed and shook her head. "Alice, open your eyes and ears. Use all your senses. There's far, far more in this world and here in Brytewood that in any scientific textbook."

Chapter 20

This expedition was really far too obvious, but what else could she do? Even with June and the children moving out this afternoon, Alice couldn't take Peter home and march him upstairs under Gran's eye. Trusting to weather and the seclusion of the countryside was her best bet.

Hence the two blankets rolled up in the back.

Picking up Peter wasn't the snag. Even the sharpest-tongued gossips couldn't see much awry with the doctor picking her new assistant to make house calls. And to be honest, the way the village viewed Peter, they'd still smile indulgently at him even if he sprouted wings and talons.

Oops! Give the conversation with Gran last night, that last thought wasn't too soothing.

"You know," Peter said, breaking into her thoughts. Probably a good thing, too. "I used to think Devon was the most beautiful part of England, but these hills come an awfully close second."

"I might be biased, but I love it here. Mind you, Devon's nothing to sneeze at. Mum and Gran used to take me down there for a few weeks every summer. You've got coastlines, which we don't."

"Probably a distinct advantage right now. Here we've got Sussex between us and the Channel."

"Sussex didn't stop William the Conqueror." Not the conversation she'd envisioned, but was anyone not worrying right now? "Who's to tell? Beats me why they're delaying. If they really had their socks pulled up they'd have come over right after Dunkirk when everyone was at sixes and sevens. It's like a cat playing with a mouse."

"Sometimes the mouse gets away if the cat gets too confident."

"I hope you're right!" Not that she really fancied likening the entire defense force to a bunch of mice.

They were approaching Fletcher's Woods and after last time, she might do well to drive on past, but it was a nice secluded spot. She pulled the car over to the grass verge. She was being unbelievably forward, but darn it.

As she turned off the engine, he gave her a very pregnant look.

"I thought you might like to explore the beauties of the countryside."

He nodded, a rather lovely smile turning up his mouth as his dark eyes gleamed. "Smashing, and by the way, I have a couple of rubber raincoats with me."

Very provident of him. "Where did you get them?"

"Nicked them last night. For reasons best known to the great organizers of the world, there was a case of them in the village hall among the ARP boxes."

Better not ask about that one. Especially as now, in the cool of the mid-afternoon, she wasn't too sure how good an idea this really was. Yes, she yearned for him, and ached for his touch ever since yesterday afternoon, but was she completely insane in addition to being indescribably fast?

Peter settled the point by jumping out of the car and going round to the back. "Want me to carry the blankets?"

So he'd noticed them. "Let's take one each."

They climbed over the fence and she deliberately led them in the opposite direction from last time. If there was another strange individual hanging around, she didn't want to meet him. Maybe a shirking of her Hippocratic Oath, but did it apply to Others, as Gran called them?

They found a sheltered hollow surrounded by trees and undergrowth but lying in a pool of afternoon sun. Peter spread his blanket. She sat down, putting the second one to the side, and wondered if she really wanted this. It was sudden, it was mad, and it was . . .

"Alice," Peter said, sitting close but not touching, "just because I brought the rubber goodies doesn't mean I expect to use them. You tell me. Nothing wrong in a nice cuddle in the sunshine. It's a lovely spot and the company is the best. I feel we're playing truant."

"We are. Perhaps I should report you to your superior."

"Go ahead, Doctor. I'll say I was following your directions."

She rolled on her tummy and leaned up on her forearms, looking up the slight incline to the ridge of ferns just beginning to turn brown. "You know," she said, "if someone had told me a few days ago that I'd be sneaking off in the middle of the day like this, I'd have been sorely affronted."

"I'd have considered myself the luckiest man in England."

"Mmm." His arm, warm around her shoulders, felt absolutely perfect, and what else was there to do but lean into him? "I'm glad we ran away." Most irresponsible and all that, and very selfish but . . .

"You won't ever regret it."

It was a promise. It didn't negate the sheer wildness of skiving off and lying in the sunshine, but after the last couple of days, and particularly her conversation with Gran last night, a few hours alone with a man she fancied was the perfect escape. "I know. After all, it was my idea, wasn't it?"

"Yes, Doctor."

Yes, Doctor indeed! If that was a trace of levity, she'd fix him. Without wasting time or breath on a reply, she leaned in and kissed him, intending a soft, friendly, teasing kiss.

He had other ideas. Holding her head steady, he kissed back: hard, sweet, and probing. She parted her lips, or perhaps he parted them for her. The touch of his tongue had her sighing and then moaning and kissing back with a heat and passion that was alien and marvelous and sent wild tremors down to her very core.

When they paused for breath, she pulled back. He let her, releasing her head and smiling. He didn't say a word. Didn't need to. The fire in his eyes matched the heat in her soul.

"Peter," she said, if only to make sure she could still breathe and speak. "This really is insane, but . . ." Dammit, why waste breath over "I've never done anything this lunatic before"? What she had or had not done before this moment didn't matter. It was NOW that she cared about. She grasped his shoulder, pushed him on his back, and stretched out half on top of him.

She wanted to tell him he was beautiful, sexy, and had her losing her reason, but even that was too much effort.

She had better uses for her mouth—and his.

This kiss was slower. At first. As if he wanted to string it out, make it last, keep her mind and body humming with longing for more. And he was so flipping good at it. She must ask him where he learned to kiss. Later. If she remembered. As if it mattered.

His hand was on her breast, stroking, giving her a gentle squeeze, then it was under her sweater, inside her blouse. To make it easier, she pulled back and yanked her sweater over her head.

He smiled up at her and opened the last few remaining buttons on her blouse. "You'll catch cold," he said.

Cold? She'd forgotten what that meant. "Keep me warm."

"I will." Her blouse ended up on the blanket, along with her bra. He'd already pushed down the straps of her slip to expose her breasts to the sunlight, and his view. It was a trifle chilly but who cared? "Lie down," he said, pushing her on her back and reaching for the spare blanket.

He covered them both, draping the blanket over their shoulders as he stroked and caressed her breasts. "So beautiful. So wonderful," he muttered and closed his lips over her nipple.

Her groan came from sheer and utter pleasure and a desperate need for more. He gave her more, kissing and playing her other nipple with his lips and tongue. Desire rose in her. Desire to feel his skin as she had yesterday. Yanking his shirt from his trousers, she reached under and ran her hands over his chest, stroking his nipples and marveling how they went as hard as hers.

She burrowed under the blanket, pushed up his shirt, and licked his nipple. Seemed he like that, if the groan was anything to go by, so she tasted the other one. Yes! He enjoyed that as much as she did.

This was wonderful, but not enough. Not by a long chalk.

Seemed he felt the same way. While she'd teased his nipples, his hands slipped under her skirt.

Wearing French knickers had been an inspiration. His warm hand slid up her thigh and stroked the fur of her pussy. "God, Alice," he said, his voice tight and hoarse, just before he kissed her again.

His mouth was hot and hard, his tongue sweet and caressing, and his fingers, dear heaven, his fingers were stroking her, opening her, and now inside her. Curling as they penetrated and she let out a deep, slow groan of sheer and utter delight.

This man was incredible, magical, wondrous. His lips glorious and his touch perfection.

He was moving inside her, pressing in and out. If his fingers felt this incredible, what would happen when she had his cock?

She longed to know, but wanted this glorious intrusion to never end. Her hips rocked in rhythm with his hand and when his thumb pressed and stroked her clit she let out a whoop of utter bliss. "Peter!" she managed, but couldn't, for the life of her, remember what she intended to say.

"I know."

What did he know?

What did she know?

Nothing but this moment, this place, and this man.

She almost cried when his fingers withdrew. But his mouth on hers stopped any complaint. She was lost in a fog of yearning and pleasure, but couldn't think clearly enough to tell him she needed more.

He knew; he had her French knickers off and her legs spread. As he stroked her open, her clit was throbbing with need and urgency.

"Please," she begged, reaching for him as he moved away.

"Just a tick," he said as he unbuckled his belt. She decided to help with the buttons on his flies, and watched in admiration as he pulled his trousers open and slid down his trousers and pants.

Her hand closed around his erection. Hot and hard were woefully inadequate for the beautiful cock she held between her fingers. He was sheer beauty, and his need matched hers.

"Hang on," he said, easing her hand off him. "Better get him ready."

Yes. Definitely!

He reached for his trousers, took a little cream envelope from the pocket, and tipped out the condom. She watched as he positioned it on the beautiful head of his cock and unrolled it down his erection. Seemed to take him ages—or maybe she was so crazed with need she had no brainspace left to measure time.

When he was satisfied he had himself sheathed and ready, he met her eyes. "You're sure about this?"

Gentlemanly and considerate was all very well, but . . . "Peter, didn't anyone tell you it's not polite to keep a doctor waiting?"

"Some things are worth the wait, Alice."

"Maybe! But not right now!"

Seemed he and she were of one mind.

He rolled her on her back, settled himself between her legs, and pulled the blanket right over them.

They were enclosed in a wondrous cocoon: a private world where his mouth found hers as his cock pressed against the softness of her belly.

Kisses were lovely but nowhere near enough. Not even with his hand on her breasts or his fingertips tracing lines of heat up and down her thighs.

In dire need, her hips took up a steady rhythm, and he followed her cue, pushing her legs wider apart and opening her with his fingers. As he caressed her clit, she let out a long, slow moan. He shifted, parted her wide, and the head of his cock pressed against her. He didn't move, just leaned over her, taking his weight on his forearms as she rocked against him. Wanting more. Reaching for more. Pressing herself up to him, she needed him inside her.

And he was.

With a sudden move he was in. Deep. Almost touching her very core. She was filled, invaded, penetrated. Heat poured through her as he began to move, pressing deep and withdrawing in rhythm with her. She was lost in need. As her climax built and peaked, she was suspended in a great arc of pleasure, desire, and sensation. Sensation that built and grew until it burst in a wild paroxysm of pleasure.

She was so caught up in the rush, swept along with her body's response, she only half noticed Peter reach his climax and gently sag on top of her.

He made to shift off her but she couldn't bear to have him

withdraw. She wrapped her arms around him. "Don't go, not yet," she said in a voice that sounded taut and alien.

"I'll be too heavy."

"No. I want to feel your body on mine."

As he lay on her, she shut her eyes, the better to feel his heat and strength and to gather to her every last sensation as his erection slowly softened inside her.

"Like butterflies," she whispered. "You feel like butterflies inside me."

"You feel like heaven," he replied.

But heaven was transitory in the fading afternoon. After Peter slipped out of her, and buried the condom under a heap of leaves and last year's bracken, he fished her clothes out from a tangle of blankets and helped her dress.

Seemed only polite to return the favor.

They both looked a bit crumpled, and all that groaning and crying aloud left her thirsty.

"I wish I'd thought to pack a picnic."

"Next time."

Her heart did a little flip at that. Yes, next time.

All the stolen next times.

"There will be a next time, Alice. Lots of them."

"Good." She looked away to pull on her shoes. Conversation afterward had never been her forte. Come to that, sex had never really been either, but with Peter it was splendid. "Thank you, thank you for having me."

He threw back his head and laughed. "It was my pleasure, love. My pleasure."

"I thought it was mine."

"You know, darling," he said as they folded the blankets. "I'd like to stay here in this little dell forever. Forget the war. Forget everything. Just stay here and make love to you until we both get old and gray."

It was a thought. "Sounds like a lovely prospect, but it's Wednesday and Wednesdays I have evening surgery hours."

"Drat! That's what happens when you love a doctor."

Her heart did a skip. Love? He'd called her "my love," but that was Devon, even the bus conductors called you "my love," but to say he loved her . . .

"Was that too much?" he asked. "Am I jumping the gun? I do love you, Alice. If this isn't love, I don't know what being in love is."

She didn't either. She'd been in love. More than once, but not like this. "It's sudden, Peter." What a vapid thing to say!

"Yes," he agreed, "but I can't do a thing about that. I love you. Think you can love me back?"

Unready to commit herself, she smiled. It was a very real and distinct possibility.

Chapter 21

"Nice spot," Peter said as they climbed over the fence and headed for the car. "Come here often?"

"I might make a habit of it. We're having such a glorious autumn and while the weather lasts . . ." And when it got cold, she'd find a way to be alone with him. "Funny really," she said as they got into the car. "The last time I stopped here was last week." She told him the first part of the mysterious disappearing patient. If Peter thought she was totally barmy, he might be right.

Seemed he didn't. "Sounds like a rum do to me. No wonder you called the ambulance out. Darn glad you did as it happens, but have you checked? Called around the hospitals to see if anyone with severe arm injuries walked into casualty?"

It was a thought. "No. I've been too busy."

"What about looking around the woods? If you found him here, it might be here he got hurt."

It didn't take anywhere near as long as she'd expected. Mind you, it would have been hard to miss the broken top third of a massive oak.

It was, she guessed, about a hundred yards from where

she'd found him, and looking at the broken tree, Gran's little chat last night didn't seem quite so incredible.

"Blimey!" Peter said. "That's got to be it; there's dried blood all over the branches here but . . ." He shook his head. "At least we know where he got hurt; it's *how* that defies comprehension. Unless he dropped out of the sky and landed in the top of the tree."

Which she thought was utterly preposterous. Seemed preposterous was becoming commonplace these days.

Dash it all. He'd seen this much, might as well tell him the rest. It would no doubt convince him she was loony. But if he loved her, he'd better get used to the idea. She shared her conversation with Gran last night, omitting the bit about being Pixies. He was from Devon and all that but really . . .

"You think we're going loopy?"

"Believing there is a vampire in the village." Yes, that was pretty much the gist of it. "Alice, my grandmother believed in Pixies. What's a lone vampire compared to legions of Pixies dancing on the lawn at night."

Now was not the time to mention that Pixies ran in her family.

"But looking at this, I don't see how a single, normal man could snap the top of a hundred-year-old oak."

"Tell me," he went on. "Did Mrs. Burrows tell you how to recognize a vampire?"

"Not really, other than the holy water and crosses stuff was fiction. Seems—at least according to Gran—vampires go back to the days of the Druids, and if this person is one, they don't disappear into a whiff of smoke and ashes in the sunlight." A thought struck her. "But it seems daylight weakens them. I had to practically drag him to the car, and I needed help to get him out as he was barely conscious."

"But he was injured."

He was treating this as possible and reasonable. Maybe she should. "Yes, badly, or so it appeared. A great chunk of wood was jammed in his arm as if he'd impaled himself. Took me forever to get it out." And now looking at the snapped branches and splintered wood . . .

"But you'd recognize him?"

"Without a doubt, and I've not seen him since."

They started walking back to the car.

"Anything else Mrs. Burrows said?"

She'd skip the bit about Pixies fleeing the Romans. "Vampires are strong. That much in the myths seems to be true at least according to Gran."

"Strong?'

"Yes, extraordinarily strong. Sort of superhuman, I gather."

He went silent. A glance in his direction showed he wasn't just silent. He was silent and ashen. "What's the matter?"

"Strong," he repeated. "Unnaturally strong?"

"Yes."

"Alice, I promised I'd keep this to myself, and Lord knows I hate to break my word, but there's something you need to know about what really happened Sunday night at the vicarage."

She listened intently. What he was saying was incredible, but no more incredible than what Gran claimed.

"Peter, the man, or whatever he was I found, wasn't Sergeant Pendragon, but I really think you need to tell Gran this."

"Hello, my loves." Mrs. Burrows was in the kitchen, ironing and listening to Music While You Work. She turned off the radio and included Peter in her smile. "How nice to see you, Mr. Watson. You'll stay and have a cup of tea, won't you? And how are things at the Watson farm?"

"Babies thriving, everyone else half dead on their feet," Alice replied.

Her grandmother smiled. "They'll survive, other parents

have." She filled the kettle and put it on the stove. "Fetch the milk from the larder, please, Alice, there's a love."

In the twenty seconds it took Alice to fetch a bottle of milk, Mrs. Burrows set her eyes square on Peter. "Have something you need to tell me, do you, young man?"

So compelling and clear were her eyes, Peter found himself fighting the urge to confess to her all that had happened up in Fletcher's Woods. He stopped himself in time, but shook himself at the weird feeling. "I'd rather wait until Alice gets back. It sounds a bit odd."

"Well and good." She spared him another searching look and set out cups and saucers. "Thank you, my love," she said, taking the milk from Alice and pouring a little into a jug. "Won't be long." She sat down at the kitchen table, nodding at Peter to follow suit. He made a point of taking the chair nearest Alice. Which was no doubt advertising how they'd spent the afternoon.

"Well then?" Mrs. Burrows asked.

He told her.

She paid him the courtesy of listening, but a smile tweaked the corners of her mouth. Had Alice been stringing him along? No, he couldn't believe that of her.

"So, Mr. Watson, you believe in vampires, do you?"

"I'm not sure." Might as well tell the truth. "But my grandmother and aunts believed in Pixies, and who's to say vampires aren't just as a real." That sounded positively wet but she just nodded with the same little smile as if holding in a secret.

"As you say, young man, vampires are as likely as Pixies." He caught the glance she exchanged with Alice, but she didn't pause. "I'll keep the full story of the rescue to myself, as Howell wants, but he's not your vampire. I can promise you that."

"You're certain?" How could she be?

"I've know him years. We're looking for someone dead. Without an aura. Howell's is unusual, but it's alive and flowing with goodness. He's not an evil doer. I promise you that."

This talk of auras was a bit strange. Heck, the entire conversation was beyond reason, but here they were, as the kettle boiled on the stove, contemplating and discussing the existence of the walking undead. And Pixies.

When Mrs. Burrows got up to make the tea, Peter took the chance to whisper to Alice. "It's all so far-fetched, Alice. It really is."

The old lady had sharp hearing. "More far-fetched than waiting for the invasion? No, young man, something is afoot right now. I sense it. Alice saw it. And you came in at the tag end of it all. We all need to be very vigilant, and I'm going to talk to Howell," she said as she carried the pot to the table.

"Hang on. You said you'd keep that between us."

"Don't worry, my love. I won't let on you told me anything, but he's in the heart of the village, not up on the hill like we are. He's busy with things and hears a lot. He'll keep his eyes and ears open. He's a good man."

"Yes." Good, honest, and accepting. "I'd hate him to know I'd broken the confidence. I wouldn't have but . . ."

"Alice got you thinking. That's good. You just thought in the wrong direction. We need to find that disappearing creature. I think he knows what's going on."

Sounded as possible as holding back the invasion with the wooden rifles stacked in the cupboard in the village hall.

After she'd said good-bye to Peter, resisting the urge to kiss him—a foolish move since it would be broadcast all over the village by supper time—Alice went back in the house.

"Gran," she said, stacking the cups in the sink. "What makes you think Sergeant Pendragon can help?"

"Child!" Gran shook her head "Why do you think? He's Other, like us."

She almost dropped the last cup. "What do you mean?"

"What do you think I mean, Alice? He's Other. He's not vampire, and he's not Pixie. His aura has a light in it that no pure human even had."

Better concentrate on sudsing up the saucers. Gran's Pixies stories had always seemed too far fetched. Village talk about Mother Longhurst being a witch, Alice had always dismissed aa nonsense. This vampire talk beyond was beyond reason, but she couldn't deny what she'd witnessed.

If Sergeant Pendragon really was some sort of mystical creature, what else lurked behind the tidy tile-hung and flint cottages that lined the village street?

Alice wasn't sure she wanted to know.

The old cliché about walking on air was completely, absolutely, and categorically true. Peter resisted the urge to sing as he cycled down to the village, but he did hum to himself. He was in love! Soppy, bone-tingling, and mind-scrambling love and he'd never been happier in his life. Did Alice feel the same? He hoped so. So far she didn't appear to find him too repulsive, and a man lived on hope.

He'd see her almost every day, and it would take all he had to keep his feelings tamped down. But he'd do it. For her sake. The last thing she needed was the village gossips wagging tongues about her. You'd think with invasion worries and bombs dropping people would have more on their minds than the two of them, but he knew better. He knew exactly how villages thrived on gossip.

They'd just have to be very, very discreet.

He was halfway down to the village, and trying to decide if it was worth stopping by Whorleigh's on the off chance of cigarettes, or wait until the morning when they were supposed to come in, when someone called his name.

It was Sid, out of school and with a man. "Mr. Watson! My dad's here. He came early!"

The boy's face shone with excitement, and as Peter paused and watched them walk down the lane from the station, he

saw the resemblance. Mr. Arckle was taller and broader, but
his smile matched Sid's.

"How do you do, Mr. Arckle? I'm Peter Watson."

"Oh! You're the one saved my boys. Sid's been telling me."

With a lot of help from Sergeant Pendragon. "I was glad I
could."

"Nowhere near as glad as I am, sir," he replied, taking
Peter's hand with a firm grasp. "Those boys are all I have.
Hurt me something proper to send them away but I thought it
for the best. Never thought Old Jerry would get them here."

"He didn't," Peter replied, "but Dave's still in hospital,
you know."

"So Sid's been telling me. I want to see him. Soon as I can."

"We'll have to see what we can do about transport. There's
buses."

"Then I'll get one. Just as long as I know where I'm going.
I can speak the language if I get lost."

Judging by the strong London accent, Peter wasn't too
sure. "We'd best have a word with the doctor first. She was
going to phone the hospital and see how everyone was doing.
He wasn't the only casualty."

"So Sid said; right shame about the vicar's lady. This war
is a bad business, make no mistake. Still, I'm here with my
boy and I've got two days off."

"That all, Dad?"

"Son, there's a war on. Can't be taking time off to gallivant.
I'm needed back at work." He turned to Peter. "I work in a pie
factory and bakery; feed half of London, we do."

They were passing the school when Sid asked, "Think I
should go back, sir?"

"Sir" was not a address he was used to. "How did you get
out of school?"

"I was in class when Miss Barkin came in and said the head
wanted to see me. So off I goes, thinking I might be in trouble
for taking yesterday off school, but she says the stationmaster

just called. My dad had arrived from London and didn't know where to go. She asked if I wanted to go meet him. I said 'yes' and ran all the way."

"It's only another half hour. I doubt if they expect you back. Might as well take your father home and give him a cup of tea. I bet he could use one."

"You're right there, sir. Proper parched I am."

"That's settled then. You go in and put the kettle on, Sid. I need to go up to the ARP post; I'll tell Sergeant Pendragon your father's here." And check what was needed with another mouth to feed tonight.

Chapter 22

"Would you mind answering a few questions, sir?"

Eiche looked at the police constable. Yes, he did mind, and was tempted to tear out the man's throat for his impudence, but that was ill-advised while standing in front of the village stores with half a dozen witnesses, all with ears flapping. "By all means, Constable Parlett. I do have the name right, don't I?" The yokel nodded, like the fool he was. "What can I do for you?"

"Sergeant Jones had a few questions, nothing much, but we'd be glad of your help. Would you come down to the station, please?"

The so-called police station was a lean-to built onto the brick house where Sergeant Jones lived with his numerous children. Eiche had seen them running around in circles and playing. Odd the way mortal children spent their time. Eiche had no memory of playing, but it had been a few centuries past.

"Would now suit you, sir?"

Not in the slightest. He had much better things to do with his time but . . . "Of course, Constable." Might as well find out what the man was blathering about. Another snag over dear Aunt Jane's return home, he supposed.

They walked, side by side, the hundred yards or so to the police station. It was on the opposite side of the village from the church and the damaged cottage he couldn't wait to get back to. A vampire needed a safe rest and camping out in Jeff Williams's three-roomed cottage, even if he did have the bed after relegating Williams to the floor, wasn't Eiche's idea of comfort.

"Here you go, sir." The constable opened the door for him. "Sergeant will be with you in a minute. I'll get you a cup of tea while you wait."

"Don't bother."

Mistake that. Constable Parlett stared at him. "You sure, sir? It's no bother. The pot's always ready."

Bother or mortal convenience weren't a concern. "Thank you, but I had one a short while ago." Now, if the constable had offered his veins . . .

"Very well then, sir. I'll tell the sergeant you're here."

He left Eiche sitting on a rather hard, high-backed bench. Moments later the fat sergeant appeared around a door to the left. "Afternoon, Mr. Oak. Thank you for coming in. This way, please."

Eiche found himself sitting on another hard, high-backed chair across from the sergeant's cluttered desk and very much aware of the constable standing behind him. As witness, no doubt.

"What can I do to help you, Sergeant?" Might as well act the helpful, concerned citizen.

"We've a few questions about Miss Jane Waite. Your aunt, I believe?"

Time to evade a little. "Actually she's a distant cousin. I always called her aunt growing up. A courtesy title, you understand, and the title stuck." What the hell was this about?

"I understand, sir. We all have a few extra aunts like that. You've know her for years then. Since you were a child."

Where was this heading? Damn that the constable was here, too. He could probe one mind but not two, and he certainly didn't want a witness to the event. "Yes, I was quite small when I first knew her." Damn! His cover hadn't included these details.

"So, sir, would you know where she'd worked and lived prior to retiring here?"

He had been unprepared. Damn. Better stick to the fiction he established in the pub the other night. "She lived in Yorkshire. Where exactly she worked, I'm not sure. I don't think I was ever told. People don't tell children everything." Nice touch that.

"Would you know what line of work?"

"She was a teacher." At least according to the cover he'd learned.

"Could be," Jones said, almost to himself. He looked up at the constable. "Better have that checked, Parlett. See if we can't find out where she worked and what she did in her spare time."

"Right, sir."

"Do you know if your aunt spoke German, Mr. Oak?"

This he'd been briefed on. "Yes. She was quite an accomplished linguist. Spoke French and Italian fluently, too."

"You used the past tense, Mr. Oak. She'd not dead yet, you know."

"I meant in her youth." He wasn't getting caught out there. "I'm not sure in later years how much she traveled or used those languages."

"Had she ever been to Germany? That you know of, of course."

Where was this going? If he only knew he could give the damn answers they wanted. "I'm sure she had. She's traveled widely. Even worked abroad at one time I heard."

"Did you hear where she worked—taught, I think you said—abroad?"

Damn! The old biddy should be here to answer these. "Italy, I believe." Let them try to confirm that.

"Would that be before or after she taught in Yorkshire, sir?"

Were they trying to trip him up? If so, he might just have

to dispose of two policemen. He had a mission to accomplish and these two plodders were not getting in his way. "Before, I believe. The exact years I don't know."

"Sure it wasn't Germany?"

Why keep harping back to that? "No. It could be but I never heard it said she worked there."

"Fair enough, sir." He spent a few minutes looking at a page of notes that he kept carefully angled so Eiche couldn't read it upside down. Irritating that. "You think your mother might be able to shed some more light on Miss Waite's work history?"

"I'm sure she could have, Sergeant, but unfortunately, my mother's dead." And had been for nigh on five hundred years.

"I see. So you don't know much about her as you were a child and wasn't told these things, and your mother who might know is no longer with us. Any other family members who might help us?"

This was way beyond his cover. If he were mortal, he'd be nervous. But he wasn't. "I wish there were, Sergeant, but I'm an only child and apart from Aunt Jane, I never knew any of my mother's family. They cut her off when I was born." Nicely convenient that was.

Maybe too much so. "I see. Everyone cut off contact except Miss Waite, a distant cousin." This was sounding like a Victorian melodrama, but damn, he hadn't been given this background.

"Pity you don't know more about her, sir. It really would have helped us." Helped to do what? "I'm new around here, sir, but did you visit Miss Waite much before the war?"

"No. I meant to and we exchanged letters and Christmas cards, but no, I never got down to see here."

Pause while he scribbled a note. "Oh, by the way, sir—" He spoke without looking up. "Mind if I have a look at your identity card?"

Yes, he did. "With pleasure, Sergeant." He took the card from his inside pocket and handed it over.

Was this about the old bitch or about him? Had Weiss or one of the others been caught and blabbed? How could they have been caught? They were vampire. Just as he was vampire and being subjected to an inquisition.

His ID card got a very careful going over. He'd been assured the coding in the number marked him as engaged in important, secret work. He hoped they hadn't lied.

Seemed not. He was handed back his card. "Thank you, sir. We just need to check everything, you not being a resident of these parts. You understand?

"Perfectly. And while I'm here, have you any idea when my aunt's house will be habitable again? The damage wasn't that severe."

"Not too long I don't think. Takes a while to repair roof and chimney damage these days. We're just making sure."

Of what? "Constable?"

"Yes, sir?"

The man still hovered behind. "May I take you up on that offer of a cup of tea after all?"

"By all means, sir. You want one, Sarge?"

"Yes, please. Bring two, if you would."

The minute the man was out of the door, Eiche seized the sergeant's mind and almost swore aloud. He let the man's mind go and barely noticed how he winced and sagged in his chair. They'd found a wireless. She must have had one to communicate with Zuerst and Zweiten but she should have hidden it better. At least his was safe. How many nosy policemen were going to climb to the top of the church tower?

"You alright, sir?" The constable put both cups on the table. If he knew why the sergeant looked pasty-faced, the stupid constable would keel over.

"Yes, of course!" He took the tea and drank down half in one go. "Now, sir. Let's go back to your aunt's travels. Any idea where she went to in Germany?"

They went round and round. Eiche playing ignorant and

vague, the sergeant asking questions and seeking information Eiche was never going to give. It was a bit of a temptation to tell him everything, watch him blanch, and then dine off the pair of them, but the timing wasn't right for such public carnage.

"Well then, sir," he said at last. "If you think of anything that might help us, any little detail, you'll contact us."

"Of course." Not.

"And where are you living now, sir?

He gave the address. "I'm sharing with Jeff Williams. He kindly offered me a bed." Under duress.

With affable handshaking all around, Eiche left them.

Damn, this was a crimp he hadn't anticipated. Seemed they suspected Miss Waite's loyalty and patriotism, but not her concerned nephew's. How quaint was that? He'd have to remember to be suitably horrified if anything more came of this.

Meanwhile, he had to move fast. Between Weiss wanting results and the flatfooted coppers getting their suspicions up, it was time to act.

Maybe tonight he'd get Williams drunk. Even vampires needed a little diversion once in a while. Not that Eiche had any doubt that the target was exactly as suspected. Williams had as good as told him that the first night he met him but a little inside information never hurt. The man had no sense of discretion, which suited Eiche admirably.

"I don't see why I have to stay and do homework." Sid looked from one grown-up to the other, looking for support.

He wasn't getting any. "Son, stow it away! You're staying here with Mr. Watson and I'm going along with Mr. Pendragon to see your brother, and don't try that with me. You know they won't let you in. Hospitals have rules and how you got to go with him last time, I dunno."

Peter did. He had a grown-up on his side and it was chaos.

Now would be different and hospital rules weren't likely to be bent twice.

"Don't push your chances, son. Be glad you're not the one lying in a hospital bed."

"I know, Dad, but I want to see him. You told us to look after each other."

"I know I did, and seems to me you both did that pretty nicely. Keeping together until help came." The man looked up from his supper. "And I tell you both, Sergeant and Mr. Watson, I'll be grateful to you for the rest of my life. Sid took me up to see the bomb site. I've seen enough of them to know if you'd not got my boys out when you did, we'd still be digging for them."

He went quiet, a little shudder shaking his broad shoulders.

"So you hush it, son, and eat up. I didn't bring that pie all this way to have you pick at it and whinge on me."

They all tucked in. Mr. Arckle had come bearing a vast meat pie, part of his factory's output.

"Get your homework done early and we can listen to the wireless or play cards if you want," Peter volunteered. "I'm not on duty tonight, unless Jerry comes calling again."

"If he does, I want to go with you," Sid said through a mouthful of potato.

"If he does, you're going down to the air raid shelter," his father told him. "No hanging about to have another house collapse on you, son. Understand?"

Unwillingly. "Yes, Dad," he replied with a sigh.

"And you will go, son. Mr. Watson here will see to it. You don't want him to have to dig you out a second time, now, do you?"

Might be hard without Sergeant Pendragon to hold up the house, but Peter kept that thought to himself and chewed on another mouthful of pie. "He'll do what you tell him, Mr. Arckle."

"He knows better than not to, Mr. Watson. But never hurts to remind him. I've two good boys, but they're likely lads and never miss a chance."

The man had his sons pretty much sized up.

"Seconds, anyone?" Sergeant Pendragon asked as he pushed his plate away. Even Sid seemed sated.

At Peter's cue, Sid gathered up the plates and Peter gave him a hand. Sid cleaned the plates and added the scrapings to the potato peelings and cabbage leaves in the bucket under the sink. It was almost full. In the morning it needed to go up to Mother Longhurst for her chickens.

Once Sid was busy with soap and scrubber, Peter left him to the sink and joined the other two men at the table

"You've been real good to me and my boys," Mr. Arckle said as he lit a cigarette. "Taking Sid in like this, to say nothing of saving them in the first place, Mr. Watson. Thank you."

This keeping mum about the whole truth was mind snarling. So was wondering what the sergeant was. "Other" had been how Mrs. Burrows described him. Oh well, at least he wasn't a vampire.

Sitting in a very ordinary country kitchen, with yellowed paint and a frayed hearth rug, the whole idea of vampires seemed preposterous. But no more preposterous than a man of sixty or so holding up a house.

"It's just," Mr. Arckle went on, "I'm none too sure about my boys going off to that farm. Always thought Dave would come and join me at the bakery, and Sid in his time. Not sure I can see either as farmers."

"Tom Longhurst is a good man," Pendragon said. "You'll see that when you meet him. Time then to decide for sure."

Arckle nodded, obviously still not certain.

At the sound of a car hooter outside, Sid called, "Hey, Dad! Sergeant Pendragon! It's the doctor."

Moments later there was a rap at the door and Alice's head appeared. "Sorry I'm a bit early, but I got through evening surgery much sooner than usual. Plus, Gran insists it's going to storm tonight, and I'd just as soon get back ahead of the deluge."

Holy smoke! She was lovely, beautiful, gorgeous, and he made a point of standing very close to the table so no one noticed what was happening below his belt.

And then she smiled at him. "Hello, Mr. Watson." He wanted to race across the kitchen and hug her tight. He yearned to kiss her again, to feel her sweet woman's body against his and inhale the scent of her skin and hair.

Wanting was downright painful. Literally! "Evening, Doctor."

"We'll be ready in a jiffy, Doctor," Sergeant Pendragon said. "This is Mr. Arckle, Dave and Sid's father."

Stupid to be jealous of a forty-five year-old man getting that smile, but he was. Very. "Good evening, Mr. Arckle. It's wonderful you could get down so quickly. I can't wait to see Dave's face when you walk in."

"I can't wait to see him, Doctor. He's not too beat up, is he?"

"Not really. Sid got the bruises, poor Dave got the broken bones. But he's young, he'll mend."

Not like the vicar's poor wife who still hadn't regained consciousness.

So off they went. Peter gave Sid a hand with the wiping, and while the boy spread his school books on the table, Peter lit a cigarette and turned on the wireless.

"Hey, Mr. Watson, switch it over to Lord Haw Haw, please," Sid asked, a bit of a wheedle in his voice.

"What would your father say if he knew you were listening to him?"

"He listens. You should hear him take him off. He does it to a T. 'Chairmany calling. Chairmany calling!' He laughs at him, honest he does."

Quite probably. Half the population listened to the propaganda broadcasts from Berlin. That they were a source of entertainment rather than panic and despair was a sure sign that old Hitler rather misgauged things. "Alright. If you get your homework done."

But tonight the ether failed to cooperate and the broadcast was scratchy and full of interference and they both gave up and settled for the Home Service. The talk on rabbit-keeping was boring enough to let Peter's mind wander onto more enthralling topics, notably Alice, Dr. Doyle, and the woman he was head over heels in love with. She beat out furry rodents, even edible furry rodents, any day of the week.

It was past nine when they returned; Sid was asleep in the parlor after soundly beating Peter twice playing Beggar My Neighbor, and Peter was considering stepping out into the garden for a breath of air.

"He's asleep?" Mr. Arckle asked. "Hoped he would be. I'll tell him in the morning what Dave said. It did me good to see he's mending. Chafing at being stuck in there he is. Don't blame him myself; who wants to be in hospital is what I say. But I told him time will pass and he'll need two good arms and legs if he's to work on that there farm."

"Everything alright with the others?" Peter asked.

"The girl is fine, in the same boat as Dave, chafing to get home, and as for poor Mrs. Roundhill . . ." Pendragon left that unsaid.

"Sad." Arckle shook his head. "Now, about meeting the farmer."

"Oh! Yes." Pendragon looked worn out. "Would you mind, lad? I'm ready to turn in, but Tom Longhurst is waiting for us in the Pig and Whistle. Mind going on down with him?"

Since he'd been feeling in need of a breather, no. "I'm happy to. Let me get my jacket."

Five minutes later, torches in hand, they set off down the pitch dark lane toward the Pig and Whistle.

Chapter 23

It was really quite fascinating to watch the effect of alcohol on mortals, and Jeff Williams seemed to show the effects particularly. His eyes watered, his speech blurred, and he even dribbled beer down his dingy shirt. Pathetic, but potentially very useful. A couple more beers and Eiche wouldn't even need to mind probe the fool. He'd betray King and country like the worthless creature he was.

Weiss wanted the camp rendered inoperative by next weekend. Might as well oblige and Williams was bound to help.

"You's a good shap, Oak," Williams announced, spraying beer across the table. "A bumper shap. Always good for scompany, not like that shob Barron, thinks he's a cut above the rest of us, he does."

Ah, yes. "Your not so esteemed supervisor."

Williams let out a mangled laugh. "Eshteem! Ha! Fool he is. Thinks he's running a holiday camp. Had the nerve to tell me I was too hard on the bitches! Ha! If I had my way that place would be run very different."

And when Eiche had his way, it would not run at all. "He can't be around all the time, can he?"

"S'here for the duration!" My, he was having trouble with his diction. "Shame as me!"

"Can't be that much longer." He knew for a fact Zuerst and Zweiten were planning Christmas in London.

"You tell me, Gabriel, you tell me. The way Jerry's dropping his bombs all over the place, who's to say?"

He could. Time enough later for total revelation. "Want another beer?"

"Shoo bet! Real gentleman you are, Mr. Oak, real pal. Don't mind sharing my digs with a man who knows how to treat a pal."

One more, he judged, and he could let the fool stagger home and have a little fun with him. Eiche want over to the bar, ignored the rather surly glance from the landlord. Damn, he was paying for the beer, wasn't he? In genuine counterfeit Reich pounds. Let Fred Wise look down his nose. Eiche would enjoy watching him in defeat.

"Another pint? Don't you think he's had enough? Much more and you'll have to carry him home."

Who was this mortal to question him? Eiche shrugged. "I'll get him home before he gets boisterous. He's had long day."

"So have a lot if us, sir." But he pulled the pint and poured a measure of whisky. Eiche was tempted to ask for schnapps, just to see the shock on his face, but discretion held him back. Wouldn't be long before this place was selling schnapps and German beer.

Glasses in hand, Eiche went back to the table just as the blackout curtain by the outer door was lifted and two men walked in.

Not bothering to look at the newcomers, Eiche tipped the whisky into the beer. That should settle Williams nicely. And damn, he might just carry him home. He could always drop him in the pond on the way.

"Evening, Mr. Watson. What can I get you?"

"A pint of bitter, please, Mr. Wise. This is Mr. Arckle, the father of the boys caught at the vicarage."

"The lads whose lives you saved, Mr. Watson. Don't be modest. And what can I get for you, sir?"

"The same, please. What do I owe for them?" Arckle asked, reaching into his pocket.

"No, Mr. Arckle," Peter protested. "You're my guest."

"Put your money away, sir, and you too, Mr. Watson. These are on the house. Not much for what you did the other night, Mr. Watson, and you, sir, welcome to Brytewood and the Pig. Wish it had been in better times."

"My boys are well, can't ask for much more."

"Mr. Wise, we're here to meet a Mr. Longhurst," Peter said. "Would you know him?"

"You must mean young Tom from up on Cherry Hill. He's been here an hour or more. Brought a couple of his land girls with him. You'll find them over by the fireplace. Table under the window."

Peter lead the way, weaving between standing groups and the occasional crowded table. The Pig did good business.

As they eased past a small table, a hand grasped Peter's shoulder and jerked him around. A red face peered close.

"Shou! I shot it was shou!" his assailant hissed. "Damn conscie coward. What are yoush doing here?"

Given the man was grasping the table for support with his free hand, Peter took that as a rhetorical question. But he recognized the man. Was he lurking here on the off chance of breathing warm beer fumes at him? Peter stepped back and reached to remove the hand from his shoulder. He shouldn't have bothered.

Joe Arckle beat him to to it, grabbing the man's wrist and twisting it until he grimaced. "That doesn't sound too friendly, sport. That's not the way to talk to my friend!"

Jeff Williams, Peter remembered his name now, seemed too far gone to catch the warning in Arckle's measured words.

"I'll talk to yim howevers I like. Heesh a coward. A yellow coward too scared to fight!"

The entire pub had gone silent. This entire interchange would be all over the village before dawn. Talk about hoping for the proverbial earth to open!

Joe Arckle smiled. Rather reminded Peter of a mongoose eyeing a cobra. Williams was too pickled to realize his wiry frame was no match for a man who'd spent the last twenty-odd years hefting bakery trays in and out of ovens.

Williams sat down with a thud. Arckle didn't give him a chance to realize what had happened. He just grabbed his chin and jerked his face up. "Coward is he? How interesting. And you're not, I suppose. You tell me how many children's lives you saved this week, sport!"

Peter had thought the room was silent before. He'd been wrong. Now it was deathly quiet. He could sense every single ear wagging. Even the dog by the fireplace had perked up. The man with Williams stood.

If there was a fight, Peter would stand with Arckle but . . .

Peter looked at Williams's companion. And shuddered. The look of hate, utter contempt, and loathing was enough to chill the soul, and the look was directed at Williams.

Then the man looked at Peter. Cold dark eyes seemed to burn with scorn. Peter stared back. "Sir, I think your friend needs to go home." Why was his heart racing so and damn his hands sweating?

Then the man broke his gaze.

Before Peter had time to think about that little interchange, Fred Wise came bustling up.

"Now, gentlemen, what's the trouble? Let's settle down, shall we?"

"The trouble mysh good man ish I will not strink in the shame pub as a bloody CO!"

"That so, sir? Then you'd best be on your way." He turned to Williams's odd companion. "And you, sir, take your friend home. I'll not serve him any more beer tonight."

"Come, Jeff," the other man said. "Time to leave." And

yanked him up and half dragged him out with an arm about his waist. No one helped, although someone near the door lifted the blackout curtain and slammed the door behind them.

"Sorry about that, sir," the landlord said to Peter. "And you, sir," to Arckle. "We keep a nice house here. Everyone knows better. They'll have to walk to Westhumble or Ranmore if they want to drink now. Not having trouble like that at my Pig." His glance went to Joe's beer. "Spilled some, did you? Sorry about that." He took the mug. "I'll top it up."

Beer mug refilled and the pub conversation back to pre-interruption level, they finally made their way to Tom Longhurst's table.

He rose as they approached, holding out his hand. "Tom Longhurst. Now that's what I call an entrance."

Peter took his hand. "Peter Watson, and I'd just as soon make an unobtrusive one. This is Joe Arckle, Dave and Sid's father."

"And this is Katy and Phyllis, two of my land girls." Both in their twenties. Nice enough, good-looking girls with bright complexions from working outdoors, but neither could hold a candle to Alice.

After all around handshakes, Peter motioned Joe to the vacant chair and pulled up another.

"Come to give me the once over?" Tom asked.

"That's right." Arckle put his beer down. "Can't say farming is what I had in mind for my boys, but might not be bad. Not now. At least they'll never go hungry."

Peter sat down. Gave the two girls another nod and listened to Arckle and Longhurst size each other up.

"We still need ration books," Longhurst said. "I've a dairy farm. All the milk we need that the government doesn't take first, and I've started keeping a few pigs and hens like half the neighborhood. I thought Dave could help with those, once his arm gets healed. Not heavy work and that would free the girls up to take care of the cows. Phyllis and Julia, who stayed back tonight, also split time with the home farm at Warton Lacey so we can always use another pair of hands for milking.

Arckle smiled. "Think you can teach a pair of town boys to milk cows?"

"Katy learned, and I don't think she'd ever seen a cow before she got here."

Katy, with dark hair and a heavy fringe, smiled. "That's right. Scared the willies out of me at first. You get used to them."

Arckle nodded. "Fair enough. Now what about their billet and getting Sid down to school? He needs another year, even though he doesn't think so."

"We can give them their own room in the house. My mother is getting on but she cooks for us, press-gangs one of the girls to pitch in from time to time. I'll pay Dave the going rate for a lad. We'll have the billeting allowance to cover their food."

"Pay him half. Bank the other half. Don't want the money burning a hole in his pocket. It's never too soon to start putting a bit by."

"Alright. I'll open a post office account for him. Anything else? We have a telephone if you want to call them, and any time you want to come down and help with the milking, feel free."

"Thank you, I will. Although time off isn't easy to get. I work in a bakery and pie factory and I tell you, we're making double what we did before the war. Between restaurants and the food kitchens, business is good." He paused. "Sad to say that isn't it? But that's the way of it."

"There's many a business booming because of the war. And there's others out of the jobs they held for years as factories closed down. Makes me glad I'm a farmer. People always need food." He took a drink of his almost empty beer. "Any more questions?"

"How about Sid getting to school regular. It's a few miles, right?"

"About five. If one of us is coming down to the village, we

can bring him in the lorry. If not, I have a bicycle he can use. It's not a bad ride in the morning, downhill most of the way. Not so much fun coming home. I know. I rode it back and forth when I was a boy."

"Won't do him no harm." Joe Arckle tipped his mug and went thoughtful. "Seems to me, Mr. Longhurst, you'll do right by my boys. Not that they didn't do well with the vicar and his wife, poor woman."

"If you want to come out to the farm before you go back, feel free."

"Think I might just. And they both need clothes."

"My mother will be glad to help. She can take them into Leatherhead shopping at the weekend."

"Thanks, I'll do it myself if I can. I'll feel better knowing they arrive with what they need."

There wasn't much more to say. Fred Wise called for last orders and that seemed a good point to set off home.

Peter and Joe joined the straggle of villagers fumbling their way home in the dark.

Then came the question Peter half dreaded. "You're a CO then, Mr. Watson?"

"Yes." Why elaborate?

"And who was that drunken lout?"

"He works up at the plant on the heath. Big government place."

"Parachutes or munitions?"

Peter had to smile at that. "Village opinion is divided. We don't see them much. Some are brought in by bus from Leatherhead or Dorking but most of them live at the camp. Only a few have billets in the village. I haven't been up there, yet. Running the works clinic there is part of my job."

"If that so-and-so ever comes in with an injury, be sure to use extra iodine."

Hardly ethical medical practice, but the thought was a temptation.

"I should thank you for stepping in."

"No, you shouldn't! I'll owe you forever, Mr. Watson. We all make our decisions. You made yours. Went to gaol did you?"

"Yes, nine months in Pentonville."

"Sorry you had to go through that, but for my part, I'm bloody glad you stood up as an objector. If you hadn't my boys might well be goners. Thank you, sir. Thank you."

They were turning the corner, about fifty yards from Sergeant Pendragon's cottage, when a dark shape appeared as if from nowhere.

Chapter 24

Peter lurched backward but managed to keep to his feet as the dark shape swept down on him and a wave of sheer cold terror wrung a scream from him. Or maybe that was Joe Arckle.

"What the bloody hell!"

That was Joe.

Peter didn't try to answer, just grabbed Joe and hauled him back. As they retreated, the shape reattacked, adding a wail to the swooping. Sounded like a soul in torment being strangled.

They backed away half mesmerized by the thing and the overwhelming sense of menace.

"Jesus wept!" Joe muttered.

Peter looked for help, others, a weapon, but there was was no one in sight and nothing but hedges on either side of the lane. "Christ Almighty! Help!" he yelled, hoping a straggler from the Pig might hear. Only the sound came muffled from a throat tight with fear. He was shaking and sweating when the thing laughed: a cold, tight, evil snicker that sent icy fear spiking though his veins and gut.

He wanted to run, to flee, but was unable to move and then it came at them again.

Only now there was a bright light and with it came a roar.

"A mighty rushing wind," thought Peter, only it wasn't a tongue of flame but a flash of blue and yellow fire.

And then the snicker stopped as if extinguished. In its place a wail filled the night sky.

And everything was silent. Around them was nothing but the dark and the clear night air.

"What in the blazes was that?" Peter wasn't sure if he'd said that or Joe. Hardly mattered, they were both shaking with fear and relief and if they didn't move fast the ARP would be down on them for showing a light and there was no way in heaven Peter could explain what had just happened.

If it ever had.

Joe nudged him. "Let's scarper."

A brilliant idea. Together they ran down the lane, racing for all they were worth, until the gate of the cottage appeared.

Then they ran even faster, if it were possible, and both burst thought the back door, slamming it behind them.

"Damn," Joe said. "Hope we didn't wake the boy."

The boy never stirred. Just as well. How could they explain how two grown men were terrified out of their wits and pale as bleached flour? At least Joe Arckle was and Peter had absolutely no reason to think he looked any better.

"What the hell was that?"

Good question. Peter shook his head. "Hideous."

"Right there, mate! I'd rather face the bloody Jerries than that again. Think it's still outside?"

"I think it dissolved in the flames."

"And what are they when they're at home? I tell you, Mr. Watson. My boys are coming home with me. No offense to anyone and everyone's been right good to them and me, but I'd rather they faced Jerry's bombs any day than that."

Understandable. "We couldn't both have imagined it, could we?"

Joe Arckle rolled his eyes. Good answer. Whatever it was, they'd both seen and felt it. To say nothing of the roars and shrieks. And where was Sergeant Pendragon? His tea was cooling in his mug by the fire. His worn tartan slippers still on the hearth rug. Not like him to leave with Sid asleep.

What the Hades? Peter had never been a swearing man but he'd never faced a thing like that before.

"Where did he get to?" Joe asked.

The door opened.

They both jumped, ready to face the horror again, but it was only the sergeant—a rather bedraggled sergeant. Had he faced the thing too?

"Evening," he said with a calm that belied his rumpled appearance. "Have a good time at the Pig? Meet up with Longhurst alright, did you?"

"What happened to you, Sergeant?" Peter asked. The man's jacket and shirt were torn, his hair was half on end. "You're bleeding!" A trickle of blood oozed down one side of his face.

He reached up and touched his forehead. "Oh! That!" he said. "I'm a clumsy old fool. Went out to get some more coke for the boiler. Thought we'd all be glad of the hot water in the morning and tripped in my own backyard, fell arse over heels, and landed in a tangle against the dustbin."

He had the coal hod in his hands to back up his story, but something was off. Definitely off. "Better let me have a look at that cut of yours."

"It's nothing that a bit of warm water won't cure."

Peter wasn't sure about that. Grazes didn't bleed that profusely. "Let me look at it."

He seemed too dazed to object much. He sat down and let Peter bathe the wound. It was a lot more than a graze. Whatever he'd hit had gouged a deep cut a couple of inches long.

"I think it might need stitches."

"Lad, with all the air raids, do you think hospitals have time to deal with a clumsy old man who tripped over his own boot scraper?"

"We could go up to the doctor's."

"No, we couldn't. I'm not knocking on her door for something a bit of gauze and sticking plaster can fix."

Peter gave up. Almost. "Let's get it cleaned up and I'll have another look in the morning. If it's still nasty looking—" And it was bound to be. "We'll have Dr. Doyle stitch it up."

"See how it is in the morning," Pendragon agreed. "Right now, I want my bed."

Poor Joe Arckle looked more than ready for his, too.

Peter cleaned the wound, which would definitely need stitches, and soon headed upstairs.

It wasn't until he was in pajamas and under the sheets that he paused to wonder why Sergeant Pendragon had gone out to fetch coke in bare feet.

Maybe they'd imagined the half of it. By breakfast time, the sergeant had a nasty bruise on his forehead, and a fading one on the side of his neck, and that was that. Peter could have sworn he did not imagine the deep gouge last night. In fact, the bloody gauze was still in the bin.

His conversation with Alice came back to him. Would being a vampire account for that rapid healing?

What the Hades happened?

Mrs. Burrows had thoroughly pooh-poohed the notion that Sergeant Pendragon might be a vampire but, with all due respect, what did an old woman know?

Maybe a little more than he did, but he darn well knew what he'd seen.

Or imagined with a mind numbed with fright.

No, not imagined. It had unnerved Mr. Arckle to the point of whisking his boys back to the heart of the Blitz.

Not that Sid seemed the least put out.

"You mean it, Dad? No kidding? We really get to come back with you?"

"Yes, son. I thought you'd be safe from the bombs here but

you're not. We're not safe anywhere, and if the Jerries do come, I want you both close by me."

"What happened with the farmer you went to meet in the pub? Was he queer or something?"

Peter almost choked on his porridge. The boy wasn't exactly a babe, but he'd not expected that to come out of his mouth.

Neither had his father. "Hell no, son! The things you come out with. He was a good chap. I liked him. Honest, worked hard. Not his fault he wasn't born in London." That got a grin from Sid and an anxious glance in their direction; the man obviously didn't want to offend. "In fact, when we left, we shook on it. I thought he'd be a fair man to work for and Dave could do a lot worse with a first employer, but then I got thinking, you'd have a long bike ride to school each day. Not that it would hurt you one whit, lad, but heck, you're not country boys and never will be. So . . ."

Sid smiled. Almost looked ready to hug his father but remembered to act he-man just in time. "Thanks, Dad. When do we leave?"

The laugh came from the sergeant.

Poor Sid looked mortified. "I'm sorry, sir. Really I am. Didn't mean it like that, honest, and I'll never forget how you and Mr. Watson got us out of the cellar, but I miss home so and I know Dave does. When can he get out of hospital?" The last was to his father.

"That I'll talk to the doctor about. They said last night a day or two, but when the postman came by he said they had more bombing in Dorking last night. So they might need the bed."

"I hope they do." With the words out of his mouth Sid resumed, mortified. "Didn't mean I wanted people bombed."

"We know what you meant, lad," Pendragon said. "Your dad's right. He needs you both with him. I tell you, I miss my son."

"Where's your son?" Sid wanted to know.

"That, Sid, I don't rightly know. He was in Norway, came

home on leave a few weeks afterward. Right now, I dunno. Fighting somewhere. If the war lasts long enough, Sid, you and Dave will get called up. Until then, your dad wants you both nearby."

"Will the war last that long? They said it would be over by Christmas."

"That was last year," his father said.

"And during the last one, too," Pendragon added. "No one knows, lad, and you'll be late for school if you don't stir your stumps."

Sid accepted the dismissal, gathered up his homework, and left.

Peter should have followed suit but stopped to do the dishes while Joe Arckle and the sergeant discussed bicycle availability and the possibility of a loan of one for the morning or afternoon.

Peter left them to it and resolved to talk to Alice at the very first opportunity. Maybe she'd be free for lunch. He could call her from the school or the post office. By hook or by crook, he was going to tell her about the odd events of the previous evening.

Trouble was, he just couldn't equate kindly, intelligent Sergeant Pendragon with the awful presence they'd sensed out in the lane. Yes, he'd come in bleeding and bedraggled. Maybe he'd encountered that same dark presence but wasn't about to admit it, or talk about it.

Damn, he had to see Alice now. Head lice could wait a couple of hours.

Chapter 25

"Something the matter, Mr. Watson?"

Peter didn't even want to try answering Mrs. Burrows's kindly inquiry. "I hate to barge in so early, but could I speak to Dr. Doyle, please?"

"Of course, come on in."

He now stood in the front hall as Mrs. Burrows called up the wide staircase. "Alice, dear, it's Mr. Watson and I think it's urgent."

Was it? Yes! Maybe! Dash it all, he was no doubt losing it but hadn't these two women been the first to mention vampires?

"Coming, just a tick."

She appeared in moments, a towel around her neck, hairbrush in hand, and her hair in a mass of damp curls around her face.

She was utterly lovely, totally devastating, and gave him the "come hither" just by standing there. And he had to keep his mind on the subject uppermost in his thoughts that shouldn't, at least right now, be the memory of her sweet body under his.

"Sorry to bother you, but I need to speak to you."

She was halfway down the stairs and smiling. Sweet heaven! "That's alright, what's the matter?"

How the heck did he explain that one? "Something really odd happened last night."

"How about you come into the kitchen and tell us about it? You look as if you need a good cup of tea and Alice hasn't even had breakfast yet."

He really fancied something stronger, but perhaps not at nine o'clock in the morning. "Thank you."

Alice put her hand in his. An action Mrs. Burrows registered with a raised eyebrow. Still, if Alice wasn't keeping things to herself, fair enough.

"Come and sit down, both of you."

They both followed that command, Peter holding the door for Alice and deliberately sitting beside her. "It's about Sergeant Pendragon and the things you said about vampires."

"I see." That Peter doubted, but to say so to an old lady seemed downright rude. "Since you're here and in one piece, I expect it can wait three minutes."

It was obviously going to have to. Alice gave her hair another rub with the towel and folded it over the back of a spare chair. He'd noticed before the number of chairs around the big table and realized they must be the empty seats once occupied by her brothers and father. Apart from her grandmother, Alice was alone.

Not anymore.

"Right then." Mrs. Burrows put a cup in front of them and then a toast rack and two pots of jam. "We're low on butter, I'm afraid, but the jam and marmalade is out of my prewar stock. Almost gone now, but we might have it while we're still here to enjoy it."

Very good point. Who knew what tomorrow would bring?

He wasn't dwelling on tomorrow. Talking about last night was going to be quite bad enough.

Alice handed Peter a plate and knife. "Eat up."

"Just one slice. I've already had porridge but the marmalade looks wonderful." And tasted every bit as delicious.

"Alright then, Mr. Watson, what brought you here in such a tizz wazz?"

He swallowed the mouthful of toast. "Last night Mr. Arckle and I went down to the Pig to meet with Farmer Longhurst. Now let's get it straight. We were not drunk; we'd had precisely one beer each."

Slowly, picking his words so it sounded plausible and reasonable, he gave a step by step account of the bizarre events of the previous night. Including Sergeant Pendragon's rumpled appearance and the overnight healing of a gash that had needed stitches.

When he finished he half expected them to call for a padded wagon.

Alice looked downright perplexed.

Mrs. Burrows nodded. "More tea anyone?"

"Gran! Let the tea wait a bit. What do you know? You do know something, don't you?"

"Are you admitting we have powers, Alice?"

"I'm asking what you know, Gran."

The tension between the two women practically hummed. Lost was a good word to describe how he felt caught between them.

"I know what you deny, child." She turned to Peter. "Mr. Watson, first, let me set your mind at rest about Howell Pendragon. He is not a vampire. But I think we need to talk to him. And soon. At least once Alice gets her hair dry. Is he home?"

"He was when I left to come up here, but he was going down to the village hall to meet Sir James Gregory, something to do with supplies for the Home Guard."

"I'll call him there. Ask him to come up later. Lunchtime."

He was going to have to wait until lunchtime to find out what was going on?

"Gran . . ." Alice began but was hushed fast.

"Now you listen to me, my love. Something is here and it means us ill. Howell can help, you wait and see. Now finish your breakfast and get on with your rounds. We'll all meet back here at one. And you, Mr. Watson, get on with what you need to do. It's daylight, so I don't think we need to worry."

This was getting more and more like a Saturday morning horror film, only he was living in the middle of it.

"Give Peter another cup, Gran. I'll get ready."

Mrs. Burrows couldn't miss the "Peter" and she didn't.

"I see. Would you like another cup, Peter?"

"Thanks, but I'd better get going. I should be down at the school. Since I'm here, can I have some prescriptions for the children who'll need more shampoo?"

"Send them to Mother Longhurst, she'll give them rosemary lotion, works just as well."

"I'll get you the prescriptions," Alice said. "I'll be back in half a mo."

"Is she related to the farmer Tom Longhurst?"

"His great aunt. She was his grandfather's sister. Lots of Longhursts around here. Seems everyone in the village is related."

"Just like at home." He thrust away the stab of homesickness. Devon definitely had its advantages, like no hideous presences swooping out of the night when you were walking home of an evening. Mind you, Devon didn't have Alice. Weighing it up, he'd take her and the dark looming shapes and the enigmatic Sergeant Howell Pendragon.

"Here you are."

Alice was back, a bundle of prescription forms in her hand. "Just let me know who gets them. Gloria always keeps track." She paused. "Come outside."

Who'd refuse that invitation? Even if the front door and his bicycle were in full view of any passersby.

"This is insane," she said.

He agreed. "I didn't imagine it, Alice, and I wasn't drunk, I swear."

She shook her head and smiled. "Peter, I didn't mean that!

I meant what I'm feeling. For two pins I'd drag you upstairs and keep you there all morning."

"I wish I had two pins."

"It's insane. I barely know you."

"I think we know each other pretty well." He was, no doubt, smirking, but what the blazes was a man supposed to say and think?

"Peter."

"Yes?"

"Go and take care of the nits and lice."

What a farewell. "Alright, head lice here I come."

"Come back early, if you can. I'll be here."

"So will I."

And dammit, no one was passing and if they were, it was none of their bloody business. He reached for her, held her close, planted his lips on hers, and gave her a full body contact kiss.

Now, he was as good as drunk! And it felt wonderful. Until he mounted his bicycle and had to ride downhill.

Eiche stirred on Jeff Williams's narrow bed. The blackout worked equally well to ensure him an uninterrupted daysleep and the rest he needed desperately after the attack last night. As he lay in pain and darkness, revenge burned in his mind like the fire that had seared his skin.

What had gone wrong? And exactly when?

All had been as planned until Williams made that ridiculous insult toward the new medical personage. So the fool was a conscientious objector. In Germany he'd have been in a camp. Here they let him minister to the sick. Eiche hoped he killed a few with incompetence.

But damn the fool Williams drawing attention that way and getting them thrown out of the miserable hostelry. He'd taken Williams back to their shared lodgings and fed rather adequately. The mortal still slumbered in the pile of blankets in the corner.

In the rush of strength from feeding, Eiche had planned a simple straightforward revenge, nothing permanent, just enough terror to have the two self-satisfied mortals shit in their clothes. Instead a presence with scalding fire attacked him.

It was unthinkable and intolerable, and something he should warn the others about, but to do so would be to admit his own weakness in succumbing to the attack.

No, better to bide his time, rest in the dark, and heal. Soon he'd be full strength again and then he would take care of his assignment.

There would be a terrible accident and the camp destroyed with a delightedly tragic loss of life. Sunday he'd report his success to the others and then let Weiss dare censure him.

It would happen on Friday.

Whether he'd let Williams survive or not was a moot point. Preferably not, he decided. After all, the man knew far too much.

If he muttered something about vampires in one of his drunken stupors, some fool yokel might actually believe him.

Chapter 26

"So, young Peter's worried about what happened last night."

He's forgive the sergeant the "young" bit. "Not just last night. Alice and I have been talking. There's been a series of odd events, culminating last night in something out of a nightmare."

"You never mentioned it at the time."

"You weren't there when we got in and when we did see you, you were injured." Damn, it sounded like an accusation. Not what he'd intended. He looked at Alice across the table and her grandmother sitting next to Pendragon watching him with an odd, almost expectant look on her face. "Besides, it was so fantastic, I think we both half believed we'd imagined it."

"Maybe you did."

"No. No more than I imagined you had a great gash in your forehead."

"A gash?" he asked, pushing the hair off his forehead. Even the bruise from this morning had faded. "What gash?"

"We can ask Mr. Arckle. He saw you were hurt. And he was with me in the lane." After Alice and Mrs. Burrows' ready acceptance, the sergeant's attitude was nothing short of deliberate obfuscation. Why?

"Mr. Arckle went back to London with his boys."

"What? He can't have yet."

"He did, Peter," Alice said. "I talked to the hospital this morning. They discharged Dave. Mr. Arckle came back and picked up Sid and they all were put on a train about noon. I'm not sure he's wise taking them back to town, but we're hardly safe from bombs here. Seems he wants his sons with him."

And was as terrified last night as Peter had been. Lucky man had London to run away to.

So bang went the only other witness to what did or did not happen last night. Peter shook his head. This wasn't getting anywhere.

"I know what Peter just said sounds ridiculous, and I'd be inclined to agree if I hadn't seen what I saw last week. That seems to have been the beginning of the odd things."

She gave a concise but pretty complete account of it all. Mrs. Burrows underscoring the lack of a living aura, which she'd initially put down to his seemingly terrible injuries.

"And his injuries, at first, were odd. Great splinters deep in the flesh of his arm and side, as if he'd impaled himself on a tree and it so happens that up in Fletcher's Woods, where I found him, a massive oak tree has the top half broken off.

"But that's only the beginning," Alice went on. "We have the death of Farmer Morgan in rather strange circumstances, and the weak condition of his prize sow, cows on the local farms appearing wasted."

"Don't forget Susie," Mrs. Burrows added. "We found her dead the same evening. Didn't make too much note of it at the time as she was an old dog, but seems she was the first animal in the village to die mysteriously."

"What's all this leading up to?" Pendragon asked.

"Alice and Mrs. Burrows think there may be a vampire in the village. This man who disappeared might be one." Peter scarcely believed he'd actually said that.

Pendragon laughed. "Really?"

"Why not?" Mrs. Burrows asked. "That one had no aura; I said so at the time."

"We thought maybe you could help us," Peter said.

"You think I'm a vampire?"

"No, you stupid old twerp!" Mrs. Burrows all but yelled. "It's time to tell them!"

"It is, is it, Pixie?"

Peter knew then and there he'd slipped a couple of cogs.

"Yes, it is! We need your help. Alice and I can't do it alone, and Peter with the best will in the world is only human. We need you. Do something in return for all the years you've lived among us."

The sergeant stood, leaning his strong hands on the scrubbed table top. "Been breaking a confidence, old Pixie!"

"No, I have not! It's for you to tell them!"

"Is it?" He looked at Alice and Peter. "Very well, then. I'm Dragon."

Alice let out a nervous laugh. "A Dragon!" She as good as spluttered.

It was not the right thing to do.

"Not a Dragon, little Pixie!" he repeated in a roar loud enough to rattle the plates on the dresser. "I am the Pendragon!"

He threw back his head and his face reddened as if holding his breath, the air around him moved and formed into runnels that covered his arms and chest. He let out another wordless roar and his cuff buttons burst, his arms wobbled and moved within his sleeves, his fingernails lengthened into claws, then vast talons, and his hands appeared reptilian and the skin turned gray and rough.

Peter fought back the shock but couldn't stop watching. What he was witnessing was impossible and happening right before his eyes.

As he watched, it seemed Pendragon exhaled and in moments the skin changed, hands and arms resumed normal shape, and the sergeant sat down in his chair with a thud.

"You're truly a Dragon," Alice said.

Peter kept his thoughts to himself. If he was going to share a roof with a Dragon, mum was the word.

"Well, I'm not the plastic wind-up sort," the sergeant said.

"So now you all know my secret and if one of you mentions it to a soul they'll laugh you out of the village."

"Why the dickens would we mention it?" Mrs. Burrows asked. "We need your help. You think I'd stand in front of the post office and announce, 'I'm Pixie!' They'd take me away."

"Do you change often? Completely?" Alice asked.

He shook his head. "I used to. Box Hill at night was a grand place to roam. I used to chuckle over the accounts of UFOs up there, but nowadays it's too risky to show that sort of light."

"You shifted last night!" Peter hadn't meant to say it but somehow it came out.

To silence.

Alice met his eyes and nodded.

"Last night, Sergeant. In the lane, it was you, wasn't it?"

Another long quiet.

He nodded. "It was. I'd gone out to get coke for the stove, just as I said, pulled on my boots without lacing them, and nipped out. Almost had the hod full when I sensed it: evil malevolence, horror, you name it, it was there. I was tempted to turn around and bolt the door against it, but remembered the old blood oath. I left the hod on the path, took off my clothes and shifted. I found it, and you two, at the corner of the lane and went for it.

"What it was I don't rightly know. It had claws and teeth and it took dragonfire to beat it. It went running then, just as you two did. I followed you home, shifted back behind the toolshed, and yanked on my clothes as fast as I could. Forgot my damn boots but got myself inside. Where you did your Florence Nightingale act."

"You were hurt."

"One of the thing's claws got me. But we heal fast."

So he'd noticed. "Let me get this straight. I'm sitting here with a Pixie and a Dragon?"

"Two Pixies," Alice said, reaching for his hand.

Talk about being surrounded, but her clasp was warm and, dammit, he loved her. Whatever she was. "Two Pixies and a Dragon."

"That's right," Mrs. Burrows said.

"Think you can cope, lad?" Pendragon asked.

"I have absolutely no idea."

"You can." Alice's confidence was reassuring. He thought.

"Alright then, I'll cope. After all, I'm not the one with an alternate personality."

"More's the pity," Mrs. Burrows said. "We could use a gremlin or a nice gryphon."

"Or a troll," Pendragon added.

"Lay off him!" Alice snapped. "This is a lot for me. Peter must be out of his depth!"

More like sinking fast. "I'm sure it will make sense in a while."

"Before then, lad, these women will have you swimming against the tides. Next thing you know we'll be hunting a vampire."

Peter had rather gathered that was the entire point but decided to keep quiet. He was way out of his depth here.

He should have stayed in Pentonville where all he had to deal with were crooks, felons, and fellow COs. Except then he'd never have found Alice.

Who was Pixie.

"I think we all need a fresh cup of tea." Mrs. Burrows stood and crossed the kitchen. "Alice, get the brandy. The sergeant needs a boost."

Peter was glad to see she added a tot to every cup. Pendragon wasn't the only one needing fortifying. "One other thing," Alice said as she put the stopper back in the decanter. "When I was in the hospital this morning I learned they arrested Miss Waite. Seems when they were putting a tarpaulin over her damaged roof they found a hidden wireless in the loft. Used apparently to send and receive messages from Germany. She's been arrested as a spy."

Chapter 27

"He is injured."

"Who?" Zuerst demanded.

"Eiche," Bela replied. Wasn't he the one they'd told her to connect to whenever she was awake? They didn't trust him. With good reason. Who in their right mind trusted a vampire? These servants of the Reich were so deluding themselves. Just as they'd deluded her. Once.

"How do you know this?" Zweiten asked, his voice cruelly quiet. His eyes hard and cold.

Did he think she was lying? She held back the smile. Fairies had difficulty lying. Concealing the truth, yes. Withholding truth, yes, but lying was alien to them. "Last night. He attacked." The venom and menace had stung her like a swarm of incensed bees. "And was attacked back."

"Who could attack a vampire?" Zweiten said to Zuerst. "Who would so dare?"

He turned his hard eyes on Bela. "You know?" It was almost an accusation.

"It was an attack with fire." She would not say that she sensed a very powerful Other. That would result in more interrogation and she wished to preserve the strength she had.

The attack to Eiche had drained her, but the others had fed and restored her. "He was burned."

"Some superstitious peasant," Zweiten said.

"How can that be? He was told not to reveal himself. Yet," Zuerst mattered.

"He has killed. Maybe he was discovered."

Zuerst nodded, paused, frowning to himself, then glared at Bela. "Can't you communicate with words? Send him a a message?"

He knew the answer to that. Was he dreaming? Wishing? "That I cannot do. I know when they rest, if they feed, or are injured. I feel a surge of their power if they attack or move fast but there are no words back and forth between us."

"Explain exactly," Zweiten said, "what they are all doing now."

"Eiche is resting to recover from his injury. He's still in pain."

"How do you know that?"

"I felt his pain." It made her writhe on the bed when it happened.

"And the others?"

"Schmidt has just fed. Weiss is moving, somewhere with earth under his feet, not streets, and Bloch is still, but alert. He's not resting."

"If you are lying, you will go to the camps and your family will be killed," Zweiten reminded her.

"I am not lying."

Without another word to her, they turned and left.

But with her now sharper hearing, their whispers outside the door were audible.

"What has happened? We must know. If he has gone rogue, the others must destroy him."

"Brunhilda has not reported in five days. Something must be wrong."

"Or she's being careful. Old schoolteachers don't take risks."

"Loyal servants of the Reich follow procedure and obey orders."

"You think that Fairy is lying?"

"I think not. She will do whatever we demand to protect her family. I heard they are like that."

Yes. Bela smiled. Fairies are like that, they protect their own, and take vengeance on those who dupe and abuse them. These creatures had lied and would pay for that. Not silly, childish tricks used on disrespectful villagers. Zuerst and Zweiten and that Dritten with the evil eyes merited far more than soured milk or spilled flour.

She would bide her time and build her strength. Already she could lean out of the iron-rimmed window. In a few nights she would try slipping out and clinging to the stone walls. And once she was ready, she would fly north, leaving havoc behind her, and find Gela.

Together they would seek the deep woods and wait their chances.

Even fairies dream.

Chapter 28

By the next morning the entire village was buzzing with the news. A resident arrested as a German spy! Brytewood harboring a member of the fifth column had tongues wagging from the ARP and WVS center in the village hall all the way up to the most distant farms.

Andrew Barron, the supervisor of the munitions plant, received a call from the war office insisting on increased security precautions. Whorleigh's store was full of gossiping villagers and the tea shop did unprecedented business as customers lingered over the shocking news. Even the teachers, enjoying their morning tea break, shook their heads at a member of their profession turning traitor.

There had been a cursory mention of the altercation in the Pig between that Mr. Williams from up at the camp (who'd been three parts drunk, everyone agreed) and Dr. Doyle's brave new assistant. But a fight that fizzled didn't hold a candle to the arrest of an enemy spy, and that little snippet was soon forgotten.

There had been brief mention of Miss Waite's nephew, or cousin, or whatever he was, a passing acknowledgment of the shame and horror he must be feeling, but he wasn't a villager after all, so he got little attention.

The sudden departure of the two London boys rescued from the vicarage barely got a passing mention.

Except by Tom Longhurst, who'd sighed as Mr. Arckle rode away on his borrowed bicycle. Good of the man to ride all the way up here to offer his explanations and apologies. Tom had been looking forward to having a pair of lads about the place, but that wasn't to be. He did vaguely wonder what had changed the man's mind; he'd seemed more than agreeable the previous evening, but Tom had three fields of meadow grass to cut before the good weather broke and no time to worry about the Arckles. They were Londoners after all, a different breed altogether.

Alice left the house early to go on her rounds. Peter, armed with directions and a little trepidation over entering Jeff Williams's bailiwick, headed to the camp. It was his first day to take over from Gloria, leaving her to spend the morning helping the WVS organize supplies.

An hour or so after Alice left, Helen Burrows rode her bicycle down into the village, picked up their week's ration of cheese and a bag of flour, lingered long enough to catch the wave of gossip, and reminded her special cronies there would be another knitting evening the Sunday after next, before setting off in the direction of Howell Pendragon's cottage.

She paused briefly at the corner, her sharp Pixie eyes noticing the battered and charred hawthorn hedge, then pedaled the last hundred yards or so and wheeled her bicycle up his garden path.

He was waiting at the door for her. "I thought you'd be down this morning."

"You thought right, old man."

"Come on in then, Pixie."

She let that pass—he could breath fire after all—and finding out his Other nature after twenty-odd years was satisfaction enough to ignore the teasing gibe in his voice. "We need to talk. Those young people have courage, but it's going to take much more than bravery to overcome this."

He shut the door, took her coat and hat, and held a chair for her. He had been expecting her, tea was already made, the pot covered under a knitted cozy, and he'd even put out a plate of shortbread.

"What do you have in mind, Helen?" he asked as he poured milk into the cups. "I'm not going around the village breathing fire. I need to live here afterward."

"Let's first make sure we have an 'afterward.'"

"You've a point there." He put down the milk jug and picked up the teapot. "It does seem more than a coincidence that just as we're bracing ourselves to repel invasion, this thing appears, and on top of it all, we find we've had a spy in our midst for years." He handed her a cup.

"No coincidence at all, is it?" She took a sip; hot and strong. The man knew how to make a good cup of tea. Perhaps he heated the water by breathing on the kettle. "I wonder what else we need to watch out for."

"One problem at a time, Helen. Let's take care of this one first."

"Who is it? Did you see his face?"

"In the blackout, with no moon? Once I breathe that fire, it dazzles me so I'm half blind. No. Besides, I'm not even sure it had a face; it was more like a dark, nasty presence."

"Then, assuming it is the suspected vampire, it shifts, changes."

"So it would seem."

"But it's here in Brytewood, living among us. We have to work out who it is."

"With all the newcomers we've had the past year? All those up at the plant, evacuees, those French refugees over in West-humble, the guests who come and go over at Wharton Lacey. Could be anyone."

"Was it male or female?" If he could tell.

"Male!"

That seemed certain enough. "How did you know?"

He shook his head. "I don't know. Just felt it was."

She, for one, wasn't about to question feelings.

"That's where we start then: consider every male who's come to the village recently. Particularly anyone injured. No one had called Alice about burns, but they might have gone to hospital."

"Helen, how often do you need medical help? I bet he's already healed himself. Like I did."

Drat! The man was right. "We need a list. I'll get it from Sam Whorleigh; he has everyone who's registered for rations."

"He'll give it to you? Just like that?"

She smiled. "Not just like that, but he'll give it to me. Why don't you come up to The Gallop and have a cup of coffee tomorrow morning and we'll see what we can find out."

"You're going to steal it! Somehow you're going to steal his records."

"All's fair in love and war, Howell Pendragon. And this is war!"

Peter wasn't sure if a nice sharp shower wasn't preferable to a bright sunny morning, at least when pedaling uphill. He was going to arrive with sweat pouring off his face. Smashing when he'd then have to face insults, antagonism, and rudeness.

Oh well, since he had no choice, might as well keep going, and the countryside, if not exactly Devon, was beautiful. It might be a good place to settle once the war was over. If Alice would have him.

Would she? It wasn't much of a trade-off for her. She had an established practice, position in the village, brothers coming home one day, God willing, and a future. She could probably have any man in the county.

What did he have to offer? A disrupted education. He could go back and qualify once the war was over. He still had money left to him by his grandmother, but he'd carry the stigma of being a CO, and a family who, if not actually wishing him ill, wouldn't miss him if he never went home again.

He was getting downright maudlin. No way to spend a sunny September day. He had a job, a good place to live, and the finest woman in all of God's creation fancied him. What man was ever better off?

With that thought in mind, he was ready to face Jeff Williams and, if need be, that creepy pal of his to boot.

Once at the top, the road curved through a hundred or so yards of woodland and then he was through the trees, and the camp lay ahead. From here it was unmistakable. Corrugated iron huts, iron framed and asbestos buildings, and row upon row of wooden huts. All covered with camouflage.

This wasn't just a small munitions camp, it was major processing plant.

He rode his bike up to the gate and, dismounting, showed his identity card to the uniformed guard.

"Thank you, sir," he said as he handed it back after consulting a clipboard. "The clinic is down on the right almost at the end, but the superintendent asked that you report to him first. His office is in the second hut on the left, right down the middle."

So he had to report, did he? Not unreasonable, but not his idea of fun. Best get it over with; after all, he was going to have to work with the man. Peter thanked the guard and wheeled his bicycle through the gate.

The second hut on the left was easy enough to find and SUPERINTENDENT stenciled on the door was clear enough. Damn! He was not going to quail before a weasly bully. He had the authority of His Majesty's Government behind him and so . . .

The door was ajar so Peter opened it cautiously. He was in a small office and a sandy-haired young clerk in civilian clothes sat behind a rickety deal desk.

"Can I help you, sir?"

"I'm here to report to the superintendent. I'm the new first aid assistant."

"Smashing, sir. Welcome, we need you. I'll let him know you're here." He opened the inner door. "The medic's here, sir,"

"Send him in, please, Millard." Sounded downright friendly. He must be a different man sober.

Good.

He was a different man.

"Grand to meet you. I'm Andrew Barron." A tall, broad-shouldered man with dark hair graying at the temples and wide bright eyes came around the desk holding out his hand.

Peter took it. "Peter Watson." A nice firm handshake. Went along with the honest open face and the genuine smile. A nice chap but . . . "You're the superintendent here? I was never given a name, but I met someone called . . ."

The man shook his head. "You've met my assistant, I gather, Jeff Williams?" Peter nodded. "Much as he'd like to, he doesn't run the place, not while I live and breathe." He paused. "Aren't you the chap who saved a bunch of children from the vicarage the other night?"

"I was on the team that got them out, yes, sir."

"Not quite what I heard. Not given to false modesty are you, Mr. Watson?"

"Not at all, sir. Two of us worked together. I could never have done it without Sergeant Pendragon's help."

"Ah!" Barron smiled. "Pendragon told me about it. He gave me the impression he stood by and watched."

Interesting about them knowing each other. "It was team-work, sir."

"I'm all in favor of teamwork. Look, I'll show you around. You don't have any staff, I'm afraid. But you've a mountain of supplies. Arrived yesterday. The result of six months of Nurse Prewitt's requests, I suspect. Looks as though they sent half a field hospital. See what you can use. If anything vital is missing, ask Millard for requisition forms and I'll sign them. No saying when we'll get it, but I'll do what I can."

Peter followed him out of the hut and they walked side by side down the middle of the camp. As Barron talked, Peter looked around and began to get an idea of the size of the place. "We work round the clock. Mostly women, some live up here—they consider themselves semi-prisoners and envy the ones who live down in Dorking or Leatherhead. I think they both have it hard. It's dangerous work, the pay is something no man would work for, and they risk injury every day of the week.

"Mostly our injuries are minor stuff: jammed fingers, twisted ankles because someone ran without looking where they were going, and the usual colds, flu, and headaches. I hope to God we never have a real disaster, and we constantly stress safety."

They'd reached a corrugated iron hut, one with CLINIC stenciled on the door.

"Here you are." Barron handed him a key. "Keep it locked whenever you're not there or stuff will grow legs and walk. You're not here officially until tomorrow. Gives you time to sort out the supplies and get your requisitions in."

Peter unlocked the padlock, which looked old enough to date from the Boer War, if not the Crimean. The inside wasn't a lot better.

Equipment, yes: boxes of it stacked against the walls. There was also a camp bed behind a screen, and a small desk and a couple of mismatched chairs and a battered filing cabinet.

"Not too hot, I know," Barron said, "but hopefully the boxes have supplies you can use. And I'm darn glad you're here."

When he left, with a final handshake and a nod, Peter sat on the better-looking chair and looked around. He had a day to get this straight? He'd need a week and a team of removal men.

Better get to it. He'd promised to take Alice out tonight.

Seven hours later he had a semblance of order. Seven long hours punctuated by numerous cups of strong tea and one weak cup of coffee and a lunch in the canteen that was reminiscent of boarding school cuisine. But he had a clinic ready to open for business tomorrow. He'd already treated several headaches, cuts, and one rather nasty gash on a shin that had needed stitches. He was getting ready to lock up and drop the requisition forms off on his way out of the gate when the door opened.

It was Jeff Williams.

"You're here then, Watson?"

It was better than previous greetings but hardly the essence of conviviality and friendliness. "Good afternoon, Mr. Williams. What can I do for you?"

"You got something for burns."

Peter took it as a question. "You need treatment for a burn?"

"Not me, someone else. You must have something. You've got boxes of stuff here."

Yes, he had. "What sort of burn?"

"On his arm, not bad, but thought with all you've got here, you could spare what I need."

"I meant, what caused the burn? Is it a worker? I really need to see them first. If it's a serious burn, we'd best get him to hospital."

"For pity's sake! It's a pal of mine, not one of the workers. Burned himself last night. All I want is some of that yellow stuff and a bit of bandage. Is that asking too much?"

No. He could spare a tube of Aquaflavine in the interest

of future coexistence. "I'll get you some, but I really urge you to have him see a doctor."

Peter failed to see what was so amusing about that. The smirk on Williams's face was even nastier than his scowls. But he handed over a tube of ointment and a roll of gauze, and closing the door behind Williams, double-checked the windows, secured the antique padlock, and headed on home.

The day had cooled, it was a wonderful ride downhill, free-wheeling most of the way. Seemed he had a good and reasonable superintendent in Andrew Barron. Alice was waiting and they were going out tonight. Life was good.

Chapter 29

Gloria tossed her hat and bag on the table, kicked off her sensible shoes, and plonked herself on the easy chair by the empty fireplace. She really wanted a cup of tea; she was dry as a bone and worn to a frazzle, and would stay that way until she settled her restlessness.

She knew exactly what was wrong with her and she knew what to do to restore the balance in mind and body, but she had never, ever shifted when she had the curse. Stomachaches and bloating were bad enough in human form, but she did not fancy shifting into a vixen in estrus. The last thing she was in the mood for was an encounter with a randy dog fox.

When she stopped roaring with laughter at that thought, her spirits had lifted. She was turning into a proper Moaning Minnie. She should darn well count her many blessings and cease this pointless maundering. She had a job in a reserved occupation and was as safe as anyone was these days. She had a roof over her head and a roof to herself now June had moved in with another teacher, in a pleasant village that accepted her. Might be different if anyone suspected she turned furry at intervals and spent nights racing over the Downs and through the woods, but who would ever know? She was ultra careful when shifting and changing back.

Until a few days ago she'd been as contented as any woman or werefox could ever hope to be.

What had changed?

She pondered that as she got up and poured herself a glass of milk from the remainder in the bottle. Might as well drink it. This warm weather, it would be sour by morning.

Why was she so unsettled?

It was if there were shifts and ripples in the atmosphere, sending things off kilter. Considering that twice this month German bombers had thought fit to drop their spare bombs on Brytewood on their way home, a little disruption in the atmosphere was hardly surprising.

But she had to run.

No doubt about it. And no point in worrying about her physical condition. The mood she was in, if she did encounter an interested dog fox, she'd take his ears off. She should call Alice and mention the outbreak of mumps up on Ranmore, but that could wait until morning.

Meanwhile, she had to do something productive until night fell. Ironing was surely boring enough to settle her restlessness. At least for a little while.

Peter made it down to the village in record time. He was a bit late but had time to give himself a wash and brush up and change clothes.

"Afternoon," Sergeant Pendragon said as Peter walked in. "How are things up at the place we can't talk about?"

"Interesting. They've enough medical supplies to service a battlefield. We could have used some of them the other night when we were measuring out bandages."

"That's always the way. Government has supplies when they want them, the rest of us . . ." He shrugged.

"Let's hope we never need that much. Ever," Peter said. "Everything fine in the village?"

"Seems so. We finally got rifles for the Home Guard, but they sent ammunition for officers' pistols. If anything happens, I swear, we'll end up using pitchforks." He shook his head. "I left Major Gregory to deal with it. You'll be out this evening then?"

"I'm taking Alice out to dinner. Thought we might go into Leatherhead and eat somewhere and then go to the cinema." Darn, was he blushing? "I'd be obliged if you'd keep it to yourself. No point in starting talk."

"Son, if they see you on the bus together, they'll have you wedded and bedded within the month. Gossip helps them keep their minds off the major worries."

Maybe, but did it have to be about Alice? "I just thought it might be awkward for her." And him, come to that. But he could cope.

"She's used to scrutiny. Half the village thinks she should marry. At one point I think they were taking bets on young Tom Longhurst. But nothing came of it. Then there was another doctor she'd known when she was in medical school, but he didn't last long." Was the sergeant trying to warn him or reassure? "The other half want their doctor to be theirs exclusively and without life distractions. Seems to me, though, our good doctor will make up her own mind when she's ready."

Smashing! Was she ready? Only one way to find out. "Know of anywhere good to eat?"

"Ask Alice, don't think I've eaten there in years. I know a couple of good pubs."

He was not taking Alice to a pub for a pork pie and a bag of crisps. "I'll ask her. Best go and get ready."

"Right you are, lad. Oh, by the way, I'm spending the evening in the Pig, will be there until closing. If you decide to skip the film and want somewhere to sit, feel free, Peter. That way you won't disturb Mrs. Burrows; she likes to turn in early."

"Yes, er, thanks!"

Crikey! Wasn't this exactly what he wanted, the chance of

private, undisturbed time with Alice? But he could hardly tell her the coast was clear and they could have more than coffee blissfully undisturbed in the Pendragon parlor. And what if they did? Someone would surely see her car, or notice her leaving late. Or would they? They were up a lane, well off the main village street, the only other cottage up here was unoccupied.

Maybe, just maybe, it might work.

God bless Sergeant Pendragon.

Peter went up to change his shirt and put on his suit and it hit him: he'd just been having a conversation with a Dragon and was about to take a Pixie out to dinner.

He certainly wasn't in Devon anymore. Or was Devon full of Dragons as well as Pixies and he'd been too self-absorbed to notice?

Better get ready for his particular Pixie.

Alice sat by the window watching. She hadn't done this since she was fifteen and one of Simon's friends had taken pity on her and invited her to the Tennis Club dance.

Today she'd rushed home, praying there'd be no emergencies, and spent the better part of two hours gussying herself up. She'd changed her dress three times, wanting to look smart, not wanting to look too dressed up, and definitely not wanting to look as if she'd spend half the afternoon wavering over what to wear.

Gran had been worse, if possible. She'd passed the afternoon baking custard tarts. "He really liked them that afternoon you first met him," she'd said. "I'll just make a small batch and leave them out, in case you ask him in for a cup of coffee."

"Gran, I'm not being that obvious."

What was Gran suggesting?

"Don't be silly, Alice. No one ever got what they wanted by being shy. That was always your trouble. Your brothers overshadowed everything so you never got in the habit of getting what you wanted."

Hardly fair. "I was the one who got the medical training, Gran."

"Only after they both made it clear they weren't interested. My love, now's the time to think of what you want and go out and get it. Life's too uncertain these days to put anything off." She paused. "You do want him, don't you, dear?"

"Yes." Why try to deny it? Gran always found out everything in the end. "But I barely know him."

"What's that got to do with it? Your instincts won't let you down, girl. You're Pixie. You know good from bad and right from wrong by instinct. And if you love him . . ."

Did she? He was on her mind constantly. Even to the point of distracting her from her patients. She'd been on edge all day, knowing she was seeing him tonight.

Gran came downstairs. Slowly, Alice noticed. More slowly than she used to. "All set, my love?"

"Yes, Gran." Alice stood, crossed the hall, and kissed her. "I'm set, only thing delaying me is the non-appearance of a certain young man."

"He'll be here, my love. Just you wait and see. You enjoy yourself and when you come in, be quiet, please. I'm going to bed early."

Gran had clearly made her point. So it was now up to her, Alice, to set the pace for the evening. Should she be sensible, or throw caution to the winds and follow Gran's not exactly subtle suggestion?

If she did, she might just scare him off for good. If she didn't, he might think she was indifferent to him. After their wild lovemaking the other day? No, indifferent would never describe what happened between them. Ever.

She looked in the mirror again, smoothed her hair, and decided she hadn't chewed off her lipstick. Yet. She checked her bag for keys, purse, and clean handkerchief, and heard footsteps coming up the front path.

Damn caution! She threw open the front door.

"Peter!" He was handsome, beautiful, smiling, and hers. At least for this evening.

"Hello," he said. "Ready?"

"Oh, yes." But ready for what?

Chapter 30

"Gabriel?" Jeff Williams called as he entered his cottage. He knew his new friend, if he could call him that, much preferred being addressed as "Mr. Oak," but damn it all. He was getting board and lodgings all found, so he'd get called by his Christian name.

And on top of that, Williams had brought back ointment and gauze to dress his burns. That smarmy little CO had been downright stingy and unwilling to part with as much as a sticking plaster, but Williams had grabbed a few extra tubes when his back was turned. Serve him right!

The burns had looked a lot better this morning than they had last night; they'd looked hideous then, but the last thing Williams wanted was his guest ending up with some sort of skin infection. By rights he should have gone to hospital, but the suggestion last night had been met with outright refusal and this morning, when Jeff left for work, his guest had been fast asleep.

Alright for some.

And come to that, what was he doing hanging around Brytewood? Since his damn aunt was arrested, you'd think he'd scarper off home. Mind you, he was generous at the Pig, always buying the first round and most of the later ones, too.

A few tubes of Aquaflavine and a roll of gauze wasn't a lot when all's said and done.

But where was he?

Tossing his coat and hat on the sofa, Williams went up the narrow stairway and pushed open the bedroom door.

The bedclothes lay in a heap in the floor. Oak never made the flipping bed. They'd had more than one argument over it, dammit, and Oak was the one sleeping in it but no matter what was said or agreed or demanded, Williams always ended up making it. Well, he wasn't this time.

Gabriel Oak stood looking out of the dormer window, intent on something outside and totally oblivious to Jeff, who'd raced up with the medicine.

"Hey, Gabriel!"

He turned. He was only wearing trousers. How he wasn't freezing to death up here without a shirt or sweater beat Williams, but that passing thought went in a flash as he stared at the man's arm and shoulder and then up at his face and neck. This morning they'd been red and blistered.

Now not a trace of injury remained. Unbelieving his eyes, Williams stepped closer. "Your burns?" he asked.

"What burns?" Oak asked, a note of cold amusement in his voice.

"The ones you came home with last night, you arse!" He had the sense to be scared as he looked up at his so-called friend. "Hell! I even brought back ointment for them."

Oak looked at the tubes and the roll of gauze. He slapped them out of Williams's hand. "Unnecessary."

"Hey! Look here . . ." Williams began.

He never got any further.

Eiche lifted him by the shoulders so they were eye to eye, and the mortal wilted under vampire will. As the man went limp between his hands, Eiche said, "I never had burns. You never saw them."

Williams blinked, struggled as his mind was compelled to

accept something contrary to his belief, then nodded, his face slack.

Really, he was so easy to compel, it was no fun. Now the stringy old Miss Waite, she'd resisted. It had almost been fun, but this specimen was good only for fodder. Eiche let out a sharp, dry laugh that had Williams wincing, bent his head, and bit into the mortal's neck.

He didn't take much. No point in depleting him completely. Not yet. But he needed more blood; healing had sapped his strength. Tonight he'd go hunting. Under cover of dark, he'd be discreet enough to even keep Weiss happy.

Eiche tossed the unconscious Williams over his shoulder, carried him downstairs, and dropped him in one of the shabby chairs by the cold stove. As the mortal stirred, Eiche compelled him once again. "If anyone asks, I was here with you all evening. I never left the house. Understood?"

Williams looked up; his eyes rolled in his head. "Understood?" Eiche repeated. "I'm in the house with you, and was all evening. I never left!"

Williams gave a weak nod. "You never left the house. Stayed in tonight."

He was barely conscious as Eiche slung a heavy satchel over his shoulder, opened the back door, and slipped out. It wouldn't be dark for an hour or so, but he could move fast enough to pass unseen and he had work to do. And dinner to find.

"So," Alice asked, "do we get the bus in the village and advertise instantly to the entire population that we're off somewhere together, or walk down to the corner of Bell Lane and get the bus there so the news will have to wait until all the other riders get home to pass it on?"

"It's really that bad, isn't it?"

"Yes." Her grin suggested it wasn't too much of a concern.

"Which is closer?" He was still getting the hang of village geography.

"Bell Lane, but it's uphill."

They headed for Bell Lane and waited a good twenty-five minutes. "Darn it," Alice said. "Maybe I should have driven, but I'd have a sticky time claiming a trip to the flicks was 'travel essential to the medical practice.'"

"I don't mind waiting with you." And dash it all, they were alone in a fading an autumn evening. Not a soul for miles and the only sign of life the crows heading home overhead.

Why waste the moment? He touched her neck. She smiled, angling her head to rub her face against his shoulder. It would be insufferably churlish to refuse her invitation. And stupid to boot.

He stroked her check, then took her face between his hands, wondering what magic had happened that this wonderful woman wanted him. "Alice," he whispered, and brushed her mouth with his. She was all sweetness and warmth and glorious woman and, for this wonderful moment in time, all his.

And had her hands on his neck pulling him closer as her lips parted and her tongue found his. Dear heaven!

She let out a little sexy sigh and deepened the kiss and he felt her desire in every fiber of his body. He was halfway tempted to let dinner and the flicks go hang and take the good sergeant up on his oblique offer of privacy. Her touch was sheer magic and her lips like potent wine.

She pulled away. "The bus is coming." Her eyes were gleaming with desire, and yes, she was right. He heard the engine change gears as it came up the hill. By the time it rounded the bend they were standing decorously side by side, and he was trying his damnedest to wipe the satisfied grin off his face.

"Evening, Doctor," the driver said as they got on. Any pretense that they were chance passengers neatly destroyed as Peter paid for two tickets. "Just visiting are you then?" he asked Peter.

"Bert, this is my new assistant," Alice explained.

"Well then, welcome to the big city of Brytewood. Where did you come from?"

Even greeted with such friendliness one hesitated to say, "Pentonville Prison." He didn't have to.

"This here is the lad who saved all those children in the vicarage," a voice called from the back of the bus. "You got a flippin' hero on your bus, Bert Sharp!"

Peter couldn't see the helpful informant, but seemed half the population of the village was on the bus, and most of them added endorsements.

"Good to meet you," Bert said with a nod as he handed back change for a half crown. "Time to get going and I'll have you in Leatherhead in record time."

"Would help if we left on time," a woman with a large basket on her lap said.

"Give the man a break, Mildred," a man across the aisle from her said. "There's a war on, you know."

Alice got a seat at the back after a tall man stood and offered her his; Peter settled for standing near the front. No one took too much notice of the Only Five Standing Passengers sign.

Amazing really, the chatter and banter that went back and forth. It was more like a crowded bus in Spain or Italy than England. Not for the first time, Peter realized how the war seemed to break down reserve between strangers. Heck, he ended up talking about badger hunting with his two neighbors and he didn't know the first thing about identifying an occupied sett.

Not that he was fooled—he was only too aware that every single passenger was formulating wild and wonderful opinions as to what Dr. Doyle and her new assistant were doing going into Leatherhead on a Friday night. He was tempted to announce to the entire bus that he was in love with Alice Doyle.

But that might be a bit much even in these not quite usual times.

Bert Sharp did his best, taking a few bends at a speed that

belonged on Brooklands Race Track, but they arrived safely and got off the bus to good wishes for the evening.

So much for discretion.

Still, Alice didn't seem too worried, so why was he?

"Any idea where you want to eat?" she asked as the bus moved on and most of the alighting passengers headed up High Street toward the Ace theater.

"Since this is the first time in my life I've been here, I was rather hoping you'd have an idea." At first glance the town looked half dead and the great gap, like a missing giant tooth between two buildings on the other side of the road, showed only too clearly that Jerry left his calling card here as well as Brytewood.

"Would you go for good food in a not frightfully fashion-able establishment?"

If she was with him, he'd happily eat at a soup kitchen. "You know somewhere?"

"Run by an old friend. Her husband got called up but she keeps it going. I like to stop by when I can."

She was right about the unfashionable bit. The Blue Parrot was a narrow restaurant at the bottom of the town but the food was good: great servings of steak and kidney pie and masses of potatoes and carrots. Nothing elegant, but delicious. Of course he was subjected to the scrutiny of Alice's friend, Beryl, her mother, and sister, but he seemed to pass muster.

"Let's skip pudding," Alice said as they were finishing.

"They're not good?" He'd rather liked the look of the apple crumble and custard a man at a nearby table was wolfing down.

"They're marvelous, but will still be just as good next time we come and it just occurred to me, we're late for the cinema anyway, and if we leave now, we can walk down to the bus station and get the bus that leaves on the hour.

"We could always have pudding at my house," she added.

"Would that be alright?" What about her grandmother?

Alice nodded, the light of promise in her eyes.

* * *

They got the bus, although it was closer to a quarter past the hour when it set off. Seemed they were beating most of the population of Brytewood home, which may well have been part of her idea.

It was close to pitch dark when the bus dropped them off, but they both had torches in their pockets and it was an easy walk downhill. They didn't talk much, just strolled hand in hand. Somewhere in the distance a vixen cried out, there was a smell of cut grass in the air, and the odd waft of manure.

Country smells.

A wondrously peaceful evening stroll with the woman he loved. He tightened his grasp on her hand, drew her close, and kissed her.

"Be home soon," she said.

"Yes!"

As they rounded the bend a dark shape swooped down on them. Damn! It was the thing! The . . .

Peter was shaking as sheer terror washed over him, setting his teeth on edge as his skin itched and tightened around his face.

He reached out to Alice, who'd stumbled, intending to put her behind him, but she'd regained her feet and stepped away. Toward the thing, the it, and was standing tall, facing it, and in the beam of his torch he caught her face pale in the shadows and her arms high, her finger pointing at it.

"Go away, you have no place here! Go! Take your turmoil with you!"

She was unbelievably brave, utterly courageous, and totally insane. "Go!" she repeated. "Go back to where you came from!"

Amazingly, against all logic, odds, or possibilities, the dark shape reared up and stumbled.

"Begone!" she called, sounding like a wild woman or an ancient goddess. The shape disappeared.

Peter caught her as she stumbled. "Alice, are you . . ."

"I'm alright, honest, but let's get home. Fast."

They ran as if the wild hunt pursued them.

Perhaps it did.

Chapter 31

They covered the couple of hundred yards to the house at record-breaking speed, running hand in hand, and Alice slamming the door behind them and bolting it before collapsing into his arms.

She was shaking. So, come to that, was he.

Talk about terrifying! What had been frightening walking home with Joe Arckle was a soul-freezing horror with Alice. What if that hideous presence had harmed her?

Not, he reflected, a real worry. "What did you do back there?" Was this Pixie magic? Was everything his grandmother and his old nanny said true after all?

Alice looked up at him, not moving one inch from his tight embrace. "Honestly, Peter, I don't know. I felt the malevolence and the sheer ill will in that . . . thing, and knew I wasn't going to let it hang around here. My home. Brytewood."

A couple of days ago he'd have thought that statement fanciful. Not anymore. "But what did you do?"

"I could feel it in my mind and told it to take a running jump. It did."

She was so wobbly he took her over to one of the easy chairs by the fireplace and led her gently into the chair. "You're upset." What a pointless statement. Surely he could do better than that.

She shook her head and smiled. A weak smile that seemed to take a lot of effort, but it was a smile. And directed at him. "I feel as though I were run over by a steamroller."

"What happened, child?"

Alice jumped and Peter turned around in surprise. Mrs. Burrows stood in the doorway, a shawl around her shoulders and oddly incongruous bright purple slippers on her feet. "Alice?" She came into the room. "Were you hurt?"

Alice appeared to consider the question several seconds. "I don't think so. Peter was with me and we got home alright."

Peter had done nothing helpful that he could see, but wasn't about to argue the point. "It was the same as two nights ago," he said. "I swear it was the same."

"It's getting arrogant and troublesome," Mrs. Burrows said.

He'd have used a stronger word, but that wasn't really the point. "Alice did something to it and it fled."

Her old face lit up, her eyes glinting with delight and a wide smile creasing the corners of her eyes. "Wonderful! At last, my love. At last." Peter felt he was missing something vital.

Mrs. Burrows crossed to where Alice sat and took the hand Peter wasn't holding. "At last, you understand, don't you, Alice?"

"I'm not sure." Neither was Peter. "I didn't think about it. I just wanted the thing to go away. Gran, I was terrified. If it hadn't been for Peter I don't know what I'd have done."

"I think I ought to say I didn't do anything. It was Alice. She was incredible."

"She was being herself."

That too, but . . . "What happened?" This was all getting a bit too much for a half-trained vet to handle.

Mrs. Burrows gave an odd, lopsided smile. "She was herself. Used her Pixie powers. We can call on quite a bit of strength when driven. It just needed you to convince her to do it."

"I didn't say anything."

She chuckled. "You didn't need to say anything. You were

there, that was enough. Honestly, young people nowadays." She shook her head as she walked over to the stove and lit the gas under the kettle. "You need a warm drink. Both of you."

"Maybe I should be going," Peter said. He could hardly suggest Alice hoof it down there with him after all this. There would be other nights.

"No!" Alice tightened her hold on his hand. "Don't go. That thing may be lying in wait for you."

Possibly, but he'd have to get going at some point and maybe now whatever it was (he still could not think of it as a vampire, for heaven's sakes) was still reeling from Alice's on-slaught. "Doubt it, love, I think you thoroughly unmanned it." If that was the right word to use.

"Don't leave, Peter, please. I don't want to be alone."

She could hardly call it that with her grandmother in the house now busily pottering around putting cups on saucers and searching through a row of tins on the top shelf of the dresser.

"Alright, for a while."

"I think you'd best stay, Peter," Mrs. Burrows said looking up from filling a muslin bag with dried herbs and petals. "Alice needs you far more than you realize. You can have Simon's room. The bed's made up. Alice will show you where to go."

That sort of settled things. Not precisely what he'd planned for the end of the evening, but a man could adapt. "Well, thank you, if it's not an imposition."

"Imposition!" She shook her head. "For the first time in her life, Alice chose to use her powers. I think we all owe you, Peter Watson, not the other way around."

"I still don't understand what I did."

"You were there, Peter, that's all was needed." She put the muslin bag in the pot and poured on water. It was, he noticed, a small, white, china teapot, not the Brown Betty they usually used. "Alice has never used her powers," Mrs. Burrows went on. "She's ignored them, even tried to suggest it was all bunk and a bunch of superstition. I tried. I truly tried, but she's always been as stubborn as a boy. This evening, she finally tapped into her Pixie strength." She put the pot on the table and covered it with a cozy. "Know what wrought this big change? You, Peter. She drew on the power of all the Pixies to protect you. Now, give that tea ten minutes to brew, it's a herb blend. It'll help calm you both down, and I'm off to bed. At my age I need my sleep. See you both in the morning."

Before Peter had time to grasp what she was saying, she was gone, leaving them staring at each other in the empty kitchen.

"You will stay, won't you?"

Hell, yes! "Seems your grandmother has made sure of it."

"Oh! Gran!" Alice gave a weak smile. "She's matchmaking, you know."

Fine by him. "Does that bother you?"

"Since she's never done it before in my life, I'm not sure. I think it's rather funny."

And how was he to take that? "Want some of this tea?"

"Do you? It's one of the weird brews Gran gets from Mother Longhurst. Might as well give it a try."

He poured two cups and added honey from the jar sitting by the pot. "Here." He carried Alice's over to her and drew up the other easy chair.

They both sipped. "Weird" was a good way to describe it. Not exactly unpleasant, but he'd rather have a nice pot of Typhoo any day. Still, it was warm and wet, and oddly soothing. "Alice, what did your grandmother mean: all that about using your powers because I was there? What have I got to do with it?"

She took another drink, creasing her forehead, as if trying to pull out the right words to explain. "You really want to know?"

"Alice, seems I'm up to my neck with vampires, Dragons, and Pixies. I'm out of my depth here."

"I was brought up on tales of Pixies and what we could do but weren't allowed to. As a little girl it struck me as point-less: why have these so-called powers if you couldn't use them? As I got older they all ended up in the compartment as fairies, Father Christmas, and Guy Fawkes, but I knew Guy Fawkes had been real once. My teenage rebellion was rejecting the lot as superstition and old wives' tales.

"I was a scientist. From the time I was ten, I wanted to be a doctor like Dad. Pixies are unscientific. I knew it upset Gran, but I wiped all the old tales out of my mind. Gran gets on at me from time to time about using what I have and I let her go on.

"Tonight I was scared witless that thing would hurt you. I wouldn't let it. Gran called it using my powers. Maybe she's right."

She took another sip of tea, paused, and smiled at him. "I didn't think about it, I just wasn't going to let that thing hurt you."

Yes, well . . . "I thought I was the one supposed to do the protecting."

"You're not Pixie." Alice gasped. She'd said it aloud and just for the heck of it repeated the words she never thought she'd ever utter. "I'm Pixie, Peter. I'm still really vague about what that means, but I'm not your average girl next door."

"You never were, Alice, and besides, I never did fancy the girl next door."

He had no idea what was involved and neither, come to that, did she. "I mean, I'm really different. I think that's why I denied it for so long. I wanted to be like everyone else."

"I'm glad you're not." He scooted his chair forward so their knees touched. "I love you, Alice. You're the best thing that ever happened to me. I still can't believe my luck."

"Ending up deep in the middle of vampires, Dragons, and Pixies?"

"Hell, yes, bring on the elves and fairies too, if you like."

That was a thought. "You believe in elves and fairies?"

"I bet right this moment they're sitting by a fire somewhere asking, 'I wonder if Pixies really exist?'"

How preposterous. And how perfectly possible. "You don't think this is all getting a little outlandish?"

"Alice, love, it went beyond outlandish when Sergeant Pendragon sprouted talons in this very kitchen."

Just two days ago. "We have to stop this thing. It can't mean us any good."

"How? If you read *Dracula,* it was consecrated hosts, holy water, and stakes. I don't think Reverend Roundhill would go for the hosts or the holy water and they always struck me as verging on the sacrilegious."

But stakes! That was it! "It's wood, Peter. Stakes. Remember the first vampire and the tree he impaled himself on. Wood harms them. That has to be it."

"So we sharpen a few stakes, but we still have to find him."

"Maybe he'll find us again. He's gone after you twice." Dear God! That thought froze her soul. "Peter." She wrapped her arms around him. "I don't want anything to happen to you."

"Neither do I, love, but what about you? You take care."

She had to smile at that. "I'm Pixie, Peter." There, she'd said it again. Gran must be smiling in her sleep. "That thing's afraid of me."

She leaned right into him, needing to feel his body close. He kissed the top of her head and she felt it down to her toes, and a couple of interesting places in between. She eased herself from his arms and stood. "Let's go to bed."

"Yes, right. Your brother's room, Mrs. Burrows said, if you'll show me the way."

She'd show him alright. Power and confidence flowed through her like warm hope. She was Pixie. The man she loved and lusted after accepted that. He was staying the night and, judging by their recent very close contact, in the same frame of mind as she was.

"Come on, Peter."

She turned the kitchen light out and led him upstairs.

Chapter 32

They took the stairs two at a time. It was far too slow. At the top of the stairs, Alice opened her bedroom door and pulled him in.

"Are you sure?" he asked, taking in the lace bedspread and the chintz cushions on the wicker chair. "This isn't your brother's room."

"No," she replied and shut the door. "It's not."

"Good," he whispered in her ear.

Her heart raced with need and longing. "Will you stay?"

"Only if you're sure."

She stood on tiptoe, laced her hands behind his neck, and kissed him. Hard and long, opening his mouth with hers and teasing him with her tongue. "Does that feel like 'sure'?" she asked as she paused for breath.

His reply was to pull her close and set his mouth on hers—his hard, hot, and wonderful mouth. She gladly opened and met his tongue. They were wondrously matched, paired with desire and sheer and utter need. His hand was inside her blouse, stroking her breasts, sending sensations streaming through her. Her little sigh was lost in the depth of his kiss. His thigh came between hers and she opened her legs, wanting more than a strong thigh between them.

She yanked his shirt from his trousers so she could touch his skin, feel the warm, hard plane of his chest, and the soft downy pelt of hair, and tease his nipples with her fingertips.

He let out a mutter and responded by unsnapping her bra so her breasts hung free to his touch. His magic touch. His wondrous touch. She couldn't hold back the moan. Had no need to. She wanted him. Wanted his hands everywhere: on her breasts, stroking her neck, teasing her nipples. But it wasn't enough and never would be.

She wanted him between her legs.

She wanted him inside.

"Alice," he whispered. "I need you."

"Good."

She pulled up his shirt, ripping it open and resting her face against his chest. She listened to his racing heartbeat as her fingers played his nipple. It hardened satisfyingly at her touch, but she licked it anyway.

"Are you sure about this?" he asked.

Was he changing his mind? Not if his body was anything to go by. "I'm sure." She reached down and cupped her hand over his fly and the erection beneath. "I think you are, too."

"Alice, I want you so much it hurts!"

"Good," she said again. To the wanting bit at least. "You're hurting? Let me kiss it better."

His eyes grew big. "Alice . . ." he began.

"I mean it." She took his hand and led him the few feet to her bed. "You have too many clothes on," she said, unbuckling his belt.

"So do you!"

She hadn't intended to be the one on the bed, but she was on her back as he pushed her blouse and cardigan off her shoulders and tossed them aside. Her bra went with them and he stood back, smiling.

She needed more than appreciative looks, no matter how flattering his admiration might be. Besides, he had more clothes on than she did. She sat up and had his shirt off faster than she realized. She didn't remember undoing it, but it was gone. Along with his belt.

His erection was still very evident and hadn't he mentioned hurting? "Sit down," she said as she slipped onto the floor and settled between his legs.

"Alice . . ." he began.

"Shh." She unfastened his waistband and the buttons in his fly. The sheer wantonness of her actions thrilled her. He was her man, her lover. They'd faced and overcome horror and now was their moment. Time stopped as they loved. This room was a haven from the worries of war and survival. Nothing mattered but the two of them.

"Stand up," she said as the last button came undone.

His trousers fell into her hands and she eased down his Y fronts. She gazed in almost breathless awe at his wondrous erection. Such power. Such strength. Such manliness. And all for her. Because of her. She was his desire.

Her fingers stroked one side of his erection.

"Alice, love," he said in a rough whisper that became a groan as she closed her hand around him. A most satisfying groan, it sounded to her. Definitely promising. "Are you sure?" he asked.

Talking was a sheer waste of breath. She'd save hers. She settled back between his knees, rested a hand on each of his thighs, and kissed the tip of his erection. Since that seemed to make him very happy, she opened her lips and took the head of his cock into her mouth, licking the smooth skin as her lips closed around him.

In reply, he grasped her head, tunneling his fingers in her hair and groaning.

It sounded like sheer pleasure.

She took more of him in.

She'd read about doing this, talked about it endlessly in her student days, imagined it, but nothing in her wildest fancies approached the rush and thrill of kneeling, enclosed by the safety and strength of her lover's thighs, and feeling his male power between her lips. He was totally vulnerable, offering his most prized and delicate parts to her.

A great wash of loving and passion swamped her mind; she was incapable of any thought other than Peter, his cock, his love, and her need. She moved her lips up and down his shaft and her body responded with its own need. A pulse throbbed between her legs. Now she understood about "hurting." She needed him deep inside but never wanted to loose his cock from between her lips.

She'd be happy to stay like this till dawn, till morning, forever.

"Alice." He gently pulled her mouth off him. "You are marvelous, but now it's my turn. You're not even fully naked."

She knelt back on her heels, lifting her chin and chest so her breasts stood out. "Better do something about that."

He did.

Standing her up and undoing her skirt, he let it drop to the floor. He disposed of that and her slip before tossing her on the bed and opening her thighs, as he ran his hand up to the tops of her stockings and stroked the sensitive flesh on the inside of her thighs. "These have got to go, I'm afraid. Very sexy and all that but if I'm naked, you most certainly have to be." As he spoke, he unhooked one suspender and slowly, as if to tease, rolled down her left stocking, pausing to kiss the inside of her ankle just before he eased the silk off her foot and tossed it over his shoulder.

"Now for the other one." If anything, he took even longer over the second one. He spent five minutes playing with the suspenders and several rolling the stocking down inch by careful inch.

"Are you doing this deliberately slowly?"

"You noticed?"

"Yes."

"Think of is as anticipation, my love."

"More like torture if you ask me!" But delicious, wonderful torture that had her literally purring as he kissed up the inside of her legs and back again.

Felt wonderful, apart from the sweet and burning ache between her legs. "Arch your hips," he whispered, his breath warm against her skin. "Best get these sexy knickers off."

They were gone. She was as naked as he. The wildness of the night took possession of them. They kissed, caressed, and fondled each other's bodies, exploring, touching, and tasting, caught up in a mutual frenzy of passion. It was wonderful and incredible.

"You have condoms?" she asked. If he hadn't she'd kill him.

"In my pocket; I'll get them."

Nice of him. Especially since it gave her a magnificent view of his nice thighs and tight bum as he bent to retrieve his trousers from the tangle of clothes on the floor.

Also gave her the chance to pull back her bedclothes and smooth down the sheets.

For him.

He paused to sheath himself while she readied the bed.

Now she watched him. Watching her.

"You're beautiful," she said. "Lovely. I used to dream about someone like you. Dreams do come true, you know."

"I know."

Why were they ogling each other when they could be loving? Should be loving. Needed to be loving.

A wild surge filled her, flooding her brain with lust and power. She stepped toward him. He put his arms around her and toppled her onto the bed, settling between her legs as his mouth found her nipple. Only now, she was the one drawing from him as her passion soared and her need burned while he drew on her other breast, then kissed a line up between her breasts to her neck and chin and finally, after minutes of agonizing joy, he found her mouth and pressed hard.

She opened to take his mouth with hers, slaking her need and longing as their tongues caressed, but it still wasn't enough.

Driven by wanting, she rolled him over, pinning him to the bed as she straddled his thighs.

This was shockingly lewd and rather lovely and his grin suggested he agreed wholeheartedly.

Seemed a fire burned between her legs.

A wondrous fire. A great blaze of need. And all she needed was Peter.

"I love you," she said, taking his erection in her hand and holding him steady as she lowered herself.

He let out a long, slow groan and closed his eyes. Seemed his entire being, her entire being, were focused on the joining between their legs.

Need, happiness, and sheer joy flooded every fiber of her being. This was what she'd been born for. Made for. Nothing in creation would ever match their union.

She threw back her head, let out a whoop of joy, and started moving. Gently at first, just a little rock of her hips and a shift of her legs, but as need and heat grew inside her, she moved faster. She pumped her body hard and Peter moved with her, holding her hips with his hands, keeping her with him as he rocked and drove up into her and she pressed down.

Seemed they moved together forever. Sweat streamed down her face and his hands grew damp against her skin. Pleasure peaked. She was climbing, reaching, soaring. Her mind snapped as if out of focus, and with a cry, she climaxed. Pleasure bursting in great cascades of sensation rolled over her mind and soaked her being with joy. Still he went on, driving hard until he gave a grunt and a gasp and came.

She was panting, her chest heaving, her breasts rising and falling, as her body's wild ride eased and she felt him soften inside her.

"So," she said as she let him slip out and snuggled beside him. "How does it feel to love a Pixie?"

"Magic," he replied, pulling the covers over them. "Sheer magic."

She so agreed. "You are, Peter."

It was magic between them.

Outside, beyond the blackout curtains, the moon rose. Neither of them noticed.

Chapter 33

The moon was high and large in the sky. Time to be heading home but Gloria hesitated. Some instinct told her to linger in the woods and she'd long learned to trust her instincts. It was a glorious evening, unseasonably warm for September. Changing and running had settled the unease in her mind. And the only dog fox she'd encountered had backed away at her approach. So much for senseless worries.

Even the wild foxes fled at her Otherness.

Enough of that! She was alive, had a job, acceptance in the village community, and miles of open countryside to run in.

And now, she rested in the moonlight on the fringe of the woods, her head relaxed on her paws as she watched the activity of the nightshift in the camp.

They should be reported. Clusters of workers smoking on their break, each woman a small red glow in the night. And the slackness with opening doors as they came in and out. Didn't they have blackout curtains? The village ARP wardens should have a look at this. And Brytewood got the bomb, not them. Mind you, better the vicarage, even if poor Mrs. Roundhill was still in hospital, than up here where the carnage would have been horrific.

Gloria shuddered down to her bushy tail at that prospect.

But honestly, somehow she'd have to drop a word in Andrew Barron's ear that he needed to tighten things up. Not sure how to do it, though. "When I was wandering in the woods last night in my fox skin . . ." might not be a good opener.

A movement to her right snapped her senses to full alert. Someone, something, was moving under cover of the trees. Something that moved at great speed and had every woodland creature silent and watching.

And anxious.

Human and fox senses mingled. Gloria caught the menace and evil emanating from the creature, but she couldn't see it and her four-footed instincts demanded she stay concealed.

The human needed to know what it was and why it lurked in the woods. Watching.

A hunter?

It didn't carry a gun. The scent of oil and wood was distinctive enough, even at this distance. She crawled, keeping her belly to the ground. Ignoring every instinct that told her to stay put and hidden, she eased her way toward the intruder. If he turned on her, she could run faster on four feet than any mortal on two.

It was a man, his silhouette a dark outline in the moonlight.

He circled the camp, keeping to the shadow of the trees, until he was facing the back of the camp. Then he stepped out of the shelter of the woods and approached the perimeter fence, moving faster than she expected. He almost skimmed the ground.

This was no human.

What was it?

Not a shifter. Not that she'd encountered many others, but this creature never turned furry, of that she was certain. She was equally convinced he was up to no good. Who in his right mind skulked around in the shadows?

He was crouching low and pausing every so often to place something on the ground. Gloria eased as close as she dared.

Better be very careful—it would be just her luck to be seen by one of the guards at the front gate. As she watched he crept forward and a glint of moonlight caught what looked like metal in his hand.

He stood upright, and moving even faster than she could, raced around the fence toward the guards. They saw him, and a challenge rang out in the night.

She stared. Amazed. The dark shape, creature, whatever, covered the two guards and they fell to the ground.

Trouble.

Damn. What could she do? Shift and run naked toward the camp screaming? Would get attention, but not the sort she wanted.

Best stay furry. She threw back her head and let out a loud, piercing, vulpine distress call.

Someone had to hear.

The thing had. It reshaped and wavered in the air.

She backed into the woods, yowling for all she was worth. Then, wonder of wonders, a nearby vixen took up the cry and was fast echoed by several dog foxes. Seemed every fox for miles around took up the distress. And now there was activity at the camp: figures running in the dark and a cry as the two fallen guards were discovered. The intruder disappeared. Searchlights she never knew the camp possessed came on and beams lit up the woods and the open ground. She raced into the safety of the deep woods.

She'd alerted them, done her best.

Time to head home.

Alice heard the phone even in the deep sleep of sexual contentment. Peter still slept, lucky him. A phone call this hour of the night meant the doctor was needed. She shoved her feet into her slippers, took her dressing gown off the hook, and ran downstairs. No point in waking anyone else.

"Dr. Doyle?"

"Speaking. What's the matter?"

"It's Reg Dickens, I'm acting officer tonight up at the camp. There's been an accident."

"Did you call an ambulance?"

"Not yet. We've two guards just collapsed. Don't seem bad or anything. They're breathing but passed out and aren't coming round. It's been fifteen, twenty minutes and they're still out cold. Would you come up and see them?"

"Of course. I'm on my way."

"I'll alert the new guards to let you in."

"You might want to call Mr. Barron."

"I already have."

"Good. I'm on my way."

Peter met her at the top of the stairs, wrapped in her lace bedspread. It wasn't his style, aside from the fact he looked much nicer naked.

"An emergency?"

"Seems so." She told him the little she knew. "I'd better pull on some clothes and get going."

"Want me to come with you?"

Now there was a thought but . . . "No, love. By the time the milk's delivered, it would be all over the village that you were sleeping up at The Gallop."

"I hate the thought of you going out with that thing hanging around."

She wasn't too thrilled at the prospect but she had a job to do. "Peter, I don't doubt it's long back wherever it lurks by now. Besides, I'm the doctor. Two people need my care."

He nodded, unhappy but accepting.

"Doubt this has anything to do with the war. Sounds as if they got bored and started drinking. Seems they passed out. I'd be willing to bet they were swigging something suspect. Probably some of Whorleigh's under-the-counter whisky."

"What can I do?"

Dear Peter. She wouldn't want to be left sitting home alone either. "If I'm not back by the time Gran gets up, tell her what happened. I usually wake her when I have a night call, but might as well let her get her rest."

"I will. But I need to leave early myself."

"Better wait until later. That way, if anyone sees you cycling down, they'll think you came up for an early meeting." This sneaking around was ridiculous, but necessary. Village gossip could shred both their reputations. "I've got to get dressed."

She reached for her scattered underwear. Couldn't find her bra anywhere so she grabbed a new one from her drawer. Pulled on a tweed skirt and sweater and long socks. "Go back to sleep if you can," she said as she shoved her feet into her shoes.

"Oh, Peter!" She hugged him, reveling in his warmth and strength. "I love you."

"Marry me and then we can stop all this slinking around."

"Peter, I barely know you."

"You know me, love. Anyone else you want to marry?"

"You know there isn't!"

"Let's go ring shopping the next day I have off."

"We'll talk about this later. When I get back."

"I'll be here."

"I've no idea how long I'll be. Aren't you supposed to be giving first aid instruction to the WVS this morning?

"I'll be here."

He most likely would. Alice left. Did she care about the gossip? Yes, she'd seen what spiteful tongues could do. Maybe Peter was right—if they were engaged, all announced and formal, they would have more leeway in public eyes. On the other hand, darn the lot of them. If they didn't like it, they could lump it. If it bothered them all that much, they could get the bus into Leatherhead and see the doctors there.

With that most un-Hippocratic thought, she cranked the car and jumped in.

Driving through the village she passed Andrew Barron's

billet. He'd already left, but she passed him a mile or so down the road. "Put your cycle in the back," she said as she pulled alongside him. "I can get you up there faster."

"Thanks," he said as he climbed into the passenger seat. "Did you get an idea what happened?"

"Two men, the gate guards, are unconscious but breathing and otherwise alright."

"If they're drunk, I'm going to string them up! After I fire them."

"If that were the case would they have called me in?"

"I don't know. We'll find out."

Chapter 34

"Thanks for coming, Doctor." Reg Dickens, the shift supervisor, greeted her with a worried smile. "Evening, sir," he added to Andrew Barron. "Sorry to have to call you both out."

"It's my job," Alice replied. "How are they?"

"One's just coming round, the other's still out for the count. We put them down in the clinic, seeing as how it's all set up now."

Alice wanted so much to look around her, to photograph in her mind an image of where Peter worked, but she had patients, mysteriously afflicted patients at that, to attend to.

One Jim Bryant, according to Andrew Barron, was slowly coming to, and looking none too well. In the glare of the unshaded lights, his face had a grayish pallor.

"Let's have a look at you then, Mr. Bryant," she said, drawing a chair up to the narrow camp bed. His pulse was still weak and his pupils dilated, but there was no trace of alcohol on his breath. "Can you remember what happened?"

He nodded and struggled to sit up. He managed it with help, but was definitely wobbly. "Rog and me were on watch duty, like most nights. Not much going on up here, so we got to chatting a bit. Then, it happened all fast like. Something came up to us, and . . ." He broke off, leaned over the side of the bed, and upchucked.

When he stopped retching, he shook his head and wiped his mouth with the towel she handed him. "Sorry, Doctor, don't know what came over me."

"Shock," she replied. "You need a warm drink."

She sent one of the onlookers out for tea, and another to find a bucket of sand. "You'd better rest. Take it easy today. If you feel worse, come by the surgery. You know what day of the week it is?'

"Thursday, Doctor, or is it Friday by now?"

"It's Friday. What's your full name?"

"James Willoughby Arthur Bryant, named after me dad I was."

"Your birthday?'

He gave a wan smile. "That'll be telling, wouldn't it, Doctor? It were May, May 10th."

"Well, you seem none the worse for what happened. Still don't remember much?"

He shuddered. "It were like getting sucked into the pit of hell."

Clear enough but hardly helpful. If it weren't for everything else going on in the past couple of weeks, she'd brush it off, but he'd been terrified enough to pass out, and he didn't look the sort to make a habit of fainting.

"Drink your tea. If you feel like eating, have them get you some toast. Better not have too much. Do you live up here?"

"No, it's mostly the girls live here. I get the bus up from Dorking."

"I suggest you get the first one back and rest up all day."

"I'm off tomorrow, thank God."

Rog, or Roger Halifax, to give him the name on his identity card, was in much the same state. Weak, in shock, but otherwise, at least to appearances, unharmed.

* * *

"There is something else, Doctor," Andrew Barron said as she stepped outside. "It's odd, but it happened."

Odd was becoming the watchword for her life these days. "What is it?"

"You'd best hear it from the three girls who found them and raised the alarm. They're waiting in my office."

"Girls" was the word. Maybe eighteen, nineteen. Wearing overalls and their hair tied up in muslin, they'd obviously just come off the assembly line. When she was their age, she'd been just starting at Barts, studying like mad and having a ball in her free time. Seemed so trivial and frivolous compared with filling shell cases or putting fuses in bombs or whatever exactly they did up here.

"Mr. Barron said you three found the guards."

"Yes, we did."

"Yeah."

"Gave me a right turn it did."

Obviously general agreement on that point. "How about one at a time?"

"Yes, Doctor. I will." A tall, dark-haired girl seemed to appoint herself spokeswoman. The others nodded, encouraging Dawn to go ahead.

"We was on break like. So the three of us went out to have a fag and a bit of a natter."

"You were smoking outside. At night?" Andrew Barron asked.

They looked at each other and Dawn shrugged. "We have ten minutes. Takes us five to get back to our hut. We get away from the factory, there's a spot by the canteen we go to. We'd never get a break, sir, if we went back to our hut."

Dawn had a point, but it was up to Andrew Barron to sort out blackout violations. "That's not what I'm here about. What I want to know is how you found the guards, and what made you go that way?" The guards were a bit old for chatting up, but who knew?

"It were the noise, something awful. It was like a soul in the torments of hell." Dawn had a bent for drama, it seemed.

"It were a fox," one of the others interrupted. "I used to stay with my auntie in Sussex when I was little. I've heard foxes; it were a fox. A vixen most like."

More likely than a soul in torment, and definitely a sound to get attention from a city dweller. "Get many of them round here?" Quite likely now that half the hunt was called up or doing war work somewhere.

"Just the odd one. But this was different."

"How?" Alice hoped for something more specific than Dawn's hyperbole.

The occasional Sussex dweller replied, "First, it was just the one. It were louder than usual, sort of like a warning. Then the others started up. There were umpteen of them all screeching and people started coming out of the huts and then we ran towards the gate to ask Rog what was going on and . . ."

"We found them both lying there like the dead," the last one added, obviously wanting to get a word in.

"See anything at the gate?" Andrew Barron asked. "Anyone near them?"

Three heads shook in denial.

"Not a thing, sir, Doctor," Dawn said. "We saw they were down and Mary ran off to call Mr. Dickens."

"We thought they was dead," Mary said.

"They are alright, aren't they?" Dawn asked.

"They'll be fine. Just shaken up." As far as Alice knew, it was the truth.

The trio left, obviously eager to skip out before they were reprimanded for blackout violations.

"Not much help there," Andrew Barron said shaking his head. "Looks as though you were called out at night for nothing much."

She didn't think so. "They were unconscious and slow coming around. Anyone in their right mind would call a doctor. Seems they'll be well, but I'll be sure to mention to Peter Watson to keep and eye on them.

"He will. Seems a good chap."

"I think so, too." She managed not to smile too broadly.

"Something definitely happened," Andrew went on.

She wouldn't argue there. "I'll be off then. Want a lift back down?"

"No. I'll stay up here. Might as well. The minute it gets light, I'm sending crews out to see if they can find anything. This doesn't make sense."

Maybe not to him, or anyone else up here, but she bet Gran and Sergeant Pendragon would have an explanation or three.

And as for her, she was half asleep on her feet but the thought of crawling into bed and snuggling up to Peter kept her awake all the way home.

It was war, a personal declaration against all his mission. But dammit, how could these pathetic Inselaffen thwart him: a vampire with the power of the Third Reich behind him? It was insufferable, intolerable, and they would pay for their insolence. He would have them groveling for mercy at his feet. Once he found out who they damn well were.

And why the blasted wildlife had been alerted to his presence. He'd wandered the woods and open country often enough in the past week or so and nothing like that had ever happened before. Animals should cringe away at his approach. Maybe they had, but lurked nearby and set up that caterwauling as a warning to each other. They warned the stupid mortals, too.

That was another thing—no one in his briefings mentioned those searchlights.

The whole night had gone wrong.

To cap it off, he'd only half laid the explosives. No doubt Weiss would jabber on about wasting resources.

But before then, he'd accomplish his mission. As soon as it was dark, he'd be back, throttle any fox he encountered, and set the rest of the damn things. He rather looked forward to watching the explosion. Would be better than any mortal New Year display.

But until then, he had a few sticky problems to resolve.

How could anyone repel him?

First, there had been that fire-throwing something. Left him nastily marked for a few hours, too. Pity he'd been so intent on his intended quarry that the creature came on him unawares.

Then, there was that mortal woman. Only she wasn't mortal. Couldn't be. She and her paramour should have been easy pickings but she'd repelled him as if he were a newly turned fledgling.

He knew who she was: the doctor who'd attended Miss Waite. Doyle her name was, and she lived in that big house on the edge of the village.

Maybe he should pay a call. What doctor refused to see a patient?

And her paramour, the one who so stirred Williams's ire. Twice he'd escaped. Was he the one with the power? This he'd not expected. And it did not please. After he took care of his mission, he'd find a way to eliminate them both.

And meanwhile, might as well report in to the humans who considered themselves his masters. He did have some interesting news after all and his radio was safe, high in the church tower.

Didn't take long to scale the tower and make contact. "Brunhilda arrested. Repeat: Brunhilda arrested. Will observe all cautions."

That should keep them, and Weiss, off his neck for a day or two.

Following procedure, he cut the connection, waited two hours, and reconnected.

The reply message came clear and to the point.

"News received. Do not, repeat, do not delay mission. Timeliness imperative."

Damn!

Gloria gave up on sleep. Usually after a good run she slept like a contented baby but this time she tossed and turned. Mind you, it could hardly be described as a "good" run. Too many unanswered questions and too many concerns. What was the thing that lurked in the woods and was up to no good? And why, come to that, had so many foxes answered her distress call? That had never happened before. Not that she'd ever given out such a frantic alarm before, but it worked and nicely foiled the thing's nefarious schemes.

But she needed help, needed to talk to someone.

Right, she could see herself going up to Alice, or the new chap, Peter, or one of the ladies in the knitting circle and saying, "Last night, when I was running though the woods in my fox shape . . ." They'd lock her up.

She couldn't let that happen.

Peter and Gran were sitting up when she got home. Drinking tea by the boiler, which Gran had obviously stoked up. The warmth was particularly welcome after the early morning drive home.

"Alice!" Peter had his arms around her and kissed her. Twice. "Everything alright?"

Not exactly, but where to begin? "Is that tea? I could use a cup."

Gran produced it in minutes. Peter insisted she sit down, and suddenly fatigue seeped into her bones.

"Well, dear?" Gran asked. "Bad news?"

"I have no idea, but I think so."

"What happened, love?" Peter was wearing Simon's red plaid dressing gown. Gran *was* making him comfortable.

"I'm just going by guesswork here. Guesswork and little bit of hearsay, but I suspect that thing, that vampire, whatever it is, went up to the plant after I got rid of it down here." She told them, pretty much word for word, what she'd learned from Jim Bryant and the three girls.

Peter looked as puzzled as she felt.

Gran had no such handicap. "He's getting more dangerous and more confident. Must be gaining strength. Seems to me we need to trap him and destroy him before he really causes bother."

"Gran . . ." Alice began.

"Don't fuss at me, dear. We need to talk to Mother Longhurst and Howell Pendragon. One of them must surely know what to do next."

"Sharpen stakes?" Alice suggested. Facetious, yes, but really.

"Why not? We know wood slows and harms them, but there has to be something more effective. You seem to have the key, I think, dear."

"Hang on a minute. You can't expect Alice to face that thing again."

Dear Peter. "I managed alright last night."

"What if it doesn't work a second time?"

"Why shouldn't it?" What was she saying? That she had magic in her and could summon it when she wanted? She was dreaming.

Gran obviously didn't think so. "At last, my love, it took this to make you embrace your powers. We'll destroy this thing yet."

"Might it not be a good idea," Peter said, sounding a trifle testy, no doubt worried, "to identify the creature first? I mean it could be living down the road, hanging around the village green, playing whist in the church hall, and buying newspapers at Worleigh's."

Chapter 35

"Peter's right, Gran. How can we identify him?"

"You've both seen him face-to-face. Peter twice. Can't you?"

"Face-to-face is not the word for it," Alice replied. "It was more like face-to-shadow. It was like facing the dark, not a living thing."

Helen Burrows shook her head. Young people . . . "He isn't living, Alice, and therein lies our advantage. We are."

"I don't quite follow you, Mrs. Burrows."

A good lad, once he came into his own. "You two and Howell have been closest to this vampire in his strength. I don't doubt we've all seen him when he passes as one of us. But you have faced its power. You are our best hope in identifying it."

"Then, Gran," Alice replied with a sigh, "I think things are going to be difficult. We didn't see anything."

"We did, Alice," Peter said. "It's just we don't know what we saw."

The lad would do. Together they would prosper. Once they took care of this problem, and as long as the invasion never happened, and we win the war. And all that was too much for one old Pixie to contemplate. Best start with what could be done.

"Peter's right. Think about it, Alice."

"Gran, it's too much on top of no sleep."

"I'll make you some good strong coffee."

Alice stared after her grandmother. She hated to think "senile" and Gran at the same time but heaven help her. And as for Peter. "What the flaming Hades did you mean about us seeing but not knowing what we've seen?" Drat, she never swore, but the past few days were enough to set a nun cursing.

"Don't you understand, Alice?" No, she didn't, apart from the gleam of excitement in his eyes. Had to be lack of sleep was making them punch-drunk. "We, and the sergeant, have been closer to this thing than anyone. That gives us the edge—we just have to work out what we know and how to use it."

Alright. "We know it's dark, powerful, and somehow projects enough menace to instill enough fear to make healthy men pass out." She couldn't forget the two guards up at the camp.

"Right," Peter said. "Plus, we know he's repelled by fire. Or at least dragonfire and some sort of magic that you can produce."

Was it magic? "That would be handy if I knew what the heck it was."

"It's your power, girl! How many times do I have to tell you that!"

They hashed things over for ages. Gran made coffee and they drank it, but still they were back at the same, hardly helpful facts: Wood harmed it. The dead and wasted animals and poor old Farmer Morgan were presumably vampire victims. And fire and Alice's unreliable and untutored magic would repel him.

Seemed Alice's half-facetious comment about sharpening stakes was as helpful as anything.

"We need the sergeant in on this, too," Peter said at last. "He's part of it after all. That fire . . ." He broke off. "Stone the crows! It's a wild possibility but . . ."

"What?" Alice asked.

"The odds are it's purely a coincidence, there's probably dozens of people in the village who have been burned, but . . ."

He explained about Jeff Williams's demand for Aquaflavine. "He took six tubes of the stuff. Nicked five when my back was turned. Didn't make an issue of it my first day up there, but what if he really did want it for someone who was burned? I kept telling him bad burns needed medical attention, but what if he wanted it for a burned vampire?" Peter shook his head. "Far-fetched, I know."

"Maybe not." Gran might be bustling at the sink, but her old ears missed nothing. "No one in their right mind needs six tubes of the stuff unless they're planning on going into business and hawking it on the black market."

"With Aquaflavine that you can get for sixpence over the counter of any chemist?" Alice shook her head. "It's the best bet we have so far. All we need to do is find out who he got it for." Yes, very tenuous but . . . "Think he'll tell us if we ask him?"

Peter grinned. "Since he hates my guts, most likely not."

"But if I, as the local doctor, heard he needed ointment for burns and ask if there's anything I can do?"

"Worth a try, my love. Worth a try." Gran wiped her hands on the tea towel.

Alice only half heard her. Peter's reply struck her. "What do you mean, 'hates your guts'?" Darn, this was obviously some sacred male thing. Peter's mouth clamped shut.

Gran filled in for him. "The man's got a thing about Peter being a CO, goes on to everyone who'd listen and plenty who don't."

That was news to her.

Not apparently to Peter. "He made a scene in the Pig the other night. He was drunk, that's all."

Again acting the he-man, brushing it off. "You had a fight in the Pig?"

"Not really, might have had, but Joe Arckle was with me, the father of those two boys. He pretty much made him stand down. Fred Wise told him and the chap he was with to be on their way."

"Who was he with?" Gran asked. "As far as I know that creature has had no friends in the village since he accused Sam Whorleigh of giving short measure and then two days later pushed Mrs. Jackson into the road when she was waiting for a bus."

Amazing how a man could lose his reputation. "Who was it, Peter?"

"I've seen him around but don't know his name."

"Fred Wise is bound to know."

"Yes, Gran, but we can hardly knock on the door of the Pig and Whistle at . . ." She glanced at the kitchen clock. "Seven-thirty in the morning and ask."

"No, dear, let him get breakfast first, but we'll find out. That should sort things out."

More like snarl things up.

But for want of anything better to do, she might as well.

"I'm coming with you, Alice," Peter said.

Good, she'd feel less of a twit asking questions with Peter there. "Let's go soon." And get it over with.

"Right, I'll cycle down and meet you there."

At this point, did discretion matter? "I'll drive you down."

"Good idea," Gran said. "Might as well let everyone know how things stand."

"Gran!"

Peter just stared, probably didn't like to tell an old woman she was presuming.

"Don't be silly either of you. You both know you're getting married. So you might as well get the village used to the idea."

"Gran!" Dear heaven, her face burned and poor Peter looked ready to croak.

He was so bumfuzzled it took him a good few seconds to speak. "I think that's a damn good idea!"

"When you two have finished organizing my life, maybe we can sort out this vampire business."

Gran smiled. "Yes, my loves, you'd better. Can't have a

vampire messing up things around here, can we? Jerry's enough trouble."

"Could they be connected?"

At least that diverted attention from her sex life. Peter stared at her.

Gran just nodded slowly. "Why not? We've been bombed, that Miss Waite arrested as a spy, and now, trouble up at the camp, which would no doubt suit them. You could be right, child. In fact I think we should look very closely at that newly arrived nephew of hers."

"You think he's involved in all this, Gran?" Alice hadn't much cared for the man but it was a bit of a leap from mild dislike to thinking he was a terrifying bloodsucker bent on mayhem and destruction. And working for the enemy to boot.

"I think you'd best go and talk to Mother Longhurst."

Mother Longhurst? The village witch who'd scared the willies out of Alice when she was a child and tried her darnedest to filch patients with her potions and nostrums? "Honestly! Gran, no!"

"Please yourself, but she knows more about vampires than anyone in the village."

Not hard to believe. "Is she pals with them?"

"Oh, child!" Gran snapped. "Look beyond yourself! Did you never listen as a child?" She started humming one of the old songs. "Pixie songs" Gran used to call them when she sang Alice to sleep as a child.

The familiar tune triggered memories. Very nice but now was not the time to relive childhood moments. Until the name of the ballad struck him. "When Magic and Time Sundered."

"They fought and we cried, as the people's hopes died, and the timeless departed forever. And the magic was lost, to our shame and our cost, and the people fled into the heather."

Alice felt her jaw drop to her chest. Peter!

Gran smirked. "I knew there was something right about

you, young man. I knew it the minute I laid eyes on you. Who taught you the Pixie lore?"

Now he looked as puzzled as Alice felt. "Old Mrs. Norsworthy. She used to come in and take care of me when my parents went out. She sung songs and used to tell me tales of battles and magic." He want pale. "I thought they were just stories made up to entertain me."

Gran rolled her eyes. "The woman was sharing the lore of the Pixies with you, and you thought they were made-up tales. I don't know—seems you and Alice belong together. Handed the wisdom of our people on a plate and you brush it aside."

"Alright, Gran. We were both mistaken. Can we cut out the recriminations until we take care of this vampire?"

Gran stood up and took her everyday coat off the hook on the door. "You do what you please. I'm getting the bus into Epsom. But if you've any sense between your ears, Alice, and you too, young man, you'll get yourselves down to Mother Longhurst before she goes out gathering."

Gran as good as slammed the door on her way out.

"Gran," Alice called after her, but she was already down the path and in the lane.

"What now?" Alice asked.

"I think we'd better do as she told us," Peter said.

Chapter 36

Gloria exhaled with relief. Sergeant Pendragon didn't ask questions, just listened and behaved as if what she was saying made sense, rather that sounding like balderdash. She'd agonized over coming and telling him. She couldn't go to the police; they'd want to know what she was doing traipsing around the woods in the middle of the night, and even though Alice was her best friend, she'd look at her as if she'd been drinking if she heard half of what Gloria just told the sergeant.

When she'd seen the chink of light through a gap in the blackout curtains, she'd knocked on his door, knowing she had to talk to someone, and he was different, an outsider like her, not one of the born and bred villagers.

As she waited in the near dark, she'd almost turned and run, but he'd opened the door, looked at her in surprise, and said, "Come in, Gloria. Best get the door closed. You look as though you could do with a cup of tea."

He'd placed a heavy mug of strong tea and a slab of toast and marmalade in front of her. "Eat up," he told her, "then tell me what's biting at you."

She'd half eaten the toast when she realized he was spreading a second slice for himself. He'd given her his breakfast but her guilty apology was brushed aside. "Eat it up. Plenty of bread for toast, and you look as if you need it."

She was hungry.

"Want another slice?" She shook her head but when he lifted the tea pot and looked at her, she pushed her mug forward and he refilled it. "Right then," he said as he topped up his own mug. "What brings you to my door before breakfast?"

She told him.

Everything about the night before—except for the detail about being four-footed and furry at the time.

And he treated her as if she made perfect sense.

"What do you think he was setting in the ground?"

"I don't know for sure, couldn't see, but I had to think land mines or explosives of some sort, don't you?"

He nodded. "I don't know what else. Doubt he was getting an early start on Guy Fawkes."

"You believe me!"

His eyes creased as he smiled and she let out the anxious breath she hadn't realized she was holding. "It's so far-fetched."

"Nurse Prewitt, how long have I known you, five, nearly six years? You came right after Nurse Hampton retired." She nodded. "Long enough to know you're not the sort of woman to come knocking on my door before dawn with an elaborate fiction."

Tears of relief stung her eyes. "I don't know what to do. I just couldn't see going to Sergeant Jones or PC Parlett with such a story."

He chuckled. "Wise of you. Look, you've told me. I'll see it gets passed on to those who need to know. Want another cup of tea?"

"No, thank you. I ought to be going, but thank you for believing me."

"I'd believe whatever you told me, Nurse Prewitt. Truly, I would."

She didn't think she'd put that to the test and just as well

Mr. Watson wasn't up yet. She'd never have been able to tell as much as she had with him there.

The Sergeant opened the door for her.

"Thanks again," Gloria said, "for breakfast and for believing me."

"You trusted me with that, will you trust me with what you are?" he asked.

For one hideous minute she thought he meant her Other nature, but he couldn't. Impossible. "You know who I am. I'm just the district nurse," she replied. "Nothing special about me."

He smiled. "Take care of yourself, Nurse, we need you."

"Bad news," Howell Pendragon said to himself as he washed up the mugs and plates. But bad news wasn't the same as a bad end. They had time. Pity the little nurse wouldn't trust him with her nature, but he understood. It didn't do to broadcast one's Otherness. She'd trusted him with quite enough already. Now it was up to him to make sure the place was checked for land mines or whatever.

Good thing really the lad had stayed out last night. Howell gave a dry chuckle. Nothing like youth; pity they were always too young to appreciate it. Well, the doctor could do a lot worse, and the lad seemed able to handle Otherness.

Good luck to them.

Now what to do about Nurse Prewitt's news?

Someone had better be alerted. But he'd shave and put on a clean shirt first then go and talk to Helen.

She'd know how to get the word out without actually physically telling anyone.

"I feel a total and utter fool doing this."

Peter squeezed her hand. Safe enough in the car. "Think she'll refuse to talk to you?"

"Not at all. She'll be thrilled to have me coming to her for help. We've had . . ." What had gone between them?

"Confrontations?" Peter suggested.

"Nothing that far. You could say we've competed over patients. Lots of the villagers go to her first, and when her remedies don't work, they come to me much sicker."

"Could be the ones she cures don't need to come to you."

"Peter, are you on my side or not?"

"I'll always be on your side, love, but if I can open my mind to Dragons and Pixies, can't you concede herbal potions and cures might sometimes work? Isn't aspirin some sort of tree bark?"

"That would be easy. It's 'My grandmother told me to ask you about vampires' that I'm going to choke over."

"Best get on with it then. That way you get the choking over with."

Not the reply she wanted, but when had Gran ever let her down? "Alright, let's go and make fools of ourselves."

"Well, I never, it's the doctor!" Mother Longhurst grinned as she recognized Alice and Peter. "And her helper. What can I do for you? Need a linctus do you? A cure? Bad headaches? Not sleeping enough?"

That Alice would not respond to. "I don't need a cure or potion, Mother Longhurst. Gran sent me here."

"Which one does she want? More rosehip tea?"

"We're not here for your herb lore, Mother Longhurst; your Other knowledge is what we need."

She grinned, a sly look in her eyes. "And what would that be? How best to keep the greenfly off your roses?"

"I know that," said Peter. "My grandmother told me that one: soap suds."

That got a cackle from Mother Longhurst. "Sharp as you look, eh, young man? Well then, what do you both want from me?"

"Mrs. Burrows said you could tell us how magic and time sundered."

"She did, did she?" For a few seconds she seemed to ponder slamming the door on them, but seemed she liked Peter. "Best come in then."

Wasn't a gracious invitation, but they were in her cottage.

After the bright morning, the place seemed gloomy in the extreme. The table was covered with papers and packets. A pot of tea and the heel of a stale loaf sat among the mess. Mother Longhurst walked over the to fireplace where a large pot simmered on the iron range.

"Sit down," she said as she settled in the rocking chair, "This will take time."

There wasn't another chair, not even a stool.

Oh, well. Alice sat down on the rug by the fire, and Peter did the same. Mother Longhurst, obviously enjoying having them at her feet, smiled. "Ready, are you?"

Alice nodded.

"Yes, Mother Longhurst," Peter said.

He did have better manners than she had, but drat it, sitting at the feet of one's old adversary wasn't exactly comfy. Even if she did have a massive sheepskin spread in front of the fireplace.

Alice ran her fingers through the thick fleece. She'd no doubt poached it when out gathering.

"Are you here to listen or scowl, girl?"

Had she been so obvious? Alice felt the blush rise. It would be the easiest thing in the world to get up and go. But Gran insisted Mother Longhurst could help.

"Sorry, I'm a bit worried."

"Should be what with bombs dropping, people dying and breaking legs and getting arrested as spies. To say nothing of all the Other stuff going on right now."

There was the term "Other" again. The way she said it put a capital on the word. Alice shivered; she was one of those Others.

"Mother Longhurst, can you tell us the story?" Peter asked.

"You're the one rescued those children from the vicarage, right?"

"With help, yes."

She grinned a sly knowing grin. "You had good help, I'll tell you that."

"Yes."

"So you want the old story, do you?"

"Please." They both spoke at once.

"Better listen then, I'm not doing this for entertainment." She had a swig of tea from a mug perched on the fender, put the mug back down, drew herself up, took a deep breath, and began singing.

Her voice was surpassingly clear for her age and the words were easy to make out. But it was the same ballad Alice'd heard umpteen times from Gran. All this for something she already knew. But leaving would be rude in the extreme and Peter was listening, rapt. She might as well.

It wasn't quite the same. It was longer, verses added that Gran had never sung, and the ending sounded like a dirge.

"So," Mother Longhurst said in the silence after she finished. "You heard it. What did you learn?"

That the song was a lot longer that she'd thought? Better not.

"Mother Longhurst," Peter asked while Alice fumbled for something polite to say. "The timeless in the song, the ones who left. They were vampires?"

Again that cackle. Did witches practice it? "Not bad, young man, not bad. You've a more open mind than our doctor here. Some call them vampires. Once they were called timeless. The ones who never aged."

"But could die?"

"Could be extinguished."

"How," Alice asked, thinking hard, "could anyone extinguish them?"

"Wrong question, Doctor," she replied with the same

annoying cackle. It had scared Alice as a child, now it just got on her nerves. "You should have asked, 'Why?'"

Alright, if she wanted to play games, Alice could play. "Why would anyone extinguish them?"

"Jealousy, fear, hate, lust for their power, to rid the earth of them. Hard to do that since they come of the earth."

"How?" Hopefully this was the time to ask that.

"Takes more than you have, Alice Doyle."

"More than Alice and I have?" Peter asked.

She smiled and shook her head.

"What about more than Peter, Gran, and myself?"

"And why would you want to know?"

She was getting tired of talking in circles.

"Mother Longhurst," Peter said, "there's a vampire in the village bent on harm. We have to get rid of it."

"And how do you know there's one? Gossip? Drunken talk at the Pig and Whistle?"

"I've faced it. Twice."

Her old eyes all but popped. "And you sit here now and tell about it? It wasn't one of the timeless."

"I believe it was. It was a dark presence full of horror and fear."

"And what did you do, give it the hex sign and tell it to run away?"

Miserable old skeptic, but Peter wasn't put off. "No. Both times I was fortunate. Someone with powers I don't possess thwarted and repelled it."

"Then you were lucky with your choice of company, young man."

"I was." He gave Alice a sideways smile. "We think it has harmed and killed and plans to do worse."

"If it's a vampire, harm and injury are part of their nature. They're dangerous, very dangerous."

That much they'd worked out for themselves. "Will you help us destroy this one?" Alice asked.

That cackle was beginning to get on Alice's nerves. "Come to me at last, have you, Doctor? Remember that next time you fuss at one of your patients for taking my cures." And with that, she stood up and walked out of the door.

Alice turned to Peter. He turned to her. Their eyes met and as she opened her mouth to speak, he put his finger on his lips and shook his head. She'd humor him. He seemed to have a feel for all that and she was well out of her depth.

They stayed put. Just as Alice was thinking enough was enough and she was darn well going home, Mother Longhurst reappeared with a bundle in her hand.

A bundle of what looked like filthy rags.

"I wouldn't keep this in the house. Too powerful. You have to be careful, magic has a way of twisting back. But this will extinguish a vampire." She unrolled the bundle and spread the dingy cloth on the table. "Come and look at it then. I didn't climb up a tree at my age to get this for fun!"

Peter gave Alice a hand and they both stood.

Two steps brought them to the table.

Alice fought to keep back the sneer. It was a dirty old knife. "What is it?"

"A knife of power. Touch the hilt, if you will. Avoid the blade."

Both blade and hilt were covered with strange markings. Some ancient alphabet perhaps? Alice touched the hilt. "It's stone?" She'd heard tales of sacrificial druid knives. Surely this couldn't be that old?

"Petrified wood. Hard enough to slay a vampire. Drive that though his heart and he will not heal."

A knife through the heart, any knife, tended to kill. "Why this knife and not any other?"

"Any other knife he'll heal from. Only wood kills them and only if it stays in their flesh."

"If the wood's taken out they don't die?"

"As hard as it is to get it in them in the first place, who in their right mind would take wood from a vampire's flesh?"

She'd skip answering that.

"So," Peter said, guessing her confusion, no doubt. "We stab him with this and that's it?"

"If it works."

"Does it?" he persisted.

"I've never used it. That was handed to me by my grandmother, who had it from hers, who had it from hers, and back through the ages. I don't know when it was last used."

Or would even work? But the bit about wood in the flesh and taking it out certainly rang true.

"Any hints to help make sure it does?" Heaven bless Peter, he did ask the right questions.

"They say coating the blade with mistletoe adds to its power."

It would. It was poison.

"Is there anything we should do to keep this safe?" he asked.

"Safe?" Mother Longhurst shook her head. "It will never be safe. Isn't that why you want it?"

"But what if someone else touches it and gets hurt?"

"That's the risk. Power can recoil and often does but if you set out to attempt the near impossible, you take risks."

Easy for her to say, safe in her poky little cottage. For two pins Alice would tell her to keep her battered knife.

"Thank you," Peter said, rewrapping the knife in the tattered cloth. "We'll only use it for its intended purpose. And then we'll get it back to you."

"We'll see. We'll see."

What did one say after that odd comment? "Thank you" seemed the best bet.

"May the strength of the ancients be with you," Mother Longhurst said as she opened the door. "Gods and goddesses befriend you both."

"Er . . . thank you," Alice replied.

She almost ran to the car.

"Next stop, the Pig and Whistle," Peter said as he opened the car door for her.

"A pity it's so early. I could use a stiff drink."

Peter's grin suggested he was of the same mind. "That was a bit odd, wasn't it?"

"I'm still not sure how helpful all that was. Apart from lending us an ancient knife designed to kill vampires. All very well and good, but we've got to get awfully close to the thing once we identify it if we want to get a stab at it."

"If Fred Wise can give us his name, we'll have a start."

"We'd better be damn sure it's the right person. That knife would do injury to anyone, vampire or not. As for rubbing the blade with mistletoe, it's a bit early in the season for berries."

"She didn't say it had to be berries. Maybe the leaves or branches would work."

"We've still got to find it and climb and get it."

"I don't think that's the hardest job ahead of us."

Chapter 37

Helen Burrows took a seat by the window and the bus took off. It was a good thing she'd left the house in a huff. If she'd stopped to think about this, she'd still be safe in her own kitchen.

She was really getting too old for this sort of lark, but if Alice could go asking favors of Mother Longhurst, whom she mistrusted to the point of active dislike, maybe paying an unannounced social call on a vampire wasn't too much of an undertaking.

Assuming, of course, he was still there, would see her if she was, was willing to help, and let her walk away unharmed at the end of it.

That last was a bit of a worry, but in all the years since she'd lived in Surrey, she'd never heard word or whisper of any vampire doing harm. Not that it was the sort of thing they put in the local paper, but one heard these things, if one knew what to listen for.

This particular vampire had lived here quietly and unobtrusively. She was one of the few, maybe the only, living soul who knew him for what he was. That in itself was a bit of a worry. But there was no point in getting off the bus now that she was halfway there.

She did wonder how Alice and Peter were getting on, aside

from the obvious, long-term aspect, which was so clear to anyone with half an eye. She really didn't understand why it wasn't the talk of the village. It would be soon.

Good.

She always enjoyed a wedding.

Of course, first they had to dispose of this nasty vampire presence in the village. Not an easy task.

Which was why she'd jumped on the first bus to Epsom, waited the better part of an hour in the High Street, watching the hands creep on the clock tower, and finally caught a bus going to the Downs. How she was getting back, given the sketchy bus service, was another problem entirely. One thing at a time.

"Mum?" the driver called back at her. "Next stop's yours. Tatteneham Corner."

This was it.

"Thank you," she said as she alit. The bus drew away. A brisk wind blew across the Downs, making her wish she'd worn more than a short jacket.

Actually having an address also would have made it easier. But she had a name, hopefully the current one, and could speak the language. The first two houses she tried were unoccupied. The third, the door was answered by a trim parlormaid who had never heard of a Mr. Jude Clarendon. Back down the path, Helen sighed: She was indeed a very foolish Pixie to think she could find a man, alright, vampire, on the strength of a name alone.

If she knocked on every door and asked, it could take her weeks. And they didn't have weeks. As she turned left, heading up the lane, a mail van passed and stopped a few yards farther along the road alongside a bright red pillar-box.

She all but ran to catch the postman before he finished emptying the postbox. "Excuse me." She was almost out of breath. "Do you know this area?"

He looked up from catching a cascade of letters and packages into a heavy mailbag. "Indeed I do. Lost are you, mum?"

"I'm looking for a house. Someone asked me to pop in and see an old friend for them, and I lost the address. Do you know where a Mr. Jude Clarendon lives? I know it's somewhere around but my memory isn't what it was." The latter was no lie.

"Mr. Jude Clarendon, Summerhaven on Green Lane. You're close, just five minutes down the road then turn left." He stood upright and slammed the postbox shut and locked it before looping a strap around the top of the bag he held. "Tell you what, mum. If you don't tell on me, I'll give you lift down to the corner."

She gladly climbed into the van and he set off. "Know Mr. Clarendon well, do you?"

"Not well, just through friends, but I was in Epsom and promised Helen I'd look him up." Perfect truth. She had promised herself to do everything she could to find him.

Good thing she took up his offer of a lift. It was a five minute drive, and most of it uphill.

"Here you are." He pulled to the curb and reached over to open the door for her. "Go up the lane forty, fifty yards and you'll see the house on the left. A bungalow: Summerhaven."

"Thank you so much. Saved me a long walk."

"Don't mention it, mum, we've all got to stick together these days, haven't we?"

He had no idea how right he was.

She found the house easily, a pantile-roofed bungalow with a wide veranda. A dark green roadster stood in the drive and a tall, fair-haired, heavyset man was loading a suitcase into the boot.

Wasn't many times in her life Helen Burrows had been plain petrified, but this was one of them. She was either looking at the vampire, or his servant, or was completely off course and about to accost some respectable citizen. No point in delaying. At the sound of the gate opening, the man, creature, whatever he was, straightened and looked right at her.

She fought the urge to turn and run and closed the gate behind her. Her feet did not want to walk up that graveled drive. They did it anyway, while the vampire, she was certain it had to be vampire, watched her, as fascinated as if she were walking on water, not his front drive.

"Mr. Clarendon?" she asked, stopping a couple of yards away and seeing clearly he had no living aura.

"I am, madam. It seems you have the advantage of me."

Not for long. "I'm Helen Burrows, I live in Brytewood, near Box Hill. I need your help." Her heart was racing and her hands sweaty with anxiety, but she held out her hand.

He took it, his grasp firm and his hand unnaturally cold. "Good morning, Mrs. Burrows. I'm on the point of leaving." He gestured to the car.

"I'll be as direct and brief as I can. I came to you for help because you're a vampire."

He grinned. "Madam, I've had some interesting approaches in my life but that's a novel one." Dear heavens, had she been wrong? No! As he laughed, his aura stayed solid and black, not a spark of life in it.

"Maybe novel, but accurate. Please, I don't have time to play games. You can help me."

"Why would I?"

"Because there's a vampire in my village injuring, killing, and terrorizing."

That got his attention. Maybe not a good thing considering the almost feral smile that curved his mouth. "Why make these rather preposterous claims?"

"Because those I love are threatened." It was not going to work. He looked downright bored. "And I'm Pixie," she added.

That sparked his interest. "A Pixie."

She nodded. He could surely sense the truth. Either that or he'd call the police thinking she'd escaped from one of the mental hospitals.

"Come in, we can't talk out here."

Taking a deep breath, she stepped over the threshold, heart racing and mind whirling.

"You're afraid of me."

No point in denying. "Yes, but I'm more afraid that I'll fail."

His blue eyes met hers. "Don't we all have that fear?"

"You? You're so strong and powerful. Why would you be afraid?"

"I'm not indestructible and I have friends in danger. Friends I'm on my way to join . . . in France," he added after a long pause.

She understood. At least she thought she did. "Then I will not keep you longer than I have to."

"Have a seat, Pixie. You came for help, I'll not turn you away if I can help."

"You believe me?"

"Why not? You're not mortal. That was obvious when you walked up the drive. No mortal could have approached after I repelled as hard as I did. I'm curious as to why you're here. A Pixie, eh? Well, I never did believe those stories of dancing around Fairy rings on a midsummer night."

"That is fairies. I'm Pixie." Better get that straight. Some misunderstandings could not be permitted to continue.

"I beg your pardon. I must admit to being woefully ignorant of Pixies and other species."

"And I know little about vampires."

"You knew enough to find me."

"I was told a name, some years ago, and that you lived up here on the Downs."

"I should probably move then." He sat down on a chair opposite. "But since I am here and you searched me out, what about this rogue vampire terrorizing your village?"

"It'll take a while, as I really have to start at the beginning, but I'll be as brief as possible."

He nodded, steepling his fingers against his chin, and waited.

She started with the vampire Alice rescued and ended with the events of the past evening. It took longer than she'd hoped but he seemed in no hurry.

"So," he said as she finished, "what do you want me to tell you?"

"How to kill him. If we can."

He had a pleasant laugh, for a vampire. "Wouldn't that be foolish, handing you the knowledge of my own weaknesses?"

"I'm not proposing to kill you. This creature is different, it's brought havoc and destruction, and has not finished, of that I'm certain."

"I don't doubt you're right, but there is a difficulty." He raised his hand to stop her interruption. "We're of many bloodlines, all different and with varying strengths and weaknesses. If I told you how you could extinguish me, it might not work on another of unknown lineage."

"So there's no help you can give me?"

"I didn't say that. When did this presence make itself felt?"

"A few days after the disappearing patient."

"Who you'd recognize but have never seen since?" She nodded. "Some of us can change shape, become birds or wolves or bats, but I have never heard of a vampire that changed their mortal appearance. In fact, we are immutable. I've looked this way for nearly two hundred years."

"So we're talking about two vampires?" And she'd thought one was a big problem.

"I believe so. That first one may have gone to earth, or be hiding somewhere else."

"And if there's two, what's to stop three or four?" It was worse than she'd realized.

"Nothing, I'm afraid. And since I would know if another of my bloodline were here, this or these are outsiders. There's another point. I told you I was going to France."

"You did. War work I imagine?"

"Precisely. If our side is using vampires, we should no doubt assume the Germans are, too."

Holy smoke! "That's it! At least I think it is. They just arrested someone in the village as a German spy."

"But she's not there."

"No, but very recently she had this nephew arrive one evening. An evening when there were no buses." That had to be it.

"I wish I could stay and help you but I do have to get a plane."

"Thank you so much. Do you have a telephone? May I use it?" She'd better warn Alice and Peter.

"By all means."

No reply at the house. She couldn't call Mother Longhurst; she didn't even have electricity, much less a telephone. The Pig and Whistle. She had to call directory enquiries first. She would be owing this nice man, vampire, a pocketful of change, but . . . "Hello."

Fred Wise wasn't much help. "Yes, she were here with that young assistant of hers, left half an hour ago."

Nothing for it but to wait until she got back, which could be hours.

"No luck?" Jude Clarendon said.

"I couldn't catch them. I want to warn my granddaughter. I'm afraid she'll do something rash."

He reached for his coat off the hall rack. "Come on. I can give you a lift into Brytewood. It's not much out of way."

Definitely faster than the bus, but vampires obviously didn't worry too much about having a car accident. The way he took the zigzag bends down Box Hill was enough to give her a heart spasm. But he got her to Brytewood, dropping her by the bridge on the outskirts of the village.

"Can you walk from here?"

"I can and thank you."

"By the way," he said, "the old stories of sharpened stakes are all true. Oak works best. Just don't take it out, or he'll heal over. And don't ever tell anyone I told you."

"Thank you, Mr. Clarendon. Best of luck where you're going."

"You, too. Seems we fight the war on our own doorsteps as well."

Unfortunately, that was proving all too true.

Now she had to find Alice and Peter and tell them she'd identified the vampire.

Chapter 38

"So we have a name," Peter said as they drove away from the Pig. "Your grandmother was spot-on about looking very hard at Miss Waite's nephew. Seems he's our boy. Beats me how it took us so long to work that out."

"Most people don't assume that someone a bit odd is automatically a blood-sucking vampire."

"True. What do we do now? Knock on his door and ask if he speaks German?"

She had to smile at that. "Doesn't mean a thing. Lots of perfectly patriotic English people speak German. I do."

That surprised him. "You do?"

"Yes, don't broadcast it nowadays, but between getting my Higher Certificate and starting at Barts, I spent a year in Germany. I made some good friends. Odd isn't it? I try not to think about them, as I imagine they try hard not to think about me." Enough of that. Better to concentrate on how to dispose of a vampire than what had happened to her friends.

"What should we do now then?"

"I don't want to do anything until Gran gets back." From wherever she'd rushed off to. That was another worry. Gran didn't go off like that. But she had.

"While we're waiting, we could get engaged. How about it?"

"This is hardly the time or the place. We're on a vampire hunt." And didn't that just prove how off kilter her life was? "Peter . . ." What next?

"I know." She truly believed he did.

"There's so much going on I feel I'm pulled from all directions and it doesn't help in the least that we seem to be walking around with 'we had fantastic sex last night' written on our faces."

"Doesn't bother me."

That deserved a jab in the ribs but since she was driving, she settled for a scowl.

"Does that bother you now?" He sounded so hurt.

"Not what we did, Peter, but the whole village is talking about it does. This is my home."

"Fair enough. Seems your grandmother is right. The sooner we get married the better."

"Aren't you jumping the gun a bit? How long have we know each other? Two weeks?"

"How many weeks do you want?"

One? A hundred? Twenty years? Would she feel differently? She'd never felt for anyone else what she felt for Peter. Come to that, she'd never leapt into bed with anyone quite as fast either. Was that it? Sex? Rather magnificent sex with the loveliest man she'd ever known. "I don't know. Can we take care of this vampire problem first? Then I'll have time to think about us."

At least she was seriously considering the possibility of an "us." "Fair enough, love. Should I start avoiding you to mislead everyone?"

"No!"

"Where are we headed, by the way? I was supposed to help Gloria out at the mothers' morning and then go up to the camp."

"Gloria can cope on her own. She has for years. We'll run by the village hall and tell her you have to go up to the camp early. I need to go and check on those two men."

"And see what's going on?"

"That, too."

He wouldn't complain at spending the morning in her company.

"Going up there early with Alice are you?" Gloria asked with a grin that had Peter completely understanding Alice's reservations.

"Er . . . yes. Can you manage?" Silly question.

"Of course. Although the mums who were hoping to give you the once over will be disappointed."

"I'm sure they'll survive."

"I don't know. Not much happens around here." He'd disagree with that statement. "Is everything alright up there after the trouble last night?"

News did spread fast. "That's what Alice is going up to check."

Half a mile from the camp it was clear something was up. The lane was blocked by a barrier manned by soldiers, not home guard.

"Sorry, madam, access is limited. If you keep on and take the road by Wharton Lacey you can get through."

"I'm Doctor Doyle." She dug into her handbag for her identity card. "I was called up to the camp during the night to check on two injured men. I'm on my way back to make sure all's well."

"And what about you, sir?" the guard asked, looking into the open window.

"Peter Watson." He handed over his identity card. "I run the clinic at the camp."

"That's right, sir. We have your name on the list. Let me check yours, Doctor."

With the window still open and several people within

earshot, Alice kept the questions boiling inside to herself. What was going on? She'd find out soon. Unless they decided a doctor was persona non grata.

They didn't.

"We called through to the next post. They're expecting you." He handed back both their identity cards. "Just show them these and you'll be through."

Waved through the next barrier, they headed for the camp gates. Which were wide open with several army trucks parked outside and clusters of uniformed soldiers along the cleared swath of open ground that surrounded the camp.

"What is going on?" Peter said.

"Andrew Barron will tell us. Let's stop by his office first."

"Let me open up my clinic. Might as well do what I'm paid for. Might learn something listening to chatter."

Good point. "Your cycle's still in the back. Better take it with you. I'll come by before I leave, but I should get on with my house calls."

"Just house calls, right? No dropping in on this Oak chap."

"What if he calls in injured?"

"He won't, if he's the vampire we suspect he is."

"I have that knife."

"No, you don't. It's in my pocket."

"Damn you, Peter! Now, don't you start any heroics."

"I'm not doing anything without a plan but I do think we need to stick together."

"What sort of plan?"

"Find out what brought the Army out here. Find some way of confirming this Oak chap is your vampire and then decide how to serve up his chips."

It sounded so easy.

It wasn't.

"Let's find out what's going on first."

* * *

"Land mines. Strung together but never detonated. Seems our sabotage chap was disturbed. Most likely by the wildlife chorus that woke up the whole camp." Andrew Barron shook his head. "Seems we all owe our survival to a bunch of foxes. Think I'll campaign to stop fox hunting once the war's over.

"Someone was really out to destroy the place."

"And the lot of us with it. Seems what they've defused isn't that powerful, but add what we have here and we'd have had our own blitz." He shuddered.

She would, too, at such a close call. "No bad news about those two guards?"

"Other than the poor chaps were hauled out of their beds after a couple of hours' sleep and yanked in for questioning. They seem to be prime suspects. If you could put in a word it might help. The Army won't take my word for it that they were out cold for the better part of an hour."

"I'll talk to whomever I have to." And find out more if she could.

"So that's your medical opinion?"

"Yes," Alice replied. A bit tartly, she admitted, but this young major rather got on her wick.

"A bit unscientific, isn't it?"

"Yes, but I can only report what I observe. It was thirty, forty minutes after they were found that I arrived. One was just regaining consciousness, the other did fifteen or so minutes later. They showed signs of extreme shock, even terror." How many times did she have to say it?

"Think they were victims of some sort of gas?"

Good question. "Can't say, having very limited experience with poison gas inhalation. In training, I saw patients from the last war but I've never seen victims of a recent attack. But they didn't have any breathing trouble."

He finally accepted that.

"They're here right now, I understand. I'd like to see them. Just to make sure all's well." And maybe get a few answers.

The latter she had little chance of. The major agreed to her seeing them, but he and a sergeant stayed in the room and flatly refused to leave.

She ascertained they were fine. Other than being put out at getting dragged up here on their day off after a couple of hours' sleep.

She sympathized, but other than recommending they have a chance to sleep, there wasn't a lot she could do.

But she knew the vampire had tried to destroy the camp. It was war. No doubt about it.

Heading for the clinic, she saw Jeff Williams standing outside a long hut. He appeared to be going on about something to a cluster of young women in drab overalls and turban-tied head scarves. They were all eyeing Williams with distinct dislike.

"Mr. Williams?" she called, getting his attention and that of the entire group. "A word, if I may?"

"I'm busy, Doctor."

So was she. "Just wanted a quick word about your burn victim friend."

That got his attention. "You lot stay right there," he told the group of women and strode toward Alice. "Wasn't a problem and how did you know about him?"

"Mr. Williams, any time a large quantity of medicine is issued, we have to follow up." A lie, but was he likely to know? "I understand Mr. Oak had some serious burns." Bingo, it was him. His mean little face showed it as clear as speaking.

"He's fine now. Wasn't anywhere near as bad as I thought at first."

"Sure? Burns can get infected easily. Why not ask him to drop by the surgery on Monday. Let me have a look."

The idea did not appeal. "No need. Wasn't really serious at all. He's healed now."

How thoroughly interesting. "Then we'll count on you returning any unopened ointment to the clinic."

Very petty, but satisfying. Especially when a hooter sounded and the knot of women all trooped back into the hut.

"Break's over, Mr. Williams," one of the called. "Time to get back to work."

The look he gave Alice suggested he blamed her for interrupting his tirade. Good. Nasty was not the word for him. Small wonder he kept company with a vampire. Mind you, the man didn't look well.

Was his new lodger snacking off him? That thought made her stomach twist.

She waited while Peter finished with his last couple of patients. "We're going to find a quiet spot and talk strategy," she said as he packed up.

"How about a quiet spot where we can find mistletoe?"

"Fletcher's Woods."

"Our place, eh? We might need a few tools." He dug into a packing case and brought out a box of folding pocketknives and a saw. An amputation saw, she suspected. "Don't expect I'll ever need to use this."

"I'm not sure you should. It looks like Boer war vintage."

"What about a dozen scout knives? What do they expect me to use them for?"

"Who cares? Let's borrow them and save having to go home."

They tucked the lot in her doctor's bag and left. Going through the same barriers before heading toward the woods.

"I'm worried, Howell. Where are they?"

He was tempted to tell her there were plenty of places a

young man and woman might be on a nice September afternoon, but Helen was obviously agitated. "They're two level-headed adults and if they're together they're safe. Why don't you tell me what's got you all in a stew. It's not just Alice missing lunch is it?"

It wasn't.

He listened to her long, rather rambling tale, then added his little installment.

"What was Gloria doing in the woods in the middle of the night?"

"Minding her own business, Helen. I didn't ask and she didn't tell. We're not the only ones with secrets."

Apparently not. Made one wonder how many Others called Brytewood home. "What now? I sent Alice and Peter to Mother Longhurst hoping she'd help."

"I know who it is, the Oak fellow, Miss Waite's nephew. Has to be. All this trouble started after he arrived. Plus he's Other. Knew that the first time I met him."

"You've known that all along and not done anything?"

"Why would I assume he's here to make trouble just because he's Other? Maybe he came for the same reason I did, for peace and quiet and to be near a line of power."

"He didn't, though, did he?"

"So it would seem."

"I don't like it, Howell, and I'm worried about Alice."

"I don't like it either."

"We need to find out what Alice and Peter have learned," Helen insisted. "We have to see this through to the finish and soon. After last night, this creature is downright dangerous and must be stopped."

"I'll come up with you if you like. I'm supposed to be checking in the shipment of rifles we just got but they can wait. Can't see Jerry coming up the Downs in the next couple of hours."

Chapter 39

Peter got the mistletoe down, at risk to life and limb, and rather mangling the amputation saw in the process, but since they both hoped never to have to use it for its intended purpose, she wasn't too worried about that. They also cut a number of stout stakes and sat on the running board of the car sharpening them.

"If anyone saw us they'd think we'd lost our marbles."

He was right there. "Maybe we have. How many people in England, let alone Surrey, miss lunch on a nice September afternoon to sharpen stakes?"

"Only those threatened by a vampire."

"Are we utterly bonkers?"

"A fortnight ago, I'd have said we were stark raving bonkers, but I've learned a lot in the past two weeks."

So had she. "I was so rude, wasn't I?"

"Yes, but much sexier that Sid Mosley. Believe me, he wrote the book on rudeness."

"I love you, Peter."

"Mutual, my dear. Will you marry me?"

Hadn't they had this conversation before? "When I was a little girl, I used to imagine getting a marriage proposal seated in a conservatory or a rose garden or perhaps a beach at midnight. Sharpening stakes was never part of the fantasy."

"Shows the difference between make-believe and reality, then. Is it yes or no?"

When it came to the crunch? She didn't know him well enough, had no idea how they'd cope, should surely at least have met his family, but . . . "Yes." She loved him. What more was there to say?

"Smashing!" Most of the stakes ended up on the ground, but for this minute it didn't matter.

She wrapped her arms around him as he hugged her and their mouths met, a great wave of searing passion engulfing them. This was nuts, beyond reason or common sense, but she loved him, and that was a darn good way to face the future.

"Once we get this business taken care of . . ." He indicated the stakes scattered at their feet. "We're going into Dorking and I'm buying you a ring."

"What are we hanging around here for?"

"To prepare the knife. I nearly killed myself getting that damn mistletoe according to Mother Longhurst's prescription."

"Do you really think she knows what she's talking about?"

"Search me, but this thing"—he picked up the knife— "looks lethal enough."

"But anyone would die from a stab in the heart, and mistletoe is a poison."

"Scientist to the bone, eh, Alice?"

"If I were truly a pure scientist I'd not be here sharpening stakes and watching you anoint a knife blade with squashed mistletoe berries." They weren't ripe but they were berries and they rubbed the whole thing with the leaves, too, just to make sure."

Peter wiped off the hilt. "Damn sticky these berries."

"I think that's how they get planted—by sticking to birds' feathers and beaks."

"Bully for the birds. Let's just hope it works. I get the feeling you don't get two goes at a vampire."

That was her constant worry. "We can't just knock on his door and say, 'Mr. Oak, we think you are a vampire.' And ask him to keep still while we shove it in his heart."

His hesitation suggested he agreed. "I want to talk to Gran before we do anything. Her and Sergeant Pendragon. Tell them what we know and see that they think. They're both a lot more up to snuff with this Other stuff than we are."

Eiche slammed the phone down so hard the cradle cracked, not that insignificant details like that mattered when faced with such hurdles. He was vampire! Stronger, faster, wiser, older, better in every way to these puny mortals. Yet, they'd attacked him with fire, repelled him with some sort of magic, and on top of it all were interrogating Williams about him and his injuries. Damn the stupid fool for giving out he was hurt, but at least the man had sense to alert him to this prying doctor woman.

He needed to find her and fast. It was going to be a very, very short meeting. If he was going to get nagged by Weiss for failing to detonate that camp, he might as well add another death to his list.

Perhaps waiting for dark, when he'd be at his strongest, might be wise. No, he might not be able to draw on the night horrors in daylight, but a puny, mortal female wasn't a match for him.

Now!

He would not delay. With the strength he'd draw from her, he'd have another attempt on the camp tonight.

But first to meet and feed off the dear meddling doctor.

"Doctor Doyle?" the fat, flabby woman waiting at the bus stop said in answer to his inquiry. "She lives up the top of Random Hill. You can get the bus; it stops right by her corner.

Big house on the right. Called The Gallop, you can't miss it. But she doesn't have a surgery on Saturdays, just emergencies."

"Thank you, I'll wait until Monday, nothing urgent."

He strolled back toward Williams's cottage, then cut across the back garden, leapt the hedge, and ran at full vampire speed over hedges and fences until he was clear of the last house. He ran on, up the hill, causing a herd of cows to scatter in fear, until he reached the crest of the hill.

The fat woman had been right. Down a short drive, behind a thick hedge, was The Gallop, with a brass plate on the brick pillar announcing Doctor Alice Doyle's surgery times.

And the damn house was empty!

No matter, he had time on his side in a way these mortals never would.

Eiche found a perch on the roof and settled against a chimney. While he waited, he'd anticipate the doctor's death throes. An educated woman would be far more satisfying than that brute of a peasant.

The sun was dipping toward the horizon. If she delayed until dark, he could really give her a nasty fright. Unless . . . no, what were the odds out of all the village she was that irritating magic user who'd repelled him last night. Nil! A doctor and educated woman would have no truck with peasant superstitions. She probably pooh-poohed the notion of vampires.

He was about to round off, and terminate, her education.

A few minutes later a large, tan shooting brake appeared in the drive.

As the driver's door opened and a young woman stepped out he leapt, landing a few meters behind her. "Doctor Doyle?"

She spun around. "Yes?"

And he recognized her.

It was then Eiche noticed Williams's personal dislike getting out of the other side.

"Alice! It's him!" the young man shouted.

She went even paler. Nice. Fear always sweetened the

blood, but if she used her magic, he'd need more. Eiche leapt over the car and caught the man's neck as he landed, dragging him with him.

The aroma of fear was tantalizing.

As Eiche leapt, Alice watched in shock and amazement. As he tackled Peter, she was jolted into activity. Grabbing a pair of stakes and the knife they'd set carefully on the dashboard, she raced around the car as the monster dragged Peter toward the house. Stake in hand, she drove it into Eiche's back.

It was done!

He reared up, let out a growl like a hellhound, and turned on her. Letting Peter drop.

Peter fell like a limp rag doll. He was dead! This thing had killed him and was now snarling in her direction. And pulling the damn stake out.

"Go!" she said. "Go!" It backed away momentarily, but wrenched the stake from its back with a vicious snarl and came toward her brandishing the stake. "Go!" she yelled.

Last night it worked. Today, the vampire grabbed her arm and slammed her against the side of the car, making her drop the remaining stakes and the knife. The knife was just inches from her foot, but she was pinned against the car by the vampire.

He grinned, giving a clear view of his fangs.

Dear saints and angels!

He kept grinning as he loomed over her.

Her knee came up and jammed into his groin.

Seemed vampires hurt there, too.

His face contorted with a scream, he jerked back, and threw her down on the gravel. A hard landing, but she fell on top of the knife.

She wasn't getting another chance. Her hand closed on the hilt just as Eiche dragged her up by the collar.

"For that impertinence, you will die slowly, and your friend can watch." He reached out to kick Peter, who wasn't as helpless as he looked. He pulled himself half up and his hand closed around Eiche's ankle.

But it wasn't enough to pull him off balance. Eiche yanked his leg out of Peter's grasp and kicked him in the face before turning to Alice.

She just had time to notice the blood still flowing from the wound in Eiche's chest when he grabbed her shoulder, yanking her to standing. She shoved the knife upwards, catching him under the ribs.

He let go of her, uttered an unearthly scream that had the birds deserting the trees, and staggered, clutching at the hilt, before screaming even louder and staring at his hand.

"You witch! May you burn at the stake and suffer ten times this." Another scream and a stream of German she couldn't follow, and she noticed his hand shrivel.

But he wasn't through yet. As if marshaling his last strength, he made another lunge for her, but tripped over Peter, who was dragging himself up.

Eiche fell, his legs tangling with Peter's, and landed on his face, the force of the fall driving the tip of the blade out his back.

Not trusting it to be over, Alice grabbed the fallen stake, aimed straight for where his heart should be, and shoved.

Took all her strength to get through ribs and tissue, but fear, anger, and the heat of the horror propelled her.

She watched in fascinated horror as Eiche writhed against the knife and stake and howled to the heavens.

Peter! He was half-standing, his face bloody but he was beautiful and she loved him. She helped him up.

"Let's use the other stake," he said, reaching for the second, unused one that lay a couple of feet away, but it wasn't necessary.

Eiche shriveled before their eyes, his unearthly cries fading as his body crumbled.

"I think we did it," Peter said. "Or rather, you did. I was down and out."

"No, you were the distraction. I wonder why I repelled him last night but it didn't work now."

"Beats me. Does it matter? You did him in."

"Alice, child, what in the name of all?" Gran called, running up the drive, Sergeant Pendragon by her side.

"It's alright Gran. It's over."

The last thing they needed was Gran or the sergeant, who was even older, having heart attacks or strokes. Assuming Dragons did have heart attacks and strokes, of course. Come to that, did Pixies? She was going to have to supplement her medical training.

"I wanted to catch you, Alice, and tell you what I'd learned, but seems you managed on your own."

"Thanks to Mother Longhurst's magic vampire-slaying weaponry," Peter said, his voice still a little wobbly. "And Alice. I was all but knocked out; she attacked that thing like a Valkyrie."

Interesting comparison.

"So we got him," Alice said. "That's what matters. We're going to have to do something about disposing of the body."

"I don't think there will be a body," Pendragon said. "Look." The vampire was now a heap of fast-decaying flesh, along with an accompanying stench of putrefaction, in a pile of torn and bloody clothes. "As long as we don't have any surprise visitors in the next couple of hours, I think he'll be nothing but dust by morning."

"That's him taken care of then," Gran said. "Let's leave him to it. Nice to know that's over and no one else hurt."

"It's not over, Gran. What about the other one, remember? He might be lurking somewhere around."

"Let him lurk, you need to change your clothes and get a good wash."

"Actually, Mrs. Burrows, Alice needs to get changed and go shopping. We need to get into Dorking before the jewelers close."

"Like that is it? Good. Alright, Howell," Gran said. "Seems we'll have that cup of tea by ourselves, and Peter, the White Horse used to serve a very nice dinner before the war. Why not call them and reserve a table for after you finish your shopping?"

Chapter 40

"Eiche is gone, extinguished," Bela said, taking care to keep her voice neutral. An expression of satisfaction or pleasure would not be welcome.

They both stared in disbelief. "If you lie, your family dies. Slowly," Zuerst said.

"I do not lie. I felt his essence fade." And his strength meet hers in a mighty rush that hit her to the ground. But now that she'd absorbed his life force, she'd bide her time, test her powers and endurance, and wait to see if her increased strength was a passing or lasting thing.

"How did it happen?" Zweiten asked.

"I don't know. Maybe he confronted a stronger being."

That earned her a slap across her jaw. She stumbled from the force of it, but felt almost nothing. Interesting. She stayed down long enough to satisfy them and made a play of struggling to her feet.

"I don't know," she repeated. She just knew her hopes had risen.

Try the other books in
Georgia Evans's fantasy series . . .

Bloody Awful

In the second volume of Georgia Evans's supernatural trilogy, Gloria Prewitt must reveal her greatest secret to have any hope of saving the people she loves . . .

As the district nurse for a country village outside London, Gloria has the respect of the town and the satisfaction of helping those who need it most. She'd lose both if anyone discovered that she turns into a furry red fox and runs through the Surrey hills by moonlight. But what she sees on those wild nights suggests Brytewood is under attack— from a saboteur with superhuman powers and the force of the Nazi Luftwaffe behind him.

What can one werefox do against a predator with devastating weapons at his command—and the strength of the undead besides? What can a woman with a secret reveal without losing all she has? With the help of a couple of Devonshire Pixies, a Welsh Dragon, and two men too stubborn to admit they're outnumbered, Gloria might just find out the answers . . .

Andrew had the best spot in the house, or rather the cellar: a battered sofa tucked in one corner. He pretty much preempted it, saying she needed to keep her leg propped up, air raid or not. It wasn't a lie but Gloria stifled a twinge of guilt as she reclined on the dusty cushions and everyone else sat on upturned tea chests, rickety old chairs or the floor.

The light from the low-wattage bulbs was no use for reading, as one customer realized as he gave up on his newspaper and folded it to sit on. There was nothing to do but wait. For whatever was or was not going to happen. The group of young officers who'd been propping up the bar, now hunkered down to one side and started a game of cards. Seemed Gloria's best course of action was to lean back against Andrew and hope it was all a false alarm and they'd be upstairs again in no time, and she could finish her soup.

It wasn't a false alarm.

After the seemingly endless drone of planes overhead and ack-ack fire, there was comparative silence. The only immediate sounds being whispered conversations among the hotel staff clustered and the odd exclamation from the card players.

"Think that's it?" Gloria asked Andrew.

"Could be. Who knows? Best wait for the all clear."

Seemed it was going to be some wait. No one moved. Nothing happened. Apart from the arrival of an Air Raid warden checking gas masks.

"You know I could fine you both for not having them," he said.

"Sorry," Gloria said, before Andrew could reply. "I know we should have brought them, but I left mine at home. I always keep it with my nurse's uniform . . ." Better drop that in. ". . . and forgot it tonight. My mind was taken up with crutches and how I was getting around."

"Nurse are you then?"

"I'm the District Nurse based in Brytewood." That should be worth something, darn it. Most people had more to do that make a fuss about gas masks. Although she'd nagged her share of school children for leaving theirs in the playground.

"Well, Nurse, you know better, but . . . let's hope you don't need it tonight."

Didn't everyone share that hope? Gloria smiled at him. "Let's hope they're just flying over." Although that meant London would be getting it.

"Time will tell. They came over a couple of nights ago. Dropped half a dozen bombs that was all, but they caused a bit of trouble." He moved on to chat to the soldiers.

"He didn't even ask about yours," Gloria said to Andrew. "Just picked on me," she added with a little dig in his ribs.

"Good thing too. He wouldn't fine a nurse but I mightn't have been let off so lightly."

"Your work is important."

"But since I can't tell anyone what it is, not much of an alibi."

"Everyone in the village knows, or has guessed. Especially after the trouble back in September." When she'd raised the alarm. Not exactly easy since she'd been in her fox skin at the time.

His chest moved, as if he held in a laugh. "That's still an official secret."

"I won't tell. I promise."

"I know," he whispered it, his lips almost touching her ear, his breath warm against her skin. "Wouldn't be here with you otherwise, Gloria."

"We wouldn't down here at all if it weren't for the damn Luffwaffe."

As if on cue, another flight passed over head. More this time. Suddenly feeling hideously vulnerable, Gloria clutched Andrew's arm, now handily wrapped across her chest. His free hand stroked the back of her neck. "Hang on, old girl," he whispered. "This building's lasted centuries, you don't think it's going to crumble for the Jerries, do you?"

She hoped to heaven not. She tamped down the fox stirring inside. Stifled the instinct to run from danger. It was ten days to full moon, she didn't need to change, couldn't anyway with her leg in a cast but wanted to. She longed to shuck her human face and run free, away from this hotel and the town for the safety of the woods.

Which weren't safe in the least. Nowhere was.

Bloody Right

*It will take all of Brytewood's Others to save their village
from destruction in the climax of a Georgia Evans's
supernatural trilogy . . .*

Gryffyth Pendragon has done his bit for the war effort
when he comes back to sleepy Brytewood from the
battlefront at Trondheim. It cost him a leg, and his chance
to use his Dragon's strength against the Nazis—or so he
thinks. Until he finds out that his little village is facing a
plague of vampire spies set on delivering it to the Third
Reich. They've come up with a plan that, if they can pull
it off, might break all of Britain's will to fight . . .

But there are more allies for Gryffyth in Brytewood
than he'd ever imagined, and while a doctor, a nurse, a
schoolteacher, and a couple of sexagenarians doesn't sound
like much of a battle force to him, there's more to his
cohorts than meets the eye. Against ancient and impossibly
powerful agents of evil, they will need every man, woman,
and Dragon-shifter they can get . . .

Once the adrenaline rush from the part change faded, Gryffyth Pendragon found himself sitting on a heap in the lane. Fumbling around, he touched broken glass. So much for a torch to help him get home. And where the hell was his stick? To say nothing of what in Hades had attacked him? What now? Could he stand without his stick? He couldn't walk without it. Unless he had Mary to support him. Thinking of her brought a smile to his lips, but didn't help his current predicament. And on top of it, the sleeves of his shirt and new jacket were in tatters.

Shit! Should he hope someone would come by on their way back from the Pig? It was hours until closing time.

The narrow beam of a shaded bicycle lamp appeared in the distance.

Help, thank the heavens, but how to explain his condition? Convince them he was drunk this early?

"Hello," he called.

"Son?"

Crikey, if wasn't his father! "Dad?"

The bicycle stopped just a couple of feet away as his father leaped off, letting it fall and crouched over him. "What the flaming hell happened to you, son? You tripped? You shouldn't be walking home in the dark."

"Dad! There's a thing loose in the village." He'd probably think he'd been drinking but . . . "It grabbed me and had fangs."

"Not another one? Damn! Let me help you up." He grabbed him by the armpits and steadied him to his feet.

"What do you mean 'not another'?"

"Let's get you home first. Remember I said I had things to talk about?" Gryffyth had imagined it meant a catch-up on village gossip. "Well unless I'm mistaken you just encountered one of those things. Where's your stick?"

"I dropped it." What was the old man talking about?

"Hang on a tick. Here, hold onto the handlebars." His father stooped and retrieved his fallen bicycle. "That'll steady you. Now, let's see if I can find your stick." He pulled a torch from his coat pocket and shone the beam over the ground. First thing he found was the broken torch. "This yours, son?" he asked, bending down to pick it up.

"No, Mary lent it to me."

"Mary Chivers?"

"Lord, no, Dad. Mary LaPrioux. The girl I danced with on Saturday night."

"Oh." Amazing how much meaning and speculation the old man could pack into one syllable. "She lent it to you."

"Yes Dad, she did!" And right now he was not in the mood to share the circumstances. "I'll buy her another to replace it."

"You might have a hard time finding one, son, but never mind that right now." He'd happily change the subject too. "Hang on, let's see if I can find your stick."

Less than a minute later, Gryffyth had his stick secure in his hand. "Right, son, let's get back home and get you cleaned up."

In the light of the kitchen, Gryff looked a proper fright: His hair was on end, and his jacket and shirt were ripped to the elbow.